Healer's Touch

A Hearts and Thrones Novel

Amy Raby

Book Layout ©2013 BookDesignTemplates.com

Healer's Touch/ Amy Raby. -- 1st ed.
ISBN 978-1-940987-04-0

ALSO BY AMY RABY

The Hearts and Thrones series

Assassin's Gambit
Spy's Honor
Prince's Fire
Archer's Sin

The Coalition of Mages series

The Fire Seer

1

Marius had never seen a carriage like this one. It sat before a backdrop of sagging storefronts and fading paint, as incongruous with its surroundings as a swan in a mud puddle. Bars of gold and ivory swooped upward to outline its form, and a crystal lamp sparkled at each corner. Four dapple gray horses waited in harness. He could not imagine what even a single horse of such quality would cost, let alone four of them. A thousand tetrals? More?

He pushed open the wooden shutters of his apartment window for a better view. The carriage was escorted by two others, one in front and the other behind. The escorts weren't as fancy as the middle carriage, but they were finer than what anyone in the village could afford. Who could be the owner of this assemblage? It was rare for the nobility to pass through a backwater like Osler.

He was due back at the apothecary in a few hours, but his mother had told him that if he ever saw a rich man's carriage in Osler, he needed to tell her immediately. Apparently she'd once had a serious quarrel with a nobleman.

Marius leaned out the window in hopes of seeing the great man, or perhaps it was a great woman. But he saw only servants. A coachman stood at the lead horse's head, and a groom was draping blankets over the horses' backs. Why would a noble personage carry a grudge against his mother for so many years? It didn't make sense, but he would tell her about the carriage anyway. On his way out, he grabbed a bottle of tincture he'd been meaning to bring her.

The carriage guards paid him not the slightest attention as he climbed down the stairs. A pair of them were going into Lev's Inn and Tavern. Marius smiled. Gods help them if they tried the special.

A quarter mile down the road, he angled onto the dirt path that led to his parents' home. Once inside, he hung his hat on the rack and called, "It's me." A savory scent wafted past his nose. His mother must be cooking.

She came into the entryway and folded him into a hug.

He hugged her back gently. His mother, Camilla, wasn't young anymore. She'd borne her children later in life than most women, and Marius feared that he and his younger sister had been a strain on her. She was delicate as a bird, yet he felt strength in her small frame.

He took the bottle of tincture from his pocket and pressed it into her hands. "I brought you more of this. Promise you'll take it this time?"

She smiled, looking sheepish. "Of course."

"Your joints will feel better if you do. It's concentrated, so go easy on it, one swallow in the morning and another at night—"

She waved a hand. "I know how willow bark works. Are you off duty until evening? I've got soup on. Won't do it any harm if we take it off the fire early."

Marius shed his cloak and followed her into the kitchen, where the aroma of onions and carrots and herbs hung heavy in the air. "I'm not here for supper. I came because I saw a fancy carriage in town."

Camilla's eye flicked back to him. "The governor's?"

"No."

She walked to the soup pot over the fire, lifted the lid, and stirred. "There's no reason for the nobility to come through Osler. They take the Nigellus Road. What did the carriage look like?"

"Fancy. There were three carriages, actually. The guards are in orange livery." His stomach rumbled. He hadn't eaten since breakfast.

Camilla dropped the lid back onto the soup pot and turned. "Orange?"

He nodded.

She raised her eyes to his, and Marius became conscious of the lines on her face. She did not speak, and Marius gathered that his answer was not the one she'd wanted.

"Is it the one you're worried about?" he asked.

She blinked and stammered something that wasn't a word. Then she left the kitchen.

"Mother?" he called after her.

Her voice shook. "He's found us." From the kitchen, he heard her pounding on the door to the workshop. "Tertius, come out. The Legaciatti are here."

Marius shook his head as if to shake cobwebs loose. Legaciatti? Those were the emperor's personal guards. They lived in the imperial city and would have no reason to come to a remote village like Osler. "I'm sure they're not Legaciatti," he called to her. He cocked his head and listened. She did not answer, but he heard banging and rustling as someone, perhaps two someones, moved around in the workshop.

His mother returned to the kitchen, lugging a rucksack.

"You shouldn't be lifting that," said Marius, reaching to take it from her.

She let him have it. "Take this and go."

Marius blinked. "Where? I have a shift this evening." She had to be wrong about the guards being Legaciatti. His family was of no importance whatsoever and would have no business with the Imperium. Neither she nor his father could have committed the sort of crime that would attract the attention of the imperial seat, or, for that matter, any crime at all. His parents were the most straight-laced, law-abiding people he knew. They never gossiped or gambled. They rarely even drank.

"Forget the apothecary," said his mother. "You have no idea what you're dealing with."

"Tell me, then."

"Some things it's better not to know."

She was shaking like a twig in a storm. As absurd as her fears might seem, it was clear that to her, they were absolutely real. Marius felt an icy chill along his spine, like the time his sister had dropped a snowball down the back of his shirt. "Explain this plan to me. Where am I to go? I've no money to travel with."

"Away from Osler. Your father and I will catch up."

She tried to push him toward the door, but he wouldn't budge. "What about Laelia?" If the danger was real, they couldn't leave his sister behind.

His father entered the kitchen with a rucksack of his own heaved onto his wiry back. He moved to the larder, snatching up supplies: the rest of the day's bread, a bunch of carrots, a pair of wrinkled apples. "I'll run and fetch Laelia. You leave now and get a head start."

Marius gaped. His father was quiet and sensible by nature, the steady counterpart to his mother's fire. If his parents were united in their determination to leave Osler, the situation was serious. "What's Gratian going to say?" Laelia's live-in lover wasn't the friendliest of men.

His father shook his head. "He'll have to let her go. If he doesn't, he'll regret it. Get moving, son."

Marius went to the entryway, grabbed his cloak, and slung it around his shoulders. His parents' sincerity had convinced him to follow their directions, at least for the time being, but he could not pretend he understood what was going on. "Are you in trouble with the Imperium?"

"Yes," called his mother. "We'll explain later."

What could his quiet, reclusive parents have done that would induce the empire to hunt them down? He stuffed his hat on his head and grabbed a blanket from the nearest bedroom. "I'll help you fetch Laelia." Strength in numbers, when it came to dealing with Gratian.

A loud noise made him jump, and he turned. Someone was banging on the front door with something heavy.

"Out the back, quickly!" shrieked his mother.

Marius lost no time in following her. It appeared her lifelong fear was justified. Someone really *was* after them.

His father yanked open the back door to a wall of orange livery, and a host of imperial guards swarmed into the house.

Marius sat at the kitchen table with his mother on his left and his father on his right. Guards encircled them. His stomach was in knots, and so far nothing was happening either to alleviate or to sharpen his fears. He and his parents were being held here for some event yet to come, and the guards refused to answer his questions. His parents surely knew something about what was happening, but when he sent them desperate, questioning looks, they stared down at the table and didn't meet his eyes.

Turning from them, he looked to the guards, trying to determine if they really were Legaciatti. They did have the sickle and sunburst insignia, but did that prove anything? Anyone could make up an insignia and sew it to a uniform. The guards were intimidating, each of them carrying a sword and pistol at his belt as well as a heavy, bronze-tipped stick. Perhaps the stick was for beating people into submission. Or, now that he thought about it, for knocking on doors.

So far the guards had not been violent. One had grabbed his mother when she tried to slip away, but not roughly. Marius recognized the guard standing across from the table as the one he'd seen outside Lev's earlier in the day.

"Could you just tell us what's going on?" Marius blurted.

"The emperor will be along shortly," said the guard from Lev's.

Marius laughed. This was all a joke, surely. The emperor would not have come personally for his mother; if she were truly in trouble, he'd have sent his guards for her. "The *Kjallan* emperor?"

The guard gave him a look. "What other emperor is there?"

The Kjallan emperor—ridiculous.

His mother stared straight ahead, stony-faced, wringing her hands in her lap. His father, as always, was an open book, his face etched with worry lines, but he did not seem surprised. That was the oddest thing about this affair. Marius's parents seemed to have expected this to happen. Even *planned* for it.

Marius tried something else. "May I have some water?"

After a moment's hesitation, one of the guards looked around the kitchen, spied the water pitcher, and poured him a glass. He set it in front of Marius. "Here, sir."

Sir. Marius almost laughed. He lifted the glass and drained half of it.

All at once, the guards shifted, turning toward the front entryway and dipping their heads as another man entered the room. This, Marius supposed, was the emperor, or at least someone pretending to be the emperor. He was average in height. In fact, Marius probably had an inch on him. The emperor, if indeed that was who he was, was black-haired and fine-featured. He didn't look much like his profile on the Kjallan tetral.

The emperor was known to be crippled, but this man wasn't limping. Marius looked down at the man's feet and saw a normal boot on the right, leather and mud-spattered. On the left was a sort of wooden shoe. He'd heard that One-Legged Lucien walked with the aid of a prosthetic. Was he looking at that famous prosthetic now?

The supposed emperor turned to his mother. "Sabina," he said, holding out his hand.

Marius let out his breath in relief. This was a mistake. Sabina was not his mother's name. These people, whether imperials or charlatans, had come to the wrong house.

His mother stiffened and planted her hands in her lap, refusing to clasp wrists. "You're too late. He's grown up, and you can't have him. He's no use to you, anyway. He's got no education and no magic."

Marius blinked, stunned by this response.

The supposed emperor turned to his father and again offered his arm. "Anton."

Marius's father lowered his eyes, but he extended his hand and clasped wrists.

Now the man turned to Marius himself. "Your name, sir?"

Marius reached out and clasped his wrist. "Marius. But I think you've come to the wrong house. Those aren't their names."

"It's the right house," said the emperor. "And those *are* their names. It's wonderful to meet you, Marius. I'm Lucien Florian Nigellus, emperor of Kjall. You and I are cousins."

Marius gaped.

"You can't have him," said his mother.

Lucien's gaze slid in her direction. "I think he's old enough to make his own decisions."

Marius reeled in his seat, catching himself just in time to avoid falling out of it. He and the emperor were *cousins*? How was that possible?

Lucien turned to him. "Your mother never told you, but she's a full sister to my predecessor, Florian Nigellus Gavros."

Marius shook his head. "I think you've made a mistake. Her name is Camilla Brosus. . ." He hesitated. Maybe he shouldn't be sharing these details.

"She changed it before you were born," said Lucien. "She's been in hiding for decades. Haven't you, Sabina?"

His mother—Sabina?—stared balefully at the emperor.

"I've found your sister," said Lucien. "A couple of guards are watching her house. They'll go in once we're done here." He gestured to his guards and nodded at Marius. "I'd like to speak with you alone."

"No!" cried his mother.

The emperor ignored her. A pair of guards directed Marius out of his chair. He rose and followed them.

"Marius, he's not a friend!" called his mother as he walked from the kitchen to the entryway in the company of the emperor and a pair of Legaciatti.

They led him out of the house, where the grand carriage awaited. A footman opened the carriage door. Marius was closer to the vehicle than he had been earlier, and he looked for signs of fakery. Perhaps the lamps were cheap glass instead of crystal. Might a thin layer of gold plating be flaking off the trim? But he saw nothing of the sort. Everything looked genuine, and when he laid his hand on the carriage door, he felt its weight and its smoothness as it swung on its hinges. And those stunning dapple grays—equine quality could not be faked.

He was convinced. Everything was real, and that meant the emperor had to be real, too.

Emperor Lucien stepped into the carriage. Marius hesitated, and the guard gave him a gentle nudge. Marius had never ridden in a carriage before. He climbed awkwardly through the door.

The carriage was enormous on the inside and could easily have seated eight. Since he and Lucien were the only ones within, Marius took the seat across from the emperor. He sank deeply into the cushions and struggled for a moment to right himself. He was used to firmer seats. Was this what luxury was like, always throwing one off balance? The footman closed the door behind them, granting them privacy. Marius was alone with the emperor of Kjall. He shoved his hands into his pockets so that their trembling wouldn't show.

"I'm going to tell you a story," said Lucien. "Once upon a time, long before I was born, my grandfather Nigellus was emperor. He had two children, a boy named Florian and a girl named Sabina."

Marius made a strangled noise.

Lucien continued. "Nigellus arranged marriages for both of his children. Florian married as Nigellus directed him and had four children, of which I am the third. But Sabina did not like the man Nigellus had chosen for her. She had fallen in love with another man, a humble upholsterer named Anton who had done some work in the palace."

"My father is a carpenter, not an upholsterer," said Marius.

"Let me finish my story," said Lucien. "Sabina eloped with Anton and fled into the countryside. Nigellus tried to find her, but his health was failing, and he died before he could locate her. My father, Florian, ascended the throne, and once established, he resumed the search. He found Sabina and Anton in the city of Rodgany, and they had a child with them—a three-year-old daughter."

Marius let his breath out. This was all wrong. His parents had never lived in Rodgany, and he was the eldest child. Laelia was two years younger than he.

"Florian left Sabina and Anton where they were, but he took the daughter. You have *two* sisters, Marius. Not one."

He shook his head. "I've always been the eldest."

"You have never met Rhianne," said Lucien gently. "She was raised in the imperial palace and is now the Queen of Mosar."

Marius stared at him, dumbstruck. He had an older sister, and she was a queen? No, that could not be true. "You've got the wrong family—"

"I don't," said Lucien. "I've been searching for years, and I'm certain I've found the people I'm looking for. You are my cousin. You are also Florian's nephew and Rhianne's full brother. Rhianne has wondered for years whether her parents had more children after Florian stole her, but they moved away from Rodgany and changed their names, even their professions. They did not want to be found again."

"Why?" Marius blurted.

Lucien leaned back in his seat. "Because they didn't want their children taken away a second time."

"You're saying they moved and changed their identities because of me and Laelia?"

"They didn't want to lose you. I promised Rhianne that I would find you, if you existed. All her life, she has missed her parents and wondered about possible siblings. Florian raised Rhianne with every advantage of education and position and wealth, but in other ways he was not good to her. She's in Mosar now, and far happier than she was here. She will be happier still if she can be reunited with her long-lost family. And Marius, you and your sister belong at the palace. Your mother says you're not educated. Is that true?"

"I'm a journeyman apothecary. I work for Appius—"

"Do you know your letters?"

"No, but. . ." He'd never needed them, and never thought he would. Appius couldn't read either. His cheeks heated as realized how provincial he must seem to this man. When Lucien said *educated*, he didn't mean someone who had learned a trade. He meant someone with a formal education, a scholar like they had at the universities. Marius couldn't even read a street sign.

"I can fix all that," said Lucien.

"You're asking me to go with you to the Imperial Palace—"

"I'm not asking," said Lucien.

Marius looked into those hard black eyes. His mother's fears had been justified. The emperor *did* mean to take him away, and apparently Marius wasn't going to have a say in the matter. He glanced out the carriage windows. Could he escape? Probably not with all those guards watching. Did he *want* to escape? He wasn't sure.

"I never knew your mother," said Lucien. "She fled from Nigellus before I was born, and we met for the very first time today. I don't know why she made the choices she did, but Marius, those choices have greatly limited your opportunities in life. When she separated you from the rest of your family, she denied you the education and the magic that should have been your birthright—"

"I don't want them," said Marius.

"Are you certain? You're an apothecary. What led you to choose that calling?"

He shrugged. "I like to help people."

"How effective are your herbs and poultices?"

Marius bit his lip. For most conditions, not very.

"What if you augmented the skill you already possess with the magic of a Healer?" continued Lucien. "Think how much more you could do."

Marius was silent. He knew Healers could help the people that apothecaries couldn't. All his life, he'd envied those rare few with healing magic. The emperor had known just where to poke him to make him hurt. And to yearn for more.

"I'm taking you back with me to Riat," said Lucien. "But I won't break up your family. All of you will come: you, your sister, and your parents."

He swallowed. "My sister's. . .friend. . .may give you some trouble."

"If a situation develops, my guards will handle it," said Lucien. "Let's get started, shall we? It's time this family was reunited. Did you know your sister Rhianne has children? You're an uncle, and you didn't even know it."

Marius couldn't respond. He felt as if a dust devil had descended upon Osler, picked up the pieces of his life, and whirled them into the air, scattering them hopelessly.

2

After Lucien left to fetch Laelia, Marius was permitted to gather his things from his apartment atop the apothecary—under guard. While his parents rummaged through their home, making a more thorough packing job than the rucksacks, Marius returned to the apothecary in the company of two Legaciatti. He would be sorry to leave this place behind. Appius, the old master, wasn't getting any younger, and Marius was certain the man had meant to retire and leave the business to Marius within the next few years. Now Appius would have to start over with a new apprentice.

He sorted through his clothes, picking out the nicer items. When was he going to wake up and realize this was all a dream, or perhaps some kind of nightmare? Lucien had asked him to pack lightly; most of his things would be replaced in Riat. The emperor meant to dress him in imperial silks, apparently, but Marius doubted he would ever feel comfortable in fancy clothes. Put a mule in a fancy harness, and it was still a mule. How could a village hayseed like himself ever pass for an imperial? It wasn't just the clothes he lacked. He didn't have the right mannerisms, the right education, or even the right accent. The courtiers at the palace would laugh at him.

In coming here to take them from Osler, was Lucien rescuing his family or destroying them? His mother saw Lucien as a villain, but Marius wasn't sure anymore. She'd lied to Marius all his life. She'd claimed to be illiterate, but if she'd been raised in the Imperial Palace as the daughter of an emperor, she'd have been educated as such. That meant she could have taught him to read and write if she'd chosen to. How much did she know, how much talent did she possess, that she'd never offered to share with him? Why had she never told him the truth about his family?

He had, for the most part, been happy in Osler. He liked his job and his family. He would confess he was a bit lonely and anxious about his prospects for marriage. The selection of young women in Osler was limited. He'd courted two young ladies in succession, but hadn't fallen in love with either of them. After witnessing all his life the deep love his parents felt for each other, he knew he would settle for nothing less in his own marriage, and at twenty-two, he was starting to feel old for a bachelor.

He'd packed everything he wanted, and the travel chest was only half full. Pathetic. He closed it, and one of the guards stepped forward. "I'll get that, sir."

"Thanks," said Marius, bemused. *Sir.*

He followed the guard out of his apartment, down the steps, and along the dirt road to where the carriage waited.

His mother's forbidden love was the cause of all this mess. She had fallen in love with the wrong man—at least, one her father didn't approve of. But there was no sense being angry with her for leaving the imperial palace. If she had not eloped with his father, Marius himself would never have been born. Neither would Laelia, or apparently Rhianne. *Wait a minute, I'm half noble and half commoner.* Would he be scorned for that? Perhaps not. Lucien didn't seem to care, and his sister Rhianne had done well enough, marrying the king of Mosar.

Maybe the villain of this saga was neither Lucien nor his mother, but long-dead Nigellus, who'd tried to force an unwanted marriage on his daughter. Perhaps a single ill act spilled over from generation to generation, unstoppable, like a waterfall over rocks.

At the carriage, Marius clasped wrists with the emperor. "Your Imperial Majesty, are you going to break up their marriage?"

Lucien's brows rose. "Whose?"

"My parents'. So my mother can marry a prince or something."

"Oh, gods, no." Lucien laughed. "Has that been worrying you? The time for Sabina to make a political marriage is past, and there's no longer any need. My sister has married into Inya and your sister into Mosar. We've alliances enough to last us until the next generation, and I have no quarrel with Anton. He's been married to my aunt for over three decades, and they seem to still be in love, so why should I cause any more trouble? Obviously she chose the right man."

Marius's shoulders dropped in relief. He was sure his parents were angry about being forced to move to the Imperial Palace, and perhaps a bit frightened as well, but at least they would have each other. "What about me?"

"I thought you were single."

"I am," said Marius. "But will I be expected to make a political marriage?"

"Let's put it this way," said Lucien. "I would like you to make a marriage that befits your station. But I won't force you into anything. I want to bring this family back together, not tear it apart."

A marriage that befits your station. What did that mean? What station did he possess, as a half-commoner, half-imperial with no education and no magic?

Never mind. He wouldn't worry about that now.

At Lucien's gesture, he climbed into the carriage. His mother and father were already within, sitting on the backward-facing seat. His mother looked furious and his father terrified. Laelia sat beside them, red-faced and teary-eyed, but there was no Gratian. Apparently her live-in lover had chosen not to come, or perhaps he was not invited. Laelia might be upset about that now, but Marius was secretly relieved. He had never liked Gratian, and his sister had changed a lot when she'd gone to live with him. She'd become quiet and distant, not the young firebrand he'd known all his life. Perhaps now the old Laelia would re-emerge.

The forward-facing seat was empty. That was presumably where Lucien would sit. Marius could sit with Lucien and make the numbers a little more even, or. . .

He sat beside his parents. Awkward as it was, it gave them solidarity. His mother reached over and squeezed his hand.

Lucien climbed into the carriage, eyed the four of them sitting together for a moment, and sighed as he sat alone on the opposite seat. "Found this," he said, handing a box to Sabina. "Were you going to leave it behind?"

Sabina snatched it from him and placed it on her lap.

Marius had never seen the box before. "What's in it?"

Sabina did not answer, but after a moment Lucien did. "It's her riftstone. She's a mind mage."

"*What?*" Marius stared at his mother, whom he thought he'd known all these years and clearly hadn't known at all. Not only was she educated, she was magical. And powerfully so.

His sister gasped as well. "You mean *all this time.* . ?" She did not finish her thought but shook her head and leaned back against the seat.

"Brace yourselves. We're going to Riat." Lucien knocked on the roof, and the carriage lurched into motion.

3

Isolda repeated the code words in her head as she approached the dock at Cus, the Sardossian port city. They were her mantra, her magic words. Used properly, they could change her life.

Her legs shook with fatigue and more than a little fear. She'd never been this far from home, and she had no husband with her, no protection of any kind. A weight dragged at her shoulder, and the suddenness of it almost pulled her to the ground. Her four-year-old son, Rory, had collapsed on the wooden planking of the dock. She picked him up and heaved him into her arms.

"Wan' go home," he sobbed into her shirt. The boy was exhausted and out of sorts. If this day had been remotely normal, he'd have been in bed hours ago.

She said nothing; it was impossible to explain the situation to a child his age. He'd understand when he was older that they *had* to leave. Someday, she hoped, he would be grateful that she had undertaken this journey from Sardos to Kjall on his behalf. Rory had no future here. Few children did, now that the blood wars had begun. She was not going to see her only son recruited as a child soldier in some Heir-hopeful's army and end up spitted on a bayonet.

A man guarded the ship's gangway, and Isolda did not like the look of him. Dirty and rough, with uncombed hair and sun-darkened skin, he was clearly a stray, nothing at all like the respectable men at home. She hesitated, considering the many possible fates that could await her on the ship and beyond. Some of those imagined fates were worse than minding a shop for a husband who didn't love her.

But for Rory's sake, she stepped forward.

"Bright moons tonight," she said to the stray.

It was a long time before he turned his head. He grunted at her dismissively. "Move along. I've no use for land beetles."

"I've a letter to send to my great-aunt," she said.

That was the code phrase, and it was clear he recognized it, since his brows rose a little. His eyes roamed over her body, lingering first on her breasts and hips, then on her face, and then on the exhausted child slumped on her shoulder. "Sorry, but we don't take mail."

"I thought that in this case. . ." She trailed off, not knowing what to say. The code phrase was supposed to grant her a hiding spot in the hold of the ship. She had not prepared for the possibility of his turning her down. Why would he do that, when she had money?

"Lady, do you know how many people come here wanting to send letters to their great-aunts, now that the blood wars have started? More'n I can count."

"Yes, but. . ." She was at a loss. This wasn't supposed to happen.

"We ain't got the space. You understand? If this was an exceptional case. . ." His eyes skimmed her form again. "But it ain't. You got nothing special, lady."

His insult didn't stab, but left only a dull ache, like scar tissue built up in a wound. At least she understood now what was going on. He thought she was buying passage to Kjall with the use of her body. No wonder he'd said no; her body wasn't worth a tin slug. Even her husband didn't want it. "You misunderstand. I can pay."

"Not interested," said the sailor.

She reached into her shirt and pulled out the pouch that contained everything she owned in the world. She withdrew several heavy coins and dropped them into the sailor's hand. "Payment. And that's all I'm paying. You understand?"

He gaped at the coins. "Where'd you get these?"

"I earned them."

His brow furrowed with suspicion. She understood why. Sardossian women didn't normally have money. In a legal sense, Isolda had stolen the money from her husband, but she didn't feel guilty about her crime. The money was hers, ethically if not legally. She had earned it.

The stray looked her over again, mystified. Then he closed his hand, shrugged, and stepped aside. Coin was coin.

"The captain will show you where to put your letter," he said.

Isolda heaved a slipping Rory back onto her shoulder and walked up the gangplank. She was still frightened, but on the inside she was also singing. She was on her way to a new country and a new life. If all went well, she and Rory would soon be far from home, in the Kjallan city of Riat.

"Good news, Isolda," her mother had said, stepping into her tiny bedroom. "A man has offered for you."

Isolda gasped. She'd known something big had been in the offing when she'd been sent to her room without even a glimpse of the visiting stranger. But she had not expected this. As the youngest of three sisters, and the least pretty, she had believed she would never marry. Her older siblings had told her no man would pay a bride price for an ugly girl. Now they had flown the nest and started families of their own. Isolda had come to accept that she would not be a wife. Instead, she would be her father's assistant in the apothecary and her mother's assistant in the kitchen. Not a bad life, but it saddened her to think that she would never know love, never have a child to call her own.

Now it appeared that her sisters had been wrong, after all! Excitement rose in her, mixed with fear. Would she like the man who had offered for her? What sort of man offered for an ugly girl? She swallowed. Her parents had probably lowered the bride price. She understood how these things worked; it was supply and demand. Her husband-to-be would be a poor man, but that didn't mean he was a bad person or in any way unlovable.

Isolda's mother sat on the bed next to her and took her hand. "I want you to understand something. Jauld isn't like your sisters' husbands. He's humble."

Isolda nodded. "I understand."

"You can't expect too much."

"I don't." Isolda's cheeks heated as she said it. She knew better than to expect much, but that didn't stop her from dreaming, in the privacy of her bedroom, of a husband who was kind, loving, handsome, and if not rich, at least self-sufficient. *"What does he do?"*

"He's a shopkeeper. He owns a general store."

That sounded acceptable. She could see herself helping out in a store, thinking about supply and demand, figuring out how to eke a little bit more profit from their modest stock. She would miss her father's apothecary. But if Jauld were a good man and kind, she could imagine herself in the role of shopkeeper's wife.

"Are you ready to meet him?"

Was a woman ever ready to meet the man she'd been sold to in marriage? *"Yes."*

Isolda's mother squeezed her hand. *"Let's go show you off."*

Isolda walked behind her mother, wanting to hide herself from view. She hadn't asked how Jauld had learned about her. Had he seen her before? Was he aware she wasn't pretty? Maybe he would change his mind when he saw her.

And then they were in the sitting room, and her mother was shoving her front and center, and the stranger—Jauld—was beaming at her. It seemed he did like her, after all.

Jauld wasn't handsome, exactly. He was ordinary looking. A little plain, like her.

Isolda's heart swelled with gratitude, appreciation, and a blossoming of love. She beamed back at him. This man liked her. He'd made an offer for her hand. He owned a general store, and he wanted to build a life with her. Neither she nor Jauld were beautiful, but what did it matter? They had each other. It would *be she and Jauld against the world. She would love this man if she possibly could.*

4

FOUR MONTHS LATER

The explosion happened in two stages. The first was just sound, a bone-jarring boom. Marius crouched and covered his head, bracing for impact. But nothing happened. Everything was still. He lifted his head and saw a great fireball rising over the harbor, only a mile or two away.

Then the shock wave punched through, and every window on the street shattered at once.

When the rain of glass stopped, Marius raised his head. His bodyguard, Drusus, had moved in front of him. Past Drusus's shoulder, the ball of fire had turned into a plume of black smoke that roiled upward, alive with shining white flashes of light, like a pyrotechnic display. "Look at that."

Drusus nudged a shard of glass with his booted foot. "We should get you someplace safe."

Marius was transfixed by the glittering smoke plume. "What do you suppose happened?"

"Gunpowder explosion, I'll wager."

"In the middle of town?" Marius shook his head. There were laws prohibiting the manufacture of gunpowder within city limits. Factories were supposed to be located in remote areas so that if a disaster did occur, no one would be harmed except those working in the factory.

Drusus frowned. "It's illegal, but people set these shops up all the time. Easy to staff them without having to pay the slave taxes; just hire Sardossian sewer rats."

Marius couldn't imagine who would take a job in an illegal gunpowder factory, when a possible outcome was dying in an explosion like that one.

"Let's get you home," said Drusus. "No sense going to market now. It's going to be chaos all over town."

Marius had already forgotten about the market. "What about the injured people at the site? They'll need help." He wished he was finished with his training, but unfortunately he'd only made a beginning. Lucien had followed through with his promise of an education, supplying Marius with a small army of tutors who were teaching him not just book learning but the meditation and deep mental awareness techniques he would need to soulcast and claim his healing magic. It would be years before he was ready. But he *was* a trained apothecary, and Riat's limited number of Healers would be overwhelmed by a disaster of this magnitude.

"Sir, your cousin would not want you to put yourself at risk—"

"He'll have no objection to my helping his people." Marius had initially resisted being assigned a bodyguard, believing that

Lucien would use the guard to try to control his movements. But Lucien had addressed his concerns, assuring him that the Legaciatti were protectors rather than babysitters. While it was Drusus's job to try to keep him out of dangerous situations, Marius should always be aware that he, not Drusus, was the one issuing the orders.

Drusus's frown deepened. "Yes, sir."

They'd only just left the villa, so Marius darted back inside to collect some supplies. The explosion had not spared his home. The first floor windows were all shattered, and broken glass littered his sitting room. Nothing he could do about it now; the servants would sweep it up. He stepped around the glass, collecting bandages and a few tinctures from his storeroom, and set out with Drusus toward the plume of blackening smoke.

Though the disaster site wasn't far, their progress through the streets past crowds of townsfolk and broken glass and terrified horses was slow. It took them nearly half an hour to reach it. Between two dockside warehouses, a charred husk still flamed around the edges, and debris littered the streets. Marius covered his nose to dull the fishy smell, which mixed unpleasantly with the odors of sulfur and charred wood. The area teemed with gawkers, soot-stained survivors, and shouting city officials.

Somewhere around here would be a makeshift hospital. He pushed his way through the crowd. Pile of dead bodies to the right—that was no help.

Then he spotted it, an area the guards were cordoning off by rope. Blankets were spread on the ground, and Healers moved among the injured.

A guard gestured for him to move off. "People working here."

"I'm an apothecary," said Marius. "I'd like to help."

The guard looked him over, and Marius was glad he'd worn a syrtos today instead of his preferred tunic and breeches. The syrtos made him look respectable.

"License?" the guard inquired.

"I don't have it with me." Gods curse it, he should have thought of that. Looking past the guard, he spotted someone he knew. "Sergia!" He almost didn't recognize her; she had a cloth tied around her face.

Sergia approached. "Let him in," she told the guard. "He's one of my students."

The guard stepped aside, and Marius climbed over the rope barrier. "How can I help?"

Sergia led him deeper within the hospital area.

The patients they passed by were grievously wounded—limbs missing, bodies charred. A broken-off post protruded from one man's stomach. Marius felt sick. He could be no help to these people; his bandages and tinctures were mere toys in the face of such injuries.

"You can help Avitus," said Sergia.

Marius looked where she was pointing. Avitus was another student of Sergia's, much younger but similarly qualified in his studies. Marius, because he had begun his education late in life, often found himself surrounded by students five to ten years his junior. The patients Avitus was tending appeared to be the luckier ones, with no visible injuries.

"These have already been healed," explained Sergia. "But some are weak from shock or blood loss. They're not ready to go home just yet."

"I see." He wouldn't need his bandages, then. These patients needed only supportive care: water, blankets, and words of reassurance. He'd like to do more, but until he acquired his healing magic, he was underqualified. This would do.

Avitus, thin and gawky in his adolescent frame, rose as Sergia approached.

"I've brought Marius to help you," said Sergia.

Avitus stepped forward and clasped wrists, but there was no welcome in his eyes. He probably didn't want a helper, and Marius was equally unenthusiastic about doing the same low-grade work as a teenager.

Never mind. He could tolerate a surly youth for the sake of people in need.

Sergia hurried off.

"What have we got?" asked Marius.

Avitus introduced him to the patients, beginning at the end of the row. "This one's unconscious; I think she might be in shock. I've covered her with blankets. You might try to get some water in her if she wakes. This fellow, I think he's more scared than anything. He wasn't badly hurt, but see how he shivers."

Marius nodded. Avitus continued down the line, and Marius began thinking of ways he might be able to help beyond just blankets and water. Some of his tinctures might be of use. He had calming medicines and pain relievers.

Avitus eyed Drusus. "Is he helping too?"

"No," said Drusus. "I'm just going to stand around and watch."

Avitus boggled at those words. But Drusus was an intimidating-looking man, and young Avitus, like so many

Kjallans, lacked the courage to ask what Drusus meant by such an impolite response.

Marius was used to Drusus unnerving people. Drusus was an imperial bodyguard, but in plainclothes. Most people assumed he was Marius's servant, or a lover, or perhaps an excessively devoted friend. Drusus found their confusion amusing but was otherwise unconcerned. As a Legaciattus, he was more than a little proud, and he considered the townsfolk and their opinions beneath him.

Avitus pointed. "Look, the cart's arriving."

A horse-dragon wagon was pulling up just outside the roped-off area.

"Supplies from the surgery," explained Avitus. "Can you run and fetch us some blankets?"

Marius went to the cart and retrieved the blankets. As he returned, he noticed a group of people lying apart from the others. "Who are those people? Are they being treated?"

"Those are just sewer rats," said Avitus.

Marius handed a bundle of blankets to Avitus. "Do you mean Sardossians?" He was starting to learn the local slang. "Are they not hurt?"

"Who knows? They'll scatter when the city guard arrives."

Marius furrowed his brow. It didn't seem right to care for the Kjallan patients and not the Sardossians. Yes, they were from a foreign country, and yes, they weren't supposed to be in Kjall. But they *were* people, despite what Avitus called them. And he'd rather have patients of his own than share these with a boy six years his junior. "I'm going to have a look at them."

Avitus shrugged, no doubt happy to be rid of him.

Marius had never met a Sardossian. In his four months in Riat and at the palace, he'd heard a bit about the problem of the Sardossian "sewer rats," but they were an underground population, always in hiding. He didn't understand their reasons for coming here, only that there was some sort of "blood war" going on in their country.

He crouched down to greet the first patient and check the man's pulse. Now he regretted his syrtos; the garment was designed to be attractive and showy rather than practical, and it pulled at him, restricting his movement. He tugged at it, trying to make it more comfortable, and wished he'd worn his tunic and breeches.

The first two Sardossians were alive and conscious. They spoke to him in a language he didn't understand, but they seemed friendly, if nervous. Moving down the line, he found two that definitely wouldn't be scattering when the city guard came, because they were dead. One had a hole in his chest and had probably died before Healers had arrived on the scene. The other lay in a pool of blood, and his body was still warm. Someone had made a crude attempt at bandaging him, using a torn shirt, but it hadn't been enough. A Healer might have saved him.

Marius clenched his fist at such a pointless loss of life. There were things he hated about Riat, and this was one of them. The city had its wonders, to be sure—the food was like nothing he'd ever tasted before, and the people infinitely more varied than he'd known in Osler. The city's sophistication awed him on a daily basis. But he could not approve of big-city depravity. How could it be right to shunt away an entire class of people, denying them aid in an emergency and leaving them to die? His home village had never harbored any Sardossian refugees. He'd have to ask the emperor to explain the political situation to him next time he was at the palace. But he could not imagine that anyone in Osler would have left this man to die. Where he'd grown up, people looked out for one another.

"Hey," called a voice behind him.

Marius turned and saw Avitus.

"City guard's coming," he said to the Sardossians.

The Sardossians turned to one another and spoke in their language, looking confused.

Avitus rolled his eyes. "City guard," he repeated, stretching out the words the way one might do for a child. *"City guard.* You know. . ." He mimed pulling a pistol from his belt and firing it.

The talk among the Sardossians became agitated. Their voices rose, and after a moment, five of them dragged themselves up from the ground and ran. One favored his right leg, while two others supported an injured woman between them.

"See?" Avitus laughed. "Look at those sewer rats go."

"You sapskull." Marius rose to his feet and advanced on the youth. "What'd you do that for? Those people needed help."

"Sardossians regenerate," said Avitus. "Kill one, and two more grow in its place. Anyway, you've got a few left."

"The ones who are left are *dead.* And one of them could have been saved if someone had bothered to help him. . ." He trailed off, realizing that a third Sardossian remained, a woman. And she wasn't dead.

"I wasn't just baiting them. The guards really are here. See?"

Marius followed his gaze. Several Riat City Guards approached.

Drusus stiffened.

Marius had come to understand that there was a sort of hierarchy among guardsmen in the vicinity of the palace, with the Legaciatti at the top, the palace guards beneath them, and the Riat City Guards at the bottom. But this was complicated by jurisdiction. The Legaciatti had no authority over crimes committed in Riat, unless they affected the imperial palace or imperial family in some way. This annoyed them; they hated having to defer to the Riat City Guard about anything.

Marius ignored the guards and checked on his last remaining patient, the woman. Her eyes were closed, but she had a pulse. As he touched her, she spoke.

"*Rory,*" she said.

"I'm sorry," said Marius. "I don't speak Sardossian."

The woman was badly burned along one side of her body. Good thing she was only half-conscious, because she would be in a lot of pain when she woke. Marius turned up her palms, and when he saw the sulfur stains, his breath caught. This woman had been one of the factory workers—it was a wonder she had survived. She must have been inside the building when it blew.

Instant death would have been preferable to the slow death that awaited her if he couldn't find her a Healer. He wished fervently that he had finished his studies and could heal her himself. As it was, he'd have to move her—Drusus could help him with that—and bring her to Sergia.

"*Sith Rory teran?*" murmured the woman.

"She's asking about someone named Rory," said Drusus. "She wants to know where he is."

Marius had forgotten his bodyguard was multilingual. But the guards were coming nearer, and for now he needed the woman to be silent.

"Quiet," he told her.

"*Rory,*" she said again.

He put a finger to his lips—was that a universal gesture? "Shh."

Her eyes closed, and she said nothing.

The guards approached. Drusus took a protective step closer to Marius.

"Good evening, citizen. Are you a Healer?" asked one of the guards.

"An apothecary and a student," said Marius.

"And you?" The guard's eyes went to his bodyguard.

"Legaciatti." Drusus took the insignia that hung around his neck and showed it to the guard. Then he tucked it back beneath his shirt.

A look of alarm crossed the guard's face, but he recovered, smoothing his expression. "We were told there were some Sardossian refugees here. But I thought there were more than three."

"They ran off." Drusus pointed. "That way."

"And these three?" asked the guard.

Marius spoke up before Drusus could. "They're dead."

"Pity," said the guard. "You saw the others before they ran?"

"Briefly," said Marius.

"My name is Caellus," said the guard. "I'm a prefect in the Riat City Guard, and I may need to speak to you later about identifying the Sardossians. May I have your name?"

"His name is none of your business," said Drusus.

Caellus bristled, and for a moment it looked like there might be a confrontation. Then he seemed to decide against it. He

turned, and he and his guards left in the direction of the fleeing
Sardossians.

When they were gone, Drusus asked, "Is the woman really
dead?"

"No," said Marius. "And I think she can be saved. Help me
get this blanket under her, and we can take her to Sergia." Sergia
would do this favor for him, he was sure. She was one of the few
people who knew he was the emperor's cousin, and she would
not want to displease him. Even for a village hayseed like
Marius, there were advantages to having imperial blood.

*Jauld's General Store was not quite what Isolda had expected.
She had known it would be humble, but she had not expected it to
be so cluttered and dingy. She ran her fingertips along a shelf,
and they came away coated in grime. This would not do. Who
would shop in such a place?*

*Jauld tripped over a bag of potatoes as he came through the
aisle. He caught himself and smiled. "What do you think of the
store?"*

*Isolda grimaced. What could she say that was optimistic, yet
truthful? "It has potential." She stared at the potatoes. Why did
he leave them there in the aisle?*

*"My father ran this store, and his father before him." Jauld
followed her gaze to the potatoes. He picked them up and set
them on a shelf next to a buggy whip.*

*An improvement, but the store was so disorganized. Potatoes
didn't belong with buggy whips.*

*Isolda had a feeling that Jauld's ancestors must have run the
store more competently than this. She personally would never*

choose to shop here, not unless it was the only store in town. "What would you say to my doing a little work on the place? A little cleaning, a little organizing." The building was in passable shape, and its location on the main road was exceptional. Jauld's General Store sat roughly equidistant between the bustling city of Tinto and the growing port town of Cus. Jauld stocked farm goods, city goods, and port goods, and sold them to all three markets, as well as to travelers passing through.

Jauld stepped forward, took her gently around the waist, and kissed her.

Tentatively, she kissed him back. She was still getting used to this sort of thing. Last night they'd consummated their marriage, and while Jauld had been gentle, Isolda had found the experience painful and not as pleasurable as she'd expected. Perhaps it would get easier and more enjoyable over time.

"I was thinking you could run the counter," he said. "I'll handle stocking and inventory."

"What about the bookkeeping?"

"Do you read and write?"

She nodded.

"Then you can do it, if you like." He shrugged.

His indifference made her wonder if anyone was currently managing the books. No matter; she would do it from now on. She was familiar with bookkeeping from her father's apothecary. "I've got some ideas for organizing the place a little better. Do you mind if I move a few things around?"

"Suit yourself," said Jauld.

Isolda put herself to work.

5

Isolda woke in a soft bed, which right away told her something was wrong. Since her arrival in Kjall, comfort was no longer a part of her life. Gritting her teeth in apprehension, she opened her eyes. Light and fresh air poured in through tall, glassless windows on both sides of the room. She was in a bedroom, but she did not appear to be a prisoner. The double doors to the room were open, and she could see into the rest of the villa beyond. It was clean and spacious, though sparsely furnished. Where was she, some rich Kjallan's home?

She folded back the blankets and tried to pull herself into a sitting position. It was harder than she thought it would be, and she almost fainted as the blood rushed to her head.

A young man hurried in from around the corner. "*Na jeketh,*" he said in Kjallan and pushed her gently downward on the bed.

The gesture was clear enough; he wanted her to lie where she was. Was she a prisoner after all? Had she been assaulted?

She didn't think so. She wasn't in fetters, and she wasn't in pain, and those windows with no glass offered an easy escape route. How had she come here? She had a vague notion that something bad had happened. No, worse than bad—something terrible. She couldn't remember what it was, but nothing about this man was helping her remember.

Where was Rory?

Oh, gods. *Rory.* She struggled upward.

"*Tey. Na jeketh,*" said the young man, pushing her gently back down.

He was Kjallan, of course—she could hardly fail to notice the dark hair and strong features that were characteristic of his people. His blue eyes were less typical. Masculine beauty had a way of transcending detail. Coloration and minor features such as the shape of one's chin were accents, artistic touches painted by playful gods upon a scaffolding of the ideal human form, and this man, with his strong, firm body, possessed that form in full measure.

He wore a soft tunic and breeches rather than the syrtos most Kjallans wore. Perhaps he was a servant. He was smiling, and he had kind eyes. But she had no idea why she was here, and why he wanted her to stay in bed. And given the way most Kjallans treated her, she was wary.

"Where is Rory?" she asked, hoping he knew at least a few words of Sardossian. She'd been three months in Riat, but had spent most of it in hiding, among her own people. She wanted to learn Kjallan, but it was dangerous to mingle, and so far she possessed only a handful of words.

He looked at her blankly. Then he turned and called, "*Drusus.*"

Another man appeared from the next room, older than the first. This man wore a syrtos, so perhaps he was the master of the house. He spoke from the doorway in heavily accented Sardossian. "Do you understand me, miss?"

It came as such a surprise, the Sardossian words coming from Kjallan lips, that at first she just blinked and stared. But then she stammered, "Yes. Where is my son, Rory?"

"We have not seen him." Drusus turned and rattled off some incomprehensible Kjallan to the younger man. The younger man spoke back, at length.

Isolda's heart beat faster. Why was she in this Kjallan villa, and where had she left Rory? Could her boy still be with Emari? She would have left him with Emari before going to work. If he was still with her, he would be safe. But how long ago had she left him? And how had she ended up here?

The bigger man spoke, interrupting her thoughts. "My name is Drusus, and this is Marius. He doesn't speak your language, but he wants to know how you're feeling."

Marius spoke in Kjallan again and pointed at Isolda's right side.

She pulled the blankets closer. How long had she been here, and how much of her body had these men seen? "What do you mean, how I'm feeling?"

"Marius helped you after the explosion. Do you not remember?" said Drusus.

The explosion, gods above. The memories bowled her over like a rogue wave. The blast—she'd been standing at the mill when it happened. The force of it had flung her twenty feet. Then there had been the fire, and the screams of her friends and co-workers. She'd seen Tamlyn swallowed up by the flames. And the *sound*, gods, the sound. First an ear-shattering boom, and then *nothing*, nothing but silence for the horrors that followed.

She trembled.

Then there were hands on her, and the men were speaking in Kjallan. She heard urgency in their words, but saw only fire.

"*Tey, tey*," Marius was saying. He pressed a glass of something to her lips.

She shook her head, and the fire was gone. She took a sip from the glass and tasted bitterness. She spat it out. Was that willow bark? She couldn't drink willow bark; it upset her stomach.

Marius said something in Kjallan.

Drusus translated. "He says it tastes bad, but you need to drink it. It's medicine that will quiet your mind and body."

Isolda looked curiously at Marius. Was she in the care of an apothecary? Perhaps she had mistaken the relationship between the two men; it seemed that Marius, the one in peasant clothes, was in charge, and the slightly bigger man in the syrtos was assisting him. She set the glass on a table next to the bed. Marius protested, but she spoke over him. "How long have I been here?"

"Overnight," said Drusus. "The explosion was yesterday. You were badly burned along your right side. Marius found you and brought you to a Healer. Your burns have been healed, but you were in shock, and you need to rest for a while."

Isolda let her breath out in relief. These were unusually kind and accepting Kjallans. If she'd been gone just overnight, Rory should be fine. Emari would have heard about the explosion and kept him with her, and Caz would look in on them both. The problem wasn't that Rory wasn't being looked after; it was that Rory and Emari might think she'd been killed by the blast. "I can't stay. I have to go home to my son. He doesn't know where I am."

Drusus turned to Marius, and they had a rapid-fire conversation in Kjallan.

Isolda examined herself beneath the blanket. She'd been burned along her right side? The Healer must have been very skilled, because she could see no sign of injury at all. The skin was smooth and clean. In fact—gods, how could she be *clean*? After the explosion, she would have been covered in soot and filth. Somebody must have bathed her, perhaps these two men. Her cheeks flamed at the thought of that handsome young apothecary, and maybe Drusus as well, handling her naked body.

But she didn't think she'd been taken advantage of. These men seemed kind. Her heart twisted at the thought. Kind men such as this Marius would give her charity, because it was in their nature to do so, but not friendship. Not respect.

Once again she tried to sit up, but her limbs shook.

Marius scolded her. She may not have known the words, but his tone needed no translation.

"He says you can't get up yet," said Drusus. "Your body needs to recover its strength."

She fell back to the pillow, exhausted. Perhaps she couldn't return to Rory right away. Emari would take good care of him— she'd have to pay the girl extra, which would be painful because her Kjallan funds were limited and her Sardossian funds worthless since the war. Oh gods, now that the factory was blown up, she didn't have a job anymore! Her goal of getting Rory a proper education was dwindling away.

"Marius says we can get word to your family," said Drusus. "They can come here and fetch you."

Isolda brightened. If Rory came here, that would solve the problem of his worrying about her, and of having to pay Emari extra. Except. . .*no*. She could not send these Kjallans into the places where her people hid; it was far too dangerous.

Could this kindness toward her be a ruse, a means of finding her people and abusing them, or sending them back to Sardos? Marius's face was so open and honest. She didn't want to believe he was a villain, but she knew she was too trusting. She'd been fooled before. Lowering her gaze, she said, "I can't do that."

"He's not going to call the guards on you," said Drusus, "if that's what you're thinking."

She couldn't take the risk. Rory would have to worry for a day or two, as long as it took her to get her strength back. His life was not easy in Riat, and neither was hers, but both of them were better off here than in Sardos.

Marius spoke again, pointing at the willow bark tincture she'd set aside.

"He says you need to be a good girl and take your medicine," said Drusus.

Isolda laughed. A good girl. She'd tried that before, and it had brought her nothing but grief. "Is that willow bark?"

He blinked at her. "I'm sorry, I don't know those Sardossian words."

Marius asked him something, and they had a conversation in Kjallan.

She wished she could talk to Marius directly. He was the apothecary and would know what willow bark was. What role Drusus played, besides translator, she could not tell. "May I have some paper and a quill?"

"It won't help to write it down," said Drusus. "I can't read it any better than I can hear it."

"I want to draw you a picture."

Drusus and Marius spoke again. Then Drusus left and returned with several sheets of paper, an inkpot, and a quill.

Isolda drew a willow tree. She was no artist, but the willow, with its drooping branches, was easy to draw.

Marius leaned in to watch, and as her second set of inked branches reached the ground, he spoke excitedly in Kjallan. "*Salcius, salcius.*" He pointed first at the tree she'd drawn and then at the glass of medicine he'd given her.

She grinned and repeated the foreign word. "*Salcius?*"

He nodded. "*Salcius.*"

"Willow bark," she said in Sardossian.

"Willow bark," he repeated.

She picked up her quill and began to draw again. Marius leaned in farther this time, resting some of his weight on the bed, which drew her toward him. Isolda didn't mind. She rarely had the opportunity to be near such a handsome man, and he seemed kind as well, a rare combination. He couldn't help it that he was Kjallan. Now she sketched the vervain plant, not bothering with shading or any attempt at realism, but trying simply to capture the distinctive pattern of its leaves and branching flowers.

Marius peered at the paper. Then he tapped it with a finger. "*Verbena.*"

"Vervain." She drew a slash mark through the willow tree. Then she pointed at the vervain plant and at herself.

He nodded. "*Verbena.*" Then he rose and left the room. When he returned, he was carrying a new glass. "Vervain," he said, and handed it to her.

She sipped. Marius had gotten it right. The new drink was indeed vervain. She grinned and raised the glass, as if toasting him.

He grinned back.

She drained the glass, taking her medicine like a good girl.

Marius was fascinated by the Sardossian woman lying in his bed. And it gave him satisfaction to have a patient to look after, one who was within his limited capabilities to restore to health. All she needed was rest, sustenance, and a little kindness, which he suspected these Sardossian "sewer rats" seldom received.

Drusus had managed to get her name: Isolda. But though she was outgoing and friendly, she resisted all inquiries into her personal life. He understood her reasons. She was not a legal citizen, and she feared being harassed or abused or sent back to Sardos. But that aroused his curiosity most of all. What would drive a woman to come all this way, to a country in which she had no connections and didn't even speak the language, to live as a "sewer rat" and have trash thrown at her by his less tolerant countrymen, to have to hide and to take dangerous jobs like the one she'd held at the gunpowder factory?

She wouldn't talk about that either.

It occurred to him that he'd happened upon one of the few people in Riat who felt more out of place here than he did.

But she *would* talk about plants and herbs, and for that he didn't need Drusus to translate. He'd left his bodyguard slouched in a chair, lost in a treatise by Cinna, while he sat at Isolda's bedside, taking turns with her at sketching plants and naming them. He was getting a rapid education in the Sardossian language, at least this limited piece of it, and he was teaching her a few words of Kjallan in return.

Isolda's yellow hair was tied back from her face in a simple plait—he and Drusus had washed it while she was unconscious—and she wore no face paint at all. He didn't mind; he was used to that from Osler. In fact, the highly decorated women of Riat, especially at the palace, struck him as gaudy and artificial. But intrigued as he was by this Sardossian woman, he could not call her pretty, at least not in a traditional, knock-one-over-sideways sense. Her features were ordinary; some might call her plain. But when she smiled, her whole face lit up, and her eyes crinkled, kindling a warm glow in his chest. He would think it hard to make a woman smile when he did not speak her language, but with Isolda it was not hard. She smiled a lot.

He'd seen her naked, when he and Drusus had bathed her, but that had been business. He had not touched her in an inappropriate way, and he would not think about her in that way either. Much as it tempted him, he would not.

She was yawning. He glanced at Drusus. "Are we due at the palace soon?"

Drusus set down his treatise and nodded. "We ought to go now, in case the roads are as bad as they were yesterday."

Marius reached for Isolda.

She leaned back, alarmed, but he only touched her forehead to check for fever.

It was cool. He removed his hand. "Drusus and I have to go out for a while. You get some sleep. I'll leave food for you on the table, in case you get hungry."

Drusus translated the words into Sardossian and rose from his chair.

Marius took one last look at Isolda as she lay back in bed. Her head sank into the pillow, and she pulled the blanket up to her chin. He fixed the image in his mind, for what reason he did not know, and headed for the stable.

6

Marius preferred to ride up to the palace for his weekly visit with Lucien, even though the emperor had offered to send a carriage. This despite the fact that he was a terrible rider. Before coming to Riat, he'd never been on the back of a horse. He'd ridden a mule once, and it was an experience he did not care to repeat. But Lucien had insisted that he learn to ride. It was one of many skills Marius was receiving a rapid education in, along with reading, writing, mathematics, history, languages, and tumbling. That last was supposed to be swordplay, but so far there were no swords involved, just a lot of rolling and calisthenics and footwork.

Lucien had provided him with a quiet bay gelding named Gambler, who was now permanently stabled at the villa alongside Drusus's gray stallion. Gambler, despite his name, was predictable and steady. His best feature was that he had a habit of stopping and waiting patiently when Marius lost his balance.

Marius and Drusus rode side by side up the never-ending switchbacks to the imperial palace. The higher they ascended, the more Marius's stomach twisted. It wasn't that he didn't like Lucien and Vitala. He liked them a lot, and he appreciated the generosity they'd shown him. It was clear that they went out of their way to make him feel comfortable. No, it was the palace environment that bothered him. When he'd first arrived, Lucien had expected him to live within the palace, in a sort of suite, with servants at his beck and call. Apparently his sister Rhianne had grown up in such a suite, as had Lucien himself.

Marius had not lasted three days. He'd grown claustrophobic and stir-crazy. He simply could not feel at home amongst the berobed and bejeweled imperial courtiers. The servants made him nervous. He missed the simple comforts of village streets and small-town life.

But he still wanted the education Lucien had promised him. So he and the emperor had made a compromise: Marius would try living in the imperial city of Riat. The emperor purchased him a villa in a quiet part of town—at least, Lucien said it was quiet. Marius found it ten times more crowded, bustling, and noisy than what he was used to. Lucien also provided him with a bodyguard, and Marius took residence, with none of his neighbors the wiser that they shared a street with a cousin of the emperor. Riat was a big city, nothing at all like rural Osler, but Marius found he was better able to adapt to that environment than to the palace. And his parents had settled in Riat as well, at a comfortable but not too-comfortable distance of three miles across town.

When he and Drusus arrived at the palace gates, the horses were whisked away by grooms to be cooled out and rubbed down. Marius changed into his finery, since it would not do to appear before the emperor in a tunic and breeches, and they were escorted to the imperial gardens. There, the emperor and empress were waiting beneath an orange tree. A table had been carried out into the garden and a feast of fruits and cakes and sandwiches awaited them. It was more food than Marius could eat in a week.

Drusus saluted the imperial couple. Marius remembered his training and bowed in the way he'd been taught.

Then Vitala hugged him and Lucien clasped his wrist.

"We were worried about you," said Vitala. "That explosion in town."

"It was over a mile from the villa," said Marius.

"Too close for comfort," said Lucien. He gestured at the table. "Fill your plate and have a seat. I thought you might find the garden more comfortable than the palace."

Marius did, in fact. This little picnic reminded him of the dozens of similar outdoor gatherings he'd been to in Osler— weddings, summer festivals, reconciliations, the Triferian. But the food was fancier and the surroundings more opulent. The company was stiffer too, although perhaps that was an unfair assessment. He was the one who stiffened up when he was at the palace, not Lucien or Vitala, or even Drusus.

Imperial food was a challenge for him. It tended to be highly spiced, with unusual flavors, and he preferred simpler fare. He picked out some of the plainer items: a mushroom tart, a couple of sandwiches, and a raspberry-flavored dessert. Raspberries were one of the few novel foods he'd been able to acquire a taste for since leaving Osler.

Lucien placed an apple tart on his own plate. "Did you know that for years I didn't use this garden at all?"

"Why not?" Marius took his seat.

"Unpleasant memories," said Lucien. "Of my father—your uncle, who practically lived out here. But over the years, I've gotten past that. There's no need to blame the garden for the things Florian did, and it's a wonderful place, don't you think?"

"Indeed," said Marius.

Lucien sat across from Marius, and Vitala took the spot next to Lucien. "How do your studies go?" asked Lucien.

Marius shrugged. "Well enough." He didn't like talking about his schooling; it was embarrassing to be so far behind others of his age. He took a bite of mushroom tart. It had a strange spice in its filling, and he wasn't sure he liked it. "Do you know what caused that explosion at the harbor?"

Vitala answered. "I've got people looking into it. We feared it might be an act of sabotage, but so far we're finding no signs of that. I believe it was a simple accident."

"A common occurrence with gunpowder plants," added Lucien.

Vitala nodded. "This is why we have regulations regarding the gunpowder trade. You can't use metal shovels in gunpowder factories, only wooden ones, because metal ones might throw a spark. No boots with iron nails, no shod horses in the vicinity—"

"And even those regulations can't eliminate the risks entirely," said Lucien. "So the most important regulation is that gunpowder factories must be located well outside of town, away from population centers like Riat. That limits the damage they can do if there's an accident."

Marius nodded. "So Drusus told me."

"He's well-read, your bodyguard," said Lucien. "The factory that exploded was illegal and in violation of regulations, but so far we don't think they intended to cause trouble. They just wanted to make cheap gunpowder. Mind you, I'll still arrest the lot of them if I find them."

Marius recalled the injured Sardossians who had shown their heels when the city guards turned up. And Isolda, sketching herbs in his bed and smiling. Time for a change in subject. "How's Laelia?"

Vitala grinned. "Talk about explosive. That girl is a pyrotechnic show in the battle room."

His sister Laelia had taken to palace life more easily than Marius had. It wasn't that she liked fancy food and fancy dresses—as far as he could tell, she was indifferent to them—but that she didn't care what people thought of her. She saw the palace as a playground for her amusement. She'd enlisted Vitala and others to train her as a war mage.

Lucien sighed. "It's supposed to be the *boys* who are war mages. The girls are supposed to be mind mages."

"I want to be a Healer," said Marius.

"And so you shall," said Lucien. "Far be it from me to hew to tradition when your mother has already broken with it so dramatically. But I do wonder sometimes what will become of us."

Marius said nothing. He doubted his becoming a Healer and his sister becoming a war mage would affect the imperial family in any way at all. They were side branches in the family tree, minimally involved in politics and palace life. Which was fine with him. He and Laelia were too uneducated and ignorant to be involved in political decisions. As far as Marius could tell,

Lucien valued his presence simply because he loved family. Marius was something like fifth in the line of imperial succession, a fact that terrified him. But when Lucien died—an event that should be far in the future, since the emperor was young and healthy—the throne would almost certainly pass to one of Lucien's two sons, and both of them were being trained traditionally as war mages.

Vitala laid her hand over the emperor's. "Change isn't always a bad thing, you know."

The emperor looked into her eyes, suddenly moony, and Marius turned his attention to his mushroom tart.

After giving them a moment, he asked, "Why are there so many Sardossian refugees in Riat?"

"It's a sad situation," said Vitala.

"Eleven months ago, the First Heir of Sardos was assassinated," said Lucien, "and his loss has left a power vacuum in that country."

"Understand that the First Heir is actually the leader of Sardos," said Vitala. "First Heir is just the title they use, implying that he is heir to the gods. His power is equivalent to Lucien's."

"Did he leave no successor?"

"He left hundreds of them, sired on dozens of wives," said Lucien. "Sardos is polygynous, and because he feared a plot against his life, he never specified which son should be his heir. But the assassination happened anyway, and, as you might expect, half a dozen of those potential First Heirs are laying claim to the throne. The families are choosing sides, and there's civil war."

Now Marius understood. "And the people who want no part of that war are fleeing over the border."

"Exactly," said Lucien. "But Kjall hasn't the resources to take them in. These refugees don't speak the language, many of them have no skills, and we simply can't accommodate them."

Marius frowned. Isolda didn't know the language, but he wouldn't say she had no skills. She'd drawn a perfect vervain plant and known its purpose. He would bet she'd been an herbalist or apothecary in her former life. And he couldn't blame her for not wanting to participate in a civil war to decide which of six half-brothers held the Sardossian throne. He wouldn't want any part of that either. "Could we do something to help them? Find work for them, get them warded? They could learn the language."

Lucien's eyes went soft.

Marius tensed. "Did I say something wrong?"

"Not at all," said Lucien. "It's just that you remind me so much of Rhianne. I understand your desire to help the Sardossian refugees, but I've got Kjallans out of work, lots of them. How can I offer jobs to Sardossians when my own people need help? As for warding them, I'm all for it, but good luck getting them to come out from their hiding places."

"They don't come out because when they do, you ship them back home," said Marius.

"I wish we could do more for them," said Vitala. "But Kjall has to solve Kjall's problems. And Sardos needs to solve Sardos's problems."

"If the Sardossians are here, they've *become* Kjall's problem," said Marius.

"Kjall has enough problems as it is," said Lucien.

Later, as they made their way back down the hill on horseback, Drusus said, "You've been thinking a lot about that Sardossian woman."

"Yes," said Marius. "Not just her, but all of the Sardossians. Can you imagine? They came all this way to live in a city where people call them sewer rats or piss-heads and throw things at them, sometimes beat them up in alleyways, or worse." Last month, two Sardossian women had been raped and murdered. Their broken bodies had been hung from a street glow just five blocks from his villa.

"We can only assume conditions are worse in Sardos."

Marius nodded. "They must be." It was hard to imagine.

And yet the Sardossians were not entirely without guilt, not if they were working in illegal gunpowder factories that, in one case, had exploded and killed innocent bystanders. The regulations Lucien and Vitala had explained to him made sense; they prevented accidents and kept people safe. But what else could the Sardossians do? Legal jobs weren't available to them, and it was dangerous for them even to be seen in some parts of the city. He wished there was something he could do to help them. Perhaps if he earned Isolda's trust while she was staying with him, he could talk to her about the problems and learn more about what her people needed.

But when Marius and Drusus returned to the villa, Isolda was gone. The bed was neatly made, and the dishes she'd used had been washed. On the table was a note. It was written in Sardossian, and Drusus read it to him. It said, simply, "Thank you."

PART TWO

Four Years Later

7

Marius was measuring out powdered trigonella for his last patient of the day when the bell rang. He growled in frustration. So many people didn't bother reading the surgery's posted hours, or at least didn't want to believe them. There were all-night facilities available in Riat, but his was not one of them. "Drusus, if it's not an emergency—"

"I'll handle it." Drusus headed for the waiting room.

Marius scraped the measured amount into a bag and tied it neatly at the top. He'd thought his apothecary skills would become obsolete once he'd soulcasted and gained his healing magic, but he'd been wrong. There were some conditions, chronic ones especially, for which his healing magic could only help a little in the short term. In those cases, medicine sometimes extended the duration of his influence. As the only man in Riat who was both a licensed Healer and a licensed apothecary, he'd found himself popular since opening his surgery and dispensary. Too popular, sometimes.

He went from the dispensary back to his office and handed the trigonella to the aged man sitting on the cot. "The best way to make that cough go away would be to stop breathing so much sawdust."

The man nodded listlessly.

Marius sighed. He understood; it was the man's job. He was seeing a lot of this in Riat, more than he ever saw in Osler. Lungs damaged by breathing things that weren't air, vision stunted by work underground, joints broken down by overwork—not excessive amounts of work, necessarily, but *repetitive* work, the same thing over and over with no variation. His healing magic was powerful, but it worked best against infectious diseases, rarely seen anymore because of near-universal warding in the big cities, and acute injuries such as cuts and broken bones. Chronic damage was less responsive. His magic could improve this man's lungs a little bit, but healing magic worked by calling the flesh back to its natural, healthy state, and for that to happen, the flesh had to *remember*. When it had been damaged little by little, over the course of years, it ceased to remember its natural state. The abnormal had become normal.

Marius gave the man an encouraging pat on the shoulder. "Avoid sawdust if you possibly can, and sprinkle this on your food in the evenings. It will help."

As his patient left through the waiting room door, Drusus came back in, grinning.

"Not an emergency?" said Marius.

"It's Lady Fabiola."

"Oh, gods," groaned Marius. Lady Fabiola was the pregnant wife of a prominent local merchant who was away on business. In her husband's absence, the lady had taken an interest in Marius, and he couldn't imagine why. He lacked sophistication and dressed unfashionably, yet she would not leave him alone.

"I think she wants you to examine her again."

"She doesn't need—I mean, she's not—" Marius sputtered.

Drusus's grin widened. "What's the harm? Can't get her pregnant *now*, can you?"

Marius could feel the heat radiating from his face. "Send her away."

"As you wish," said Drusus, disappearing again into the waiting room.

Marius let out his breath. The depravity of the imperial city— he would never get used to it. He waited in his office until the bell rang, indicating the door had opened and Drusus was escorting Lady Fabiola out. Only then did he feel himself relax. When he'd soulcasted five months ago and become a licensed Healer, Lucien had purchased, on his behalf, the building adjacent to his home villa. That meant he needed only to walk next door to go home.

He touched the light glows in his office to deactivate them and headed out into the waiting room.

Where he was surprised to find Lady Fabiola standing in the middle of the room, in all her pregnant glory, while Drusus was at the door speaking to a second woman. The woman at the door held a sizable child of eight or nine years old who appeared unconscious. Did Marius have an emergency to deal with after all?

"Drusus, help the woman with her boy," he ordered.

Drusus took the child, and Marius got his first clear view of the woman's face.

It was Isolda. The Sardossian woman he'd helped four years ago, who'd left his villa and whom he hadn't seen since. She looked almost the same as before, except that her hair was loose and considerably lighter, no doubt an effect of the Kjallan sun.

His breath hitched, and his mouth went dry as he stared. He had never expected to see her again. Finally he found his voice. "Isolda."

"Marius," she answered.

She didn't sound surprised. But of course she wouldn't be; she'd come to him for a reason. Could the sick child be Rory, the boy she'd mentioned before?

"He is sick," said Isolda.

"I see that," said Marius.

Wait. Had she just spoken those words in the Kjallan language? Last he'd seen her, she'd only spoken Sardossian.

"Marius." Lady Fabiola rose to her feet and strode across the room, graceful despite her six-months-pregnant form. "I've been waiting. Surely you're not going to let that piss-head in here with her flea-ridden brat."

Marius shot her a look of irritation. "I see a woman whose child needs help. Are you bleeding at all?"

She feigned shock at his words.

"Are you bleeding?" he repeated.

Lady Fabiola shook her head.

"Then go home," he said. "If you're having problems tomorrow, come back then." Not that he was looking forward to having to brush her off again, but he'd have to look her over and make absolutely certain there wasn't a problem he was overlooking. For now, the child.

He leapt forward to open the waiting room door. Drusus brought the boy into his office and laid him on the cot. Marius reactivated the light glows to brighten the room. The windows were open, but dusk was falling, and the boy looked pale. Marius wanted all light available to him for this examination.

"Is this your son?" he asked Isolda. "Rory?"

"You remember," she murmured.

He had known her for only a couple of days, yet he remembered her well. For months afterward, he'd looked for her in every street, every shop, every corner. But he had not seen her, and eventually he'd given up. She was a ghost, she and her fellow Sardossians.

The boy was hot all over, feverish. Infectious disease was so rare in Riat as to be almost nonexistent, and yet here it was. "Is he warded?"

Isolda did not answer.

"Is he warded?" demanded Marius.

"No," she said softly.

"I want you to leave the surgery and run three blocks south to Warder Nonian's. Tell him Marius wants him immediately."

Isolda nodded and ran out the door. At least she wasn't arguing.

"Sardossians," growled Drusus. "I have a feeling you're not getting paid for this one."

Drusus was probably right, but Marius didn't care. He would help Isolda's child for free, as he'd helped her after the gunpowder explosion. He would help her any time she came to his door.

As seriously ill as the boy appeared, most fevers were easy to treat, especially in the young. He'd rarely seen one in a person, but in the course of his education he'd treated many in unwarded animals to prepare him for occasions such as this, when warding failed. The boy had the same coloration as his mother, yellow hair and green eyes. Marius skinned off the boy's shirt and found him clammy with sweat. Thin, too, and not in a healthy way. Perhaps he could come up with an excuse to keep the boy here longer, maybe fatten him up a bit, and Isolda too. He couldn't see the state of her feeding when she was layered in clothing from head to toe, but he had a feeling that if the boy was underfed, she was too, and perhaps more so.

He also needed to find out where that fever had come from. Fever was not an illness in its own right, but a symptom of some other problem. Its cause was invariably an evil spirit, whether the spirit infested a dirty wound, or contaminated one's food, or simply lurked in the air, waiting to be breathed in by its next unsuspecting victim. But evil spirits didn't arise out of nowhere. They propagated from one host to another. The boy had caught it from someone, which meant that somewhere out there, somebody else in Riat was ill. Maybe lots of somebodies.

He laid hands upon the boy and called on his magic. At once, he felt the child's youthful body respond. It wanted to return to normal—it was strong and vigorous, underfed but still healthy, and it needed only to be called to its proper state. Sometimes with older bodies he had to cajole them a bit, to persuade them back to health, but with this child, it was as if his body only wanted permission.

The boy groaned a little and shifted on the cot. His fever would be dropping, and that meant his delirium would lift. Soon he would awaken.

Marius had an idea. "Drusus, can you get some of that sleeping draught?"

Drusus raised an eyebrow at him. He knew perfectly well this wasn't called for. Indeed, after sticking to Marius's side for all four years of his education, Drusus knew everything Marius did. It made him an ideal partner and assistant in the surgery, and in playing that role, Drusus now had cover for his real role, that of Marius's personal bodyguard. The downside was that Marius couldn't put anything past the man.

"Look how skinny he is," said Marius. "You know if I just cure the fever, Isolda will disappear with him and we'll never see them again."

"Who cares if we never see them again?"

"I'd rather get a good breakfast into him tomorrow. Into both of them." He didn't mention that he planned to come up with some excuse to keep them longer. If he could feed them for a week, so much the better. And he'd really like to find out where that fever had come from.

Drusus folded his arms.

"Go," said Marius. "That's an order."

Drusus sniffed, giving his opinion of this plan with his customary eloquence, and left to fetch the sleeping draught.

The boy coughed suddenly, and his eyes drifted open. He stared woozily at Marius. "Who're you?" he croaked.

"A Healer. Sit up." He helped the boy struggle upright. "What's your name?"

"Rory. Where am I?"

"At the surgery. You were sick." The boy was still weak and a little woozy; otherwise he might object more to Marius's hands on him. Marius was still applying his magic, testing here and there to see if there were any places in Rory's body where the sickness still lurked. But he couldn't find any. And the boy's skin wasn't hot anymore.

"Where's my mom?"

"She's run to get something. She'll be back."

Drusus arrived, wearing his disapproving look and carrying a cup of what looked like weak tea.

"Did you put sugar in it?" asked Marius.

Drusus shook his head.

Marius gestured, and Drusus, rolling his eyes, disappeared again.

"How are you feeling?" asked Marius.

Rory shrugged. "Cold."

Marius gave him back his shirt, and Rory put it on. Then Marius wrapped him in a blanket.

"What was I sick with?" asked Rory.

"A fever," said Marius. "Do you know anyone else who has a fever?"

Rory suddenly looked cagey, and shook his head.

Marius sighed inwardly. How old could this child be? He'd guess eight or nine, and already Rory knew not to say anything about his people. "It's important, so think about it. If I know who's sick, I can heal them."

"I didn't know I was sick."

Looking into those wide, green eyes, Marius could almost believe him.

Drusus returned, carrying the sugared sleeping draught. Marius took it from him and offered it to Rory. "Drink this. It's medicine."

Rory took it and drank. He made a face, but drained the cup. Marius almost felt guilty.

Isolda burst into the room with Warder Nonian on her tail. Her eyes lit on Rory, sitting up and looking alert, and her worried face sagged in relief. She sent a grateful smile in Marius's direction.

He remembered that smile well.

"You need an emergency warding?" asked Nonian.

"Yes, this boy. Also her." Marius pointed at Isolda.

"Actually," stammered Isolda, "we don't have our papers on hand."

Marius snorted. Of course they didn't have papers on hand. "Payment in coin," he told Nonian.

Isolda hung her head. "I don't have that either. But I could run into town—"

"I'll pay it," said Marius.

Nonian nodded his acceptance. "Standard wards?" His fingers were already moving over Rory.

"Yes." To the untrained eye, warding looked invisible. Fingers moved and nothing seemed to happen, yet in the spirit world, things of great importance happened. Marius had seen this for himself during his magic training, when he'd opened the Rift—or rather, it had been opened for him, by mages more experienced than he—and he'd looked into the spirit world. There he had seen the great unseen which lay beyond human perception. It was the world of the gods, and he would be awed by it to the end of his days.

Nonian turned to Isolda. "Shall I prevent conception?"

"Conception?" She seemed shocked by the question. "No. . .I mean. . .it doesn't matter."

"Are you married?" asked Nonian.

Marius fussed with Rory's blanket, trying to look busy as he listened keenly to this conversation.

She hesitated before replying. "No."

"If you are unmarried, I must prevent conception. That is the law." Nonian's fingers moved over Isolda.

Marius pulled a few quintetrals from his pocket to pay Nonian, and the Warder departed.

Rory yawned.

"How is he?" asked Isolda.

"Better," said Marius. "But his body has played host to an evil spirit, and he needs rest. He'll have to stay here overnight."

Anxiety clouded her eyes. "Here in the surgery?"

"The villa is more comfortable. I've got a spare room. You could stay with him."

The worry in her eyes did not abate, and he felt a little guilty for keeping her here unnecessarily. Why did it bother her to stay? Perhaps he could draw the reason out of her tomorrow. He felt that getting a good meal into these two, preferably several days' worth of good meals, and some rest as well, would do them a world of good. And for public health reasons, he'd like to find out where the fever had come from. But he doubted he could contrive to keep either of them much past breakfast, if his experience four years ago was any guide.

Poor Rory was trying to keep his eyes open, but his lids were drooping. His body swayed on the cot.

"Drusus," prompted Marius, and his bodyguard swept the boy into his arms. Marius opened the door for Isolda and gestured her through.

Isolda rested her chin on her hands as she watched Rory eat breakfast. Her son was packing his cheeks like a squirrel storing nuts. Then the food disappeared down his gullet, to be replaced by more. The boy was completely recovered from his fever. She had never seen such an astonishing turnabout in fortune, from unconscious and burning up last night, to hale and upright and stuffing his face with fish cakes this morning. The cook Marius employed could hardly fry them quickly enough, but whenever Isolda admonished Rory to stop eating so much, Marius intervened and informed her that after a fever like the one he'd had, Rory needed to eat as part of his treatment.

Isolda knew better.

She had known few kind Kjallans, but Marius was one of them, and he was kind to a fault. He'd seen Rory's thin body, and he meant to fatten him up. He was trying to do the same with her, shoving fish cakes in her direction—they were delicious, yes—but he could not employ the same excuse in her case. She had not been sick. And she knew this was charity.

She hated charity.

Marius had taken such scrupulous care of her four years ago, and she felt the debt. She had walked by his villa many a time since then, surreptitiously, and disregarding the very real danger—poor Tanla had been beaten half to death in this neighborhood last spring. But it gave her such a warm feeling in her breast to know that here lived a man who cared. Not about her specifically, but about people in general. And unlike many Kjallans, Marius thought of her and her fellow Sardossians as people rather than as sewer rats or piss-heads.

Because she had nothing of value to offer him, and she knew he was too decent a man to turn her away, she had resolved never again to come to his door. She was in his debt already, and to ask more would be to take advantage. She would not do that.

For years, she'd only been able to guess at the happenings in his life. Was he married? Did he have children? She saw no one except his man Drusus, who seemed to be a sort of high-class servant, but her visits were rare enough that she could easily have missed a wife.

She took notice when Marius bought the building next door and turned it into a surgery and dispensary. He'd become a licensed Healer! She could not think of a better profession for him. She'd felt vicariously proud of his accomplishment.

It was desperation that had, at last, driven her to his door. That fever, three gods. At supper Rory had been fine, a little less hungry than usual, but well enough. And then an hour later he'd been flat out on the floor and delirious, and she'd been afraid for his life. Nothing but Rory's welfare would have led her to seek charity a second time—or to risk being attacked or deported—but here she was.

Now he was fine, and stuffing his face with fish cakes she'd never be able to pay for. Isolda turned away, wiping her eyes.

"Are you all right?" Marius asked, reaching for her arm.

"Fine," she said, her voice shaking. "Just relieved."

"Never you worry," he said, giving her elbow a pat. "Fevers are dangerous but, in the right hands, easily cured. You were right to bring him here. I'd like to keep him here another day or two for safety's sake."

Isolda shook her head. "We cannot. He has to work today, and so do I."

"That fever could come back," warned Marius. "I need to keep an eye on him for a while."

"*Please* can I stay?" asked Rory, who'd just drained an entire glass of lemonade. Since Rory worked at a fruit stand where expensive fruits such as lemons were sold, she had an idea of how many quintetrals had just gone down his gullet.

"He eats and drinks too much," said Isolda.

"Not at all," said Marius. "It's important to eat and drink when you've had a fever. You should do the same. To protect yourself in case you've been exposed."

She shook her head. That was nonsense; as of last night, she'd been warded, so she couldn't catch Rory's fever. Perhaps she could leave Rory here for the day while she went to work, but the idea bothered her. Rory was a bottomless pit of need and Marius an overly generous giver. Someone needed to stand between the two of them.

Marius rested his chin in his hand, as if puzzled. "Would you like to help out in the surgery while he rests?"

Isolda considered. She could supervise Rory if she did that, but she'd miss out on a day's pay at the factory, and Rory's pay as well. She supposed she could afford that.

"I could pay you," added Marius.

Accept his charity *and* his money? Gods, no. But perha compromise. "I will help you in the surgery today to compensate for your treatment of Rory."

"There's no charge for Rory's treatment," said Marius. "But I accept."

8

Isolda hoped to be of use in the surgery to repay Marius for his kindness, but she soon realized that Marius needed little in the way of assistance. His first patient was a woman with stomach pain. He bade the woman lie on the cot, and he laid hands on her, presumably using his magic. Neither Isolda nor Drusus could be of any help. When Drusus offered to go to the dispensary to mix something up, Marius said he would do it, and he asked Isolda to go with him.

Once there, he asked her to hand him a stoppered vial.

She did so.

"How did you learn Kjallan?" he asked.

She shrugged. "I live in Kjall now, so I learned it."

"Forgive me for saying this, but my impression is that ⸱ people don't mingle much with my people. Therefore they always learn the language."

This felt accusatory, and she wasn't sure what he was getting at, or how she was expected to respond. But there was truth in his assessment, and since Marius was a kind man, she gave him the benefit of the doubt. "It is true. Some of my people choose not to learn Kjallan. Also, it can be dangerous for us to mix with Kjallans."

He measured liquid into the vial. "I know, and I'm sorry about that. But you chose to learn the language anyway?"

She considered. "I am here for. . .what is the word? Forever. A lifetime. So I learned the language. And of course Rory knows it. He learned it faster than I did."

"How old is Rory?"

"He turned eight this past winter."

"A bit young to be working." Marius tipped a bit of powder into the vial, capped it, and shook it gently.

"It is light work, arranging fruit on a stand and calling to customers." Naive man. What did this wealthy young Kjallan know of a life like hers? She did what she had to do, and so did Rory. "An education is expensive."

Marius's brows rose. "Rory is being educated?"

"Not yet, but if we save our money. . .riftstones are expensive, but perhaps a warder's stone might be within reach for Rory. He works hard."

Marius leaned against the wooden counter. "It warms my heart to hear you speak of your son's education. My mother never gave me an education despite it being within her means to do so."

"If not your mother, then who?" Isolda was perplexed. "You're a Healer, so somebody must have paid to educate you. You could not have paid your own way."

"You're right. Another family member stepped in," said Marius. "It's a complicated family situation, and I won't bore you with it. I don't mean to suggest that she didn't care about me, because she did. It's just that our situation was unusual."

"You're not boring me. How was your situation unusual?"

"Oh, in a variety of ways."

He did not elaborate, so there it was, the icy Kjallan reproof. She deflated, wishing he trusted her enough to tell her his story. Clearly it was an interesting one. Now that she thought about it, his education had come later in life than most. And he dressed oddly, eschewing the fashionable syrtos in favor of a simple tunic and breeches. She liked his simple clothes; they were similar to what she'd been accustomed to in Sardos. Still, she knew that in Kjall, fashionable men wore the syrtos and servants the tunic and breeches. Despite his choice of clothes, Marius appeared to be wealthy, at least wealthy enough to live in that nice villa.

"We'd better get back," said Marius, resting his hand on her shoulder as he passed.

The memory of his touch lingered.

As she followed him out of the dispensary, she realized that all she'd done in there was hand him a vial. Had he asked her to stay with him today because he truly wanted her help? Or did he just want to question her? It was starting to look like his true interest was in the latter, yet he would tell her little of himself. She sighed and settled into a chair.

Marius spoke to his patient, giving her the vial and some instructions for its use. She departed, looking much better, and the next patient came in, an adolescent boy with a lacerated foot.

This one Marius was able to heal without needing anything from the dispensary, and both Isolda and Drusus sat idle.

The boy was dismissed, and Isolda saw a look of dismay on Marius's face when the next patient entered the room. It was the pregnant woman who'd been in the waiting room last night. Drusus smiled and leaned back in his chair, clearly amused.

The first thing the woman did—after sending Isolda a dirty look—was open her dress and show Marius her breasts. She claimed to be worried about them, but it was plain to everyone that she merely wanted to show them off. They were glorious breasts, large to begin with and now darkened and engorged by pregnancy. Isolda was jealous of them; her own could not compare. But the display did not have the desired effect: Marius's eyes were drawn to them, but he became embarrassed, and when she would not cover herself up, Isolda could see his tightened jaw, and she knew that he was angry. He conducted a cursory examination, and then ended the appointment and sent her away.

After she'd gone, Drusus glanced into the waiting room, declared it empty, and said to Marius, "Why don't you just fuck her and have done with it?"

"I haven't the slightest interest in that woman, and I can't imagine why she thinks she wants me. She's *married*." His eyes fell on Isolda. "Three gods, Drusus, we're not alone here. Apologize to the lady for your crudeness of speech."

Drusus grinned. "I'm sure the lady's heard worse, since she's Sardossian. But I apologize."

"You wouldn't believe the things we hear," said Isolda. Drusus was right, but she appreciated Marius treating her as if she were quality. It had been a long time since anybody had.

9

Marius's aggravation began to fade as he entered the villa and saw that his cook, Aurora, had managed to keep Rory occupied in an admirable way. The boy was crimping pastry with the back end of a knife, his face furrowed in the intense, single-minded concentration typical of young children. He didn't even notice when they walked in.

"Rory's helping me make tarts," said Aurora.

"I hope he hasn't been any trouble," said Isolda.

"Oh, no, he's an excellent helper."

"Mom, I'm good at this," said Rory, adding a final crimp to his tart.

The room smelled heavenly. Marius looked to the windowsill and saw that an earlier batch of tarts had already been baked.

"Carrot and potato," said Aurora, pointing at the first row. "Chicken and mushroom. Apple. Careful, they're hot."

Marius offered Isolda first choice. When she hesitated, he realized that she was probably planning to eat sparingly out of some misplaced concern that she and her son were eating too much of his food. Therefore, he stepped in and loaded a plate for her, placing one of each variety of tart on it, and assembled identical plates for himself and Rory.

"I should warn you that I've had Aurora alter the recipe for these," said Marius. "I haven't a taste for most spices, so the flavor may be simpler than what you're used to."

"It sounds perfect," said Isolda. "I've never gotten used to all the spice in Kjallan foods."

Marius relaxed a little. He'd been criticized before for his lack of sophistication in his eating habits. It was nice to have a guest who didn't think less of him for preferring the simple, earthy flavors he'd grown up with in Osler.

He offered a plate to Rory, but Rory waved the food away, saying, "I'm busy." He was crimping another tart.

"Rory," scolded Isolda.

"Never mind," said Marius, ushering her out of the kitchen and into the dining room. "He can eat later."

Drusus joined them at the table, with five tarts piled on his plate. Since Lucien had assigned him a bodyguard, Marius had never been truly alone. But Drusus, at least, wouldn't stick his nose in the conversation. Aside from a little teasing where Lady Fabiola was concerned, Drusus minded his own business.

Lady Fabiola—what a shameful episode. Especially with Isolda right there in the room. "I'm sorry about that woman this morning."

Isolda shrugged. "I have seen worse."

"Have you?" Now he was curious. "Here, or in Sardos?"

She laughed. "Here, of course. Never in Sardos."

"Why do you say that? Do you impugn the morals of Kjallan women?" He smiled to make it clear that he was joking.

"Women and men are the same everywhere," said Isolda. "But given that woman's pregnant state, surely she is married. And in Sardos, adultery is punishable by death."

Marius's skin crawled. The death penalty felt extreme, even to his small-town soul. "You mean to tell me that a woman who does what Lady Fabiola was trying to do—"

"Woman *or* man," said Isolda.

"It's punishable by *death*?"

She nodded.

Marius shuddered. "Then I'm glad I don't live in Sardos. Not to insult your homeland, and it's not that I don't disapprove of adultery. It's just that I feel it should be a private matter rather than a matter of state."

"We're of the same mind," said Isolda. "Kjall is a freer country than Sardos, and I am grateful for that. Despite the dangers my people face here, in some ways we are actually safer. But adjusting has been hard. I see things in Riat that I never saw at home." She lowered her eyes.

Something about her manner kindled his concern. "Has someone harmed you?"

She shook her head. "I have been fortunate and managed to avoid most trouble."

"Are you sure?"

She nodded.

He suspected she was not being entirely truthful, but whatever she'd suffered, he'd have to earn her trust before she'd tell him about it. "If you've only been in Riat, you haven't seen the whole of Kjall. I come from a small town in the east, and even after a number of years here, I find people like Lady Fabiola to be a bit of a shock."

"Really?" She looked up at him. "I would have guessed you city born and bred."

"Then I must congratulate myself for blending in better than I thought."

"What small town are you from, and why did you come to Riat?"

Her curiosity put him in an awkward position. He couldn't answer that second question without divulging his imperial connections, and aside from not wanting unwanted attention from fortune hunters and influence seekers, he might scare her off if she knew how highly connected he was. "I grew up in Osler, and later I moved here to be closer to my extended family. Tell me, where is Rory's father? You said you were not married. But you must have been at one time."

"My husband is dead. Killed in the blood wars."

"I'm sorry." Poor woman—a war widow, far from home with no hope of returning, and burdened with a child. Not that Rory seemed a great burden. He was a charming, cooperative boy, and already accustomed to work, but it would be hard for her to marry into a stable family when she had a child already. His heart ached for her. What was a woman in her situation to do?

He feared that her dream of buying Rory a magical education was out of reach. She was right about a few things: the high-quality jasper needed by warders was commonly available and inexpensive compared to other riftstones. Warding magic was workmanlike, the least exciting form of magic, yet it was essential to civilized society. For this reason, the empire subsidized the training of new Warders.

But no Sardossian refugee would receive one of those subsidies. They were handed out as rewards to the children of war veterans, nobles, and public figures. And while the riftstone was not too dear, the education itself was the real expense. Rory would need, at minimum, six years of university or palaestra education before he could soulcast. Marius had done it in four, but only because Lucien had provided him with full-time, one-on-one tutoring.

Still, Marius couldn't bring himself to destroy Isolda's hopes. Even if she couldn't make a Warder out of Rory, she might improve his circumstances if she could buy him an apprenticeship in a high-skill trade. Perhaps he could be a baker—he seemed to enjoy making the tarts with Aurora.

He gestured at her plate. "Eat up. You're too thin—you and Rory both. You need your strength." He cut into his mushroom tart in case she felt uncomfortable eating without him. Drusus was setting a good example. He'd polished off two tarts already and was demolishing a third.

"These tarts are delicious," said Isolda. "Much like what I used to eat back in Sardos. Did you have a cook last time I was here?"

"I did, but she was off work that day."

"I was proud of you when you opened the surgery," she said.

Proud of him? He looked at her more keenly. "You knew when I opened the surgery?"

"Well. . ." She bit her lip. "I saw the sign."

Her eyes were a deep, sparkling green, like peridots. He wondered why he had not noticed them before. He couldn't decide which was her best feature, her eyes or her smile. "Do you miss home?"

She cocked her head. "You mean Sardos?"

Did she consider Riat to be home by now? He nodded. "Sardos."

"I miss some things about it."

He waited for her to elaborate. When she didn't, he added, "What's it like? I've never been there."

Isolda shrugged. "I am perhaps the wrong person to ask. While I was in Sardos, I lived in only two places, first my parents' home in the city of Tinto, and then my husband's home and general store twenty miles outside of Tinto. I never traveled far outside that small distance, so I only knew a tiny piece of Sardos. The country is vast."

"Tell me about the small piece that you knew."

"It's cooler than here," she said. "Hilly. Forested, outside of Tinto. We got more snow. Did you know I've seen snowfall only twice since coming to Riat?"

He nodded. "Riat is seldom cold enough for snow. The sea moderates our weather."

"It moderates the temperature," she said. "But that storm last year—I'd never seen anything like it."

"It was unusual even for Riat, so I was told." The damage had been extensive. Winds and rising seas had wrecked a dozen ships in the harbor that were thought to be safe from danger. Some of them were big, expensive warships, and Lucien had been distraught at their loss. But Marius didn't want to waste time talking about the weather, and he certainly didn't want to talk about Lucien. "Rory's a charming boy. You and he seem very close."

"Thank you." She smiled fondly. "He means everything to me."

"After losing your husband, I imagine he would."

She shrugged again.

An odd response. "Did you and your husband not get along?"

She looked away. "It was complicated."

He sensed old pain there, but curious as he was about its source, it would do him no good to prod at the wound. First he had to earn her trust. "You say your husband ran a general store. What sort of work did you do there?"

She brightened. "Everything. Ordering, stocking, cleaning, organizing, bookkeeping. Jauld—my husband—was good with the customers. He had a certain charm about him."

"It sounds like you miss the store."

"I loved almost everything about it."

"Not the bookkeeping, I imagine." He made a face.

"I *especially* loved the bookkeeping."

Drusus, who'd cleaned his plate and kept silent throughout the exchange, finally spoke. "Marius thinks bookkeeping is a dirty word."

"Bookkeeping is where the magic happens," said Isolda. "You don't know a thing about your store until you run the numbers. You may think you're making all your money on sales of spirits, but then you do the books and it turns out that your profits are really coming from sales of cloth, or raw cotton. And maybe you're *losing* money on the spirits because of transport fees."

"Or maybe you're losing money on everything," said Drusus.

"If business is truly bad," said Isolda, "But that won't happen to a Healer. Not one as skilled as Marius."

Marius said nothing. The surgery *was* losing money, and he was ashamed to admit it.

"You aren't losing money, are you?" Isolda asked him.

Reluctantly, Marius nodded.

"But that's terrible! Will the surgery have to close?"

Marius shook his head without offering an explanation. The truth was that Emperor Lucien quietly covered his losses.

"But you cannot run the surgery at a deficit!" said Isolda. "Will you let me look into it for you? I'd hate to see the surgery close after all the hard work you've done."

"You mean look at the books?" Not only would that reveal his total lack of business sense, but she would see the childish scrawl of his handwriting. He'd only learned to write a few years ago, and he still found it hard going.

"Well, yes, that would be the best way to go about it. If there are books to look at."

"There are," he said.

"Marius doesn't want you to see his handwriting," put in Drusus.

Marius glared at his bodyguard.

"Is that all?" said Isolda. "Poor handwriting won't bother me at all. You should have seen my husband's."

Perhaps he should just be honest. If he wasn't, Drusus would continue to blurt out inconvenient facts. "It's not the same thing. I received my education rather late in life, so my handwriting looks like a ten-year-old's."

"Well, as long as I can make it out. I wasn't educated at all, unless you count what my parents taught me."

Marius was getting the impression her parents had taught her a great deal, far more than his own had.

"It's readable," put in Drusus.

"Please, let me look into this for you," said Isolda. "I'd hate to see your wonderful surgery go out of business. There's a reason you're not making money. I'll find out what it is, and that can be my payment to you for the help you've given me and Rory."

"Very well," said Marius.

He extended his hand, and they clasped wrists.

10

Isolda was astounded by what she found when she delved into Marius's books. The good news was that Marius, unlike her husband, Jauld, kept reasonably complete records within the surgery's thick bound ledger, and his handwriting wasn't nearly as bad as he'd led her to believe. Here, in a windowless room in the back of the surgery, she'd found everything she needed to make sense of his business, and in better order than expected. His records indicated that he kept high-quality stock in the dispensary, stored it properly, and turned it over frequently. And she'd already seen that he kept his home and place of business clean.

Marius's problems were not remotely the same as she'd found in Jauld's store before the overhaul. Marius was neither lazy nor slovenly. He ought to be making piles of money, but he wasn't. The problem was shockingly simple: Marius was treating patients for free.

He wasn't being charitable—at least, his records indicated that wasn't his intent. Marius billed all his patients. But a significant number of them had not paid those bills, and Marius had not followed up with additional letters, nor had he employed a bill collector. Worse, he continued to see the delinquent patients, who piled on more and more charges, having decided that their healing and medications were free.

Marius was too nice.

She felt a little guilty coming to this conclusion, given that she was one of Marius's charity cases herself. But Marius had not billed her thus far, in fact had told her outright there would be no charge. And there was a difference between herself, a homeless Sardossian refugee who'd come to Marius in an emergency situation, and Lady Fabiola, an apparently wealthy Kjallan who'd accumulated over thirty visits for what seemed to be trivial complaints, and who had yet to offer a single quintetral in payment.

Isolda sighed. She'd diagnosed the problem easily enough, but the cure would be difficult. She was going to have to convince Marius to be less nice.

While she waited for him to finish with his patients, she put the books in order—an easy task, since they were not terribly disordered to begin with—and wrote up some lists that would help her make her case.

Around midafternoon, Marius burst into the back room. "Do you like parsnip soup, or would you prefer bacon and barley? Aurora's heading to market soon." He glanced at the paper she was writing on. "I'm sorry about my handwriting."

"You needn't be sorry about anything," said Isolda. "If your handwriting is like a ten-year-old's, the ten-year-old in question is the neatest and most precise I've ever known. I was able to make sense of the books straightaway."

"Did you find anything?" He scratched the back of his neck. "Not to rush you."

"I'm finished, actually," said Isolda. "Do you have some time? I could go over my findings with you."

He nodded and pulled up a chair. "I'm between patients. Though honestly, I'm not sure I want to know. You know what they say about ignorance."

"It's the most dangerous thing in the world?"

He snorted. "You must be a follower of the Sage."

"You'll want to hear what I found. I think with some simple changes you could make your surgery profitable." She pulled out his ledger, opened it, and showed him the expenses column. "First, something small but significant: I think you're paying too much for some of your medicines. I could be wrong, because this is Kjall and the prices I know are from Sardos, but I'm looking at them comparatively. Poppy should not cost three times what you're paying for myrrh."

"Poppy is imported," said Marius.

"So is myrrh. I'd wager you could find a better price on poppy from a different supplier."

"Very good. I'll look into it."

"There are a few others I think you're paying too much for," she said. "I cannot be sure, again because my experience was in Sardos, but I've marked them in the margins for you—see?"

He studied the ledger. "Interesting. Most of them are from the same vendor."

"Perhaps you ought not to do any more business with that vendor, at least not without renegotiating prices. But that's a minor issue. The real problem with the surgery's finances is something more damaging. You've got a large number of patients who aren't paying their bills."

Marius looked sheepish. "The truth is I'm not sure all of them are capable of paying."

Isolda chose her words carefully. "You are a kind man and a generous one. Certainly you have been exceedingly generous to me and Rory. But let me show you the list of your patients who have not paid their bills, and I think you'll be surprised by the names you see." She pulled out the list, which was multiple pages long, and held it out to him.

As Marius took the list, he blanched at its length. His eyes darted down the first page. "Why do some names appear multiple times?"

"Because they have multiple unpaid bills," said Isolda. "I wanted you to get an idea of the scale of the problem. As you can see, this fellow Ennius Antonius has been in to the surgery twenty times—"

"His arthritis," muttered Marius. "I had no idea he was a nonpayer."

"And there are others. This fellow has been in fifteen times, this woman and her children, eighteen."

Marius turned to the second page, and the third. He snorted. "Lady Fabiola must be in here twenty-five times, at least. And she's never paid me a quintetral?"

Isolda raised an eyebrow at him. Marius was getting angry. Good.

"But there's a problem. See this fellow?" Marius's finger stabbed a name on the second page. "He's a street sweeper and half crippled. I'm not sure at all that he can afford to pay me. I can get tough with Ennius and Lady Fabiola and some of these others. But I don't want to hurt this man."

"Then don't," said Isolda. "Forgive his bill and go after the others."

"Yes, but. . ." Marius gave a grunt of frustration. "Half the people on this list I don't know well enough to have a sense of their finances. I couldn't tell you what they can and can't afford—"

"It's not your business to know that," said Isolda. "If they come to a Healer, they should expect to pay."

"I know." Marius sighed. "But I want to help them. At least the ones who aren't trying to take advantage of me."

"Look at it this way," said Isolda. "If the surgery goes out of business, you can't help anybody."

"True," he said.

He seemed not to be concerned about the potential loss of his business, which was odd.

Marius paged through the list. "Thank you. This is extraordinarily helpful. In putting this together, you've more than repaid the cost of your boy's care. Now, would you like parsnip soup for dinner? It's one of my favorites, but I find most Kjallans like bacon and barley better."

Isolda shook her head. "Rory and I have imposed upon your hospitality long enough."

Marius winked at her. "Bacon and barley it is. Your boy's got to eat, or that fever may come back. I need to go back to my patients, but I'm off duty in two hours."

Isolda sighed as she watched him leave. Who knew that kindness could be a fault? The man was incorrigible. She hoped she had gotten through to him at least a little bit, but she couldn't stay here. She was not in the habit of accepting charity, and she and Rory had jobs to get back to.

Isolda swept the aisle one last time for good measure. Jauld's General Store was clean and bright and inviting. The shelves were freshly painted, all the sales items were neatly arranged, and she'd installed a new system of weights and measures behind the counter so they could sell bulk goods in smaller, more convenient quantities.

She'd been making changes little by little over the past several months, and sales had already tripled. Her next project would be to tackle suppliers. She'd looked at the books and was fairly certain she and Jauld were being overcharged in a few areas. Worse, the quality of the goods was substandard, and she wanted the reputation of her husband's store to inspire more trust. She'd talk Jauld into making a trip to Tinto with her and then one to Cus to search for better, more cost-effective suppliers.

She put the broom away, sank into a chair behind the counter, and placed a hand on her belly. No movement there yet, but soon there would be. She'd had no moon blood for two months, and she was nauseous all the time. The signs were unmistakable.

Jauld's eyes lit on her as he came in from the back room. "Feeling all right?"

"Fine," she said, offering him a shy smile.

"You've done a wonderful job brightening this place up." He laid a hand on her shoulder.

She placed her hand on his, hoping the gesture would inspire some warm feelings. She was struggling to love her husband. He wasn't a bad man, but he was lazy. Isolda, after helping her father in his apothecary for years, had become accustomed to certain practices that she regarded as normal: cleaning and organizing, turning over stock regularly so that it stayed fresh, inspecting supplies for quality, keeping the books up-to-date. It had not occurred to her that another shop owner might not consider these things important. Jauld ran his shop in a scattershot fashion, occasionally doing a bit of work to improve things, but mostly he was just idle. She did all the work.

It wasn't all bad, though. She liked the work, and business was excellent. A good thing, now that she had a baby on the way. And Jauld was kind, at least. Her mother had warned her not to expect much from her marriage, and Isolda allowed that she could have done worse.

The bell rang, and three men entered the shop. They were rough-looking fellows in patched-up work clothes—unmarried farmers or lumberjacks, perhaps. Isolda tensed at the sight of them. Since wealthy men monopolized most of the marriageable women in Sardos, Sardossian men who lacked inherited assets generally could not afford to marry. These so-called strays had little to lose and were inclined toward violence. Isolda had been cautioned all her life to be wary of them.

"Jauld," called one of the men, and Isolda relaxed a little. It appeared these were friends.

"Rosche, Essim, Dane. How can I help you?" Jauld's gait was stiff as he moved to greet them.

His body language suggested some tension in the relationship. Isolda sat perfectly still behind the counter. Like *most plain women, she had acquired the ability, through practice, of being as close to invisible as one could possibly be.*

"We heard you got married," said Rosche. "Where's the poor girl who got stuck with a horse's ass like you?"

"Least I can afford a wife," said Jauld, positioning his body so that he blocked her from their view. "Unlike you hedge-born scuts."

"She got three tits or something?" asked Rosche.

"Hey, I see her," said one of the others, leaning sideways so he could see around Jauld. "She's behind the counter." He looked her over and laughed. "I see why you could afford her, Jauld—the parents must have given you the deal of a lifetime."

A trickle of hot shame crept up Isolda's neck. Bad enough these men should humiliate her for her looks, something she could not control. But they were doing it in front of her husband, with whom she had a new and fragile relationship, and that terrified her. She was accustomed to this sort of treatment— didn't like it, had learned to tolerate it. But for Jauld, this experience would be new.

"I paid a pretty bit of coin for her," said Jauld.

"Sure you did," said Rosche. "One coin."

The others laughed.

"The store's looking nicer," said one of the men. "Maybe you needed a little money to fix the place up, and they needed to get this ugly bitch off their hands—"

"You're not funny," growled Jauld. "Get out."

"Three gods, man, if you can't take a joke—"

Jauld advanced on them, his chest swelling. "I said get out!"

The strays fled the store, leaving Jauld and Isolda alone.

Isolda watched her husband closely. She was proud and relieved that he'd defended her, but also worried. How might he react to being humiliated on her behalf? She fought the tears that threatened to well forth, knowing she could not afford to fall apart now. Jauld might lack the strength or even the desire to comfort her. She wished he would run to her, hold her, tell her he loved her, tell her he thought her beautiful no matter what his friends said. But he did not.

She let out a shaky breath. She had to be sensible about this. Jauld didn't love her, and he certainly didn't think her beautiful. He had settled *for her. She was the best he could afford, and the men's accusations, though exaggerated and cruel, were in their essence true. Because she was plain, she had been an inexpensive bride.*

Even so, his friends were jealous. She wished she could tell Jauld that without offending him. They lashed out at Jauld for his plain bride because they had no bride at all, nor any prospects of ever having one. But she was afraid to speak to Jauld right now. He wasn't looking at her. He was looking at the door. His sides were heaving, and his face was red.

She rose from her chair and said softly, "I'll go in the back and unpack those crates."

"What?" He whipped around as if startled.

"I said I'll go unpack those crates."

He did not respond, but gave her a cold look and strode out the door. At least he had not struck her, but Jauld's cool treatment stung more than any slap across the face.

11

The carriage came for Marius the next day, just before lunch. Not the official imperial carriage, but Lucien had sent it nonetheless, and it was fancy enough to make him uncomfortable and perhaps to make the neighbors wonder. Marius climbed inside and flopped onto the seat. Lucien wouldn't let him ride Gambler to the palace today, since Marius's sister Rhianne was visiting Kjall accompanied by an entourage of Mosari nobles. As Lucien had said, "There will be dancing, and you don't want to smell like a horse."

"Cheer up," said Drusus, nudging him with an elbow. "We're going to a party, not a funeral."

He'd lost Isolda again. After he thought he'd reeled her in with his invitation to supper—he'd thought himself *so* clever with that wink and making the soup decision for her when she refused to make it herself—she'd taken Rory and absconded yet again. He had no idea where she'd gone, and no notion of how to find her. Unless she or Rory became desperately ill, he'd probably never see her again.

Why did it bother him so much that she was gone? He shouldn't be so interested in her. She was not young, rich, educated, connected, or even beautiful, yet there was something about her that fascinated him. Perhaps it was just that he felt comfortable in her presence, that he could be himself instead of pretending to be some fashionable, social-climbing scion of the empire. She'd praised his handwriting. She liked his food. She hadn't aimed any dirty looks at his tunic and breeches.

Gods rot it, why should he even care what someone's social class was? Five years ago, he'd been an uneducated journeyman apothecary in an obscure rural village. Only an accident of birth had catapulted him into the emperor's inner circle. This idea of *station*, of *class*, of one person being inherently better than another—it was an illusion. He knew that better than anyone.

When the carriage arrived at the palace, he went to the room Lucien kept reserved for him, where he changed out of his tunic and breeches into a silk syrtos. From there, he headed to the Cerularius Hall. Lucien had described this as an intimate gathering, but Marius had figured out by now that when Lucien said *intimate*, he usually meant a hundred people or more. The Cerularius was the imperial palace's second-largest and most opulent ballroom. As he walked past six Legaciatti through the double arched doorway, he looked about the room and estimated there were fifty people present already.

The polished floor of the Cerularius was so bright it was blinding. Five chandeliers illuminated the room: a grand one in the central dome lit with glows of pure white, and four smaller ones in the corners with multicolored glows, creating a more muted scene along the periphery for conversation and dining.

He heard a delighted squeal and turned just in time to catch his older sister Rhianne as she flung herself into his arms. Rhianne was a bit of a stranger to him compared to his younger sister, Laelia, but it was impossible not to like her. He'd met her for the first time soon after his arrival in Riat. She'd come all the way from Mosar to see him, and the moment he laid eyes on her, all doubts as to his heritage fell away. He could not deny the physical resemblance, not so much between himself and Rhianne but between her and Laelia. As he and Rhianne had talked, he'd observed that she'd inherited their mother's passion and their father's steady heart.

Rhianne had children, a daughter and a son, Marius's niece and nephew. They had not come for this visit, however; today they were at home in Mosar.

Rhianne's husband, Jan-Torres, the King of Mosar, joined them to make his greetings. He was more reserved than his wife, and Marius was secretly a little afraid of him. Jan-Torres clasped wrists, offered a few pleasantries, and moved off. As he departed, Marius could not help aiming a surreptitious glance at the strawberry-and-white ferret that rode on the king's shoulder. Mosari mages, unlike those of all other nations, partnered with animal familiars, in the tradition of the gods of old.

"Come and sit down," said Rhianne, gesturing at a table. "I've saved you a place, you and Drusus. Tell me all about your new surgery and dispensary. Being a Healer in the big city must be fascinating."

His parents were already sitting at the table, and Laelia too. He relaxed at the sight of them. "It is. I love it."

Rhianne was easier to talk to than most upper-class women, because she enthusiastically supported his choices and his life's ambitions. A lot of people at the palace looked down their noses at him when he told them he was a Healer. It wasn't high class, healing the citizenry. Women who sought to increase their status desired military officers, governors, or idle rich men as husbands. He could have been any of those things if he'd desired; Lucien would have set him up in whatever role he'd chosen. But he hadn't wanted to be idle or in the military, or to govern some obscure province as Lucien's puppet. He wanted to help people. And he had no patience for anyone who didn't respect that.

Laelia leapt from her seat to greet him. She was now a fully qualified war mage, working for Empress Vitala in a covert organization called the Order of the Sage. She was often away from Riat, but today she was at home, wrapped in a sparkling green dress that put him in mind of Isolda's peridot eyes.

He hugged his mother and father next. They'd reclaimed their given names upon returning to Riat, and Marius was trying his best to remember them as Sabina and Anton rather than Camilla and Tertius. His mother had calmed considerably since that fateful day in Osler, but in gatherings of this sort, Anton wore his terrified rabbit look. Marius suspected his father would never feel comfortable in the imperial palace. It had taken Marius four and a half years to warm up enough to tolerate a party like this. In that respect, he was his father's son.

Anton loosened up a little as he greeted Marius. "How's business at the surgery?"

"Good," said Marius. "*Too* good, sometimes."

"I always knew you'd make something of yourself," said Anton. "Whether here or in Osler."

His father's praise warmed him like a sunny springtime afternoon. Marius was aware that his accomplishments paled in comparison to his sisters'. Rhianne was the Queen of Mosar, and Laelia a war mage working for the empress. He was merely a licensed Healer and apothecary, and a money-losing one at that. But he knew Anton's appreciation was genuine. Marius's father did not measure Marius against his siblings, but appreciated him on his own merits.

Marius took his seat, and Rhianne plopped down beside him. A servant set a goblet of wine on the table along with a plate of sliced fruit and cheese. Marius picked up the wine and sipped. He could use a bit of liquid courage.

Rhianne smoothed her dress. "I'll have you know that I brought eleven single women with me from Mosar. All are from excellent families, and they're dying to meet you."

Laelia winked at him from across the table. "No pressure, Marius, but you're booked for the first eleven dances."

Marius choked on his wine and glared at his younger sister. "Is your dance card full yet? Because if it isn't, I'm sure I can find eleven single men to keep *you* occupied."

Laelia grinned.

"Am I putting pressure on you?" asked Rhianne, her eyes full of concern. "That wasn't my intent. I thought that the more women I brought, the more you'd have to choose from. But you don't have to dance with any of them, Marius. Not if you don't want to."

"I'll dance with them." Why not? He could dance well enough; it had been part of the education Lucien had provided him. But he didn't understand why his family was so eager to marry him off. Laelia was equally unmarried; why not focus on her? He was the elder, but at age twenty-six, hardly an old man. "Provided they understand it doesn't mean much. I'm not looking for a wife."

"Oh, they know—I mean, it's just a chance to get to know somebody. Eleven somebodies." Rhianne winced. "Perhaps I should not have brought so many."

Later that evening, when the lights dimmed and the orchestra began to play, Marius danced with each of Rhianne's imported noblewomen in turn. All of them struggled with the language, being Mosari, but each of them was a delight in her own way. All were beautiful. Most were kind, several were clever, and one had a biting wit. But when they asked what he did for a living and he replied that he was a licensed Healer and apothecary in the city of Riat, he got more than a few raised eyebrows. He sensed the usual disapproval of his choice of profession, and what would they think when they saw him in his tunic and breeches instead of his imperial silks?

Marius was no intellectual, but he did know his own mind. He could not be happy with a woman who disapproved of the way he lived. Any one of these women would be a showpiece on his arm, to be sure, but she would be constantly dissatisfied, hinting that he should give up the surgery and do something more prestigious. Then if Marius relented, Lucien would give him some meaningless job or title so that he could stomp about and act important while doing nothing of consequence. His wife might be happy, but he wouldn't be.

After the dancing, he spent some time in the washroom, not to attend to any physical need, but just because the party had become overwhelming. So many people, so much noise. He could take it in small doses, but not all at once.

When he returned to the table, dinner had been served. He'd missed the first course, soft-boiled quail eggs with chopped nuts and honey, but the plate was waiting for him, and as he sat down, a servant added a plate for the second course, scallop fritters with greens. How much of this would he have to eat in order to be polite? He scooped up some of the chopped nuts and honey in his spoon and privately hoped that bread would be served with one of the later courses.

The imperial heirs came by the table and were fawned over by all present.

"It's almost their bedtime," explained their nurse. "But they wanted to see the party."

Marius liked the imperial heirs, all the more so because their existence meant that the imperial throne had no chance of ever falling to him. Jamien, the eldest, was eight years old, outgoing, and intelligent beyond all reasonable limits. His younger brother, Maxian, age five, was a quieter and more introspective child. Maxian had a sleepy look sometimes, like he wasn't paying attention or was bored by his surroundings. Marius suspected that in truth, the boy was not dull. He had hidden depths, and when he found his voice, he would have a lot to say. But that time had not yet come.

The heirs' manners were flawless as they bowed to King Jan-Torres and Queen Rhianne. Once the formality was out of the way, they ran in for hugs with cries of "Aunt Rhianne!" and "Uncle Marius!"

Marius was not the boys' uncle any more than Rhianne was their aunt—the actual relationship was more distant—but Lucien and Vitala had taught their boys to address Marius, Rhianne, and Laelia in such a way because Lucien had been raised alongside Rhianne and thought of her as a sister, even though she was actually a cousin.

"What have you been up to?" Marius asked Maxian.

"I beat Papa at Caturanga," said Maxian.

"Well done." Knowing what he did of Lucien's prowess at Caturanga, Marius guessed that had been an act of generosity on the emperor's part.

"Lupa had puppies," said Maxian. "Two bitches and three dogs. One of the bitches is gold and white. You want one?"

"I'll think about it," said Marius.

"All right, young masters," called the nurse. "Off we go. Careful, Jamien, you're wrinkling the queen's dress."

Maxian climbed reluctantly off Marius's lap. As the boys walked away, Marius eyed Jamien, the Crown Prince. He was the same age as Isolda's boy, but what a difference in upbringing. Jamien had everything—two parents who loved him, an education, all the resources the empire could provide for its future emperor. And Rory had so little.

Suddenly everybody at his table was standing up. He knew what this meant. The emperor or empress had arrived. He stood and followed the gazes of his fellows to see who was honoring them with their presence.

It was both the emperor and the empress. Lucien was dashing in blue silk, while Vitala dazzled the eye in a mauve gown over which she'd draped a layer of glittering silver lace.

"You look stunning," said Marius to the empress when she and her husband gestured for them to sit.

"You're very kind," said Vitala. "I have always wanted to wear silver, but it's not my color."

"I beg to differ. It's very much your color," said Rhianne.

"When I combine it with something else," said Vitala.

"If anyone is unclear on this point," said Emperor Lucien, fixing his gaze on each of the men at the table, "the empress is mine."

"We were just admiring your boys," said Rhianne.

"The empress is an overachiever," said Lucien. "Produced an heir and a spare right from the start. From now on, we're hoping for all girls."

As they exchanged pleasantries, Marius's eyes were on his cousin the emperor. Lucien appeared relaxed and happy, thoroughly in his element. Marius was glad to see it.

When Marius had met Rhianne for the first time, she'd spoken to him in confidence about Lucien. Despite his wealth and position, Lucien had not enjoyed a happy childhood. His mother, an unhappy, self-absorbed woman, had died in a riding accident that might have been a suicide. And his father, Florian, had rejected Lucien in favor of his two older brothers. When those older brothers were killed by assassins, Lucien became the heir, but that hadn't made his father like him any better. Instead, it had intensified Florian's dislike, as Florian tried desperately to mold Lucien into somebody else.

Lucien had forged only one happy childhood relationship, with his cousin Rhianne. But he yearned for a big, happy family—always had. Now that his parents and older brothers were gone, he was creating that family. He'd lost Rhianne when she'd married a foreign king, and for the good of the country he'd married his sister, Celeste, to a foreign prince. But he had

Vitala and his children. In locating Marius and Laelia and bringing them to the imperial seat, Lucien was beginning to assemble the loving extended family he'd dreamed about.

"Don't worry yourself that he had an ulterior motive in bringing you here," Rhianne had told him. "He hurts inside because of his family troubles, and he's trying to heal that hurt. I can't say if it will work or not, but from your perspective it's harmless. He has no desire to hurt you, and every desire to earn your trust, your presence, even your love."

After almost five years in Riat, Marius believed it. Lucien had been wholly supportive toward him and Laelia. Now, glancing at the empress Vitala, he wondered about *her* family situation. He understood she'd had a worse childhood than her husband, but unlike Lucien, who now surrounded himself with family in an attempt to heal that wound, Vitala had isolated herself from her Riorcan family. She had not seen her father since she was two years old and apparently had no interest in finding him. Her half-siblings were probably still living, but she did not track them down. Her Riorcan mother, Treva, had sought Vitala out, only to be rejected. Treva now lived at the palace, having been granted a place there by Lucien. Marius had met her on two occasions, and he knew she had some contact with her grandsons. But Vitala would have nothing to do with her.

Marius felt that Lucien's way of dealing with his childhood family trouble was healthier than Vitala's. But who was he to judge? Vitala had been extraordinarily kind to him since he'd come to Riat, so much so that he felt she'd adopted Lucien's extended family as her own.

"How goes the harbor project?" Marius asked Lucien.

Lucien grunted his displeasure. "Not as well as I'd like."

"What's wrong?"

"The imperial treasury is drained," said Lucien. "So I've had to go looking for investors, and I don't have a lot of takers yet."

"Don't the shipping companies want a better harbor?"

"Some of the larger companies don't," said Lucien. "Because it will also be a *bigger* harbor, and that means more room for competitors."

"It will be more sheltered, though. Won't it? Less risk of losing their ships to the next storm."

"Yes, it will be more sheltered and more inland," said Lucien. "But the big shipping companies seem willing to risk a few lost ships."

"That's unconscionable." He remembered last year's storm. It hadn't been only ships that were lost. Hundreds of men had also lost their lives. For weeks afterward, their bodies had washed up on the shores of Riat.

"Never mind," said Lucien. "I've turned my attention elsewhere. The smaller shippers, as well as shipping customers and potential competitors, have more to gain than they have to lose. Imagine, for a moment, that you import coffee from Mosar and sell it to general stores throughout Kjall. Won't you benefit if there are more ships bringing coffee? More importers?"

"I would imagine." He wished Isolda were here—she understood this business stuff.

"More importers means lower prices for you, and potentially more profit," explained Lucien. "Even better, maybe you could buy a ship or two of your own and import the goods yourself. Cut out the middleman."

"Of course."

"So that's who I'm going after," said Lucien. "Smaller shipping companies looking to expand, and wealthy families who buy imported goods. I'm offering them a share of harbor profits plus exclusive berthing."

"I would think they'd jump at that." He hoped his comments sounded intelligent, given that he had no idea what he was talking about.

Lucien shrugged. "The harbor will take a decade to build, at least. That's a long time to wait for a turnaround on one's investment. But we'll get there."

"When you break ground, I imagine there will be a lot of new jobs in Riat."

"Undoubtedly. But that won't happen anytime soon."

Marius didn't fully understand the economics behind Lucien's harbor project, but he was impressed. Lucien was thinking big, the way an emperor should. Kjall did need a world-class harbor, and Riat seemed the perfect place to locate it. Furthermore, the project would have a number of side benefits. A flood of new jobs in Riat might mean opportunities for many. Maybe even for Isolda and her people.

12

Marius climbed wearily into his carriage with Drusus. The imperial party had retired for the night. It was late, and he was drowsy from dancing, conversation, and rich food. He rested his head on the back on the seat and closed his eyes. "What did you think of those Mosari women?"

"The ones you danced with?" asked Drusus.

"Yes."

"They were beautiful."

"I know *that*," said Marius. "At imperial events, all the women are beautiful."

"Then what are you asking?" said Drusus.

"Gods, I don't know."

"If you're asking whether I think you should marry one of them," said Drusus, "my answer is no. You need time to get to know a woman, and those Mosari women are only going to be here a few days. Better you should look for a Kjallan."

"Do you have one in mind?"

"No."

Marius sighed. He wasn't in a hurry to get married, yet there was something about his visits to the palace that tugged at his soul. It wasn't the lavish parties, and it certainly wasn't the fancy clothes or food. It was the people. Lucien had surrounded himself with a loving family: his wife, his two boys, Rhianne and Jan-Torres, Laelia. And now Marius was heading home to his bachelor lifestyle in Riat. It seemed a stark comparison. Marius had never felt lonely, exactly, but he did feel that something was missing from his life. "What about a Sardossian?"

"You'd be inviting a great deal of trouble," said Drusus. "Broken windows, pranks. You'd lose business at the surgery."

"I don't care," said Marius.

Drusus was silent a moment before speaking again. "The Sardossian you are thinking of is considerably below your station, and she has a child already."

"I like Rory, and I don't care about her *station*," said Marius. "What about you—are you going to marry when your contract ends?"

"Of course," said Drusus.

Marius hated to think of it, but Drusus had only a year and a half left on his contract. Men in the Legaciatti served twenty years and were then granted a generous retirement stipend. Drusus had begun his work at the age of sixteen, so he'd be thirty-six when his contract ended. "You have anyone in mind?"

"Legaciatti aren't allowed to fraternize."

One reason the contracts for Legaciatti were relatively short was that they demanded so much of the men and women involved. It was a round-the-clock job, and while an occasional visit to a bawdy-house might be overlooked, romantic relationships were forbidden. "You must get lonely."

"The work is hard." Drusus shrugged. "But the opportunities afforded a Legaciattus are extraordinary."

Marius nodded. Drusus, like all Legaciatti, was an orphan, recruited in childhood so that his loyalty to the throne would be absolute. He had no family, no *station*, and if he had not joined the Legaciatti, his future would not have been bright. "You want children, when you retire?"

"Maybe."

"You'd make a great father." His thoughts turned to Isolda. Like Drusus, she had no family to support her, but in her case there was no retirement stipend coming her way. Her prospects were severely limited, and she seemed to know this, since she was concentrating all her energy on Rory. "Do you think the emperor and empress would approve of Isolda?"

"Of course not," said Drusus. "She isn't even legal."

Marius sighed. Lucien and Vitala had given him so much, and he didn't want to anger or disappoint them. Lucien wanted Marius to make a marriage that befitted his *station*—gods, that hated word again—and Marius granted that this wasn't much for Lucien to ask. Lucien was building a family, and the woman Marius married would become part of that family. Isolda had little to recommend herself to the emperor. She wasn't wealthy, or connected, or magical, or educated. As Drusus had pointed out, she wasn't even legal. She had street smarts, business smarts. But what use was that in the imperial palace?

He supposed it made little difference what the emperor would think of her. She'd run away again, and he hadn't the slightest idea where to find her.

Isolda scooped Rory up from the storeroom floor before he could reach a stack of wrought-iron lanterns. He could now walk a few steps unassisted, but when he really wanted to get somewhere, he dropped to all fours. His crawl was so fast, and his curiosity so insatiable, that she had to keep a close eye on him all hours of the day.

"No lanterns for you," she scolded, and carried him out into the general store. Tiwar, who was manning the counter, gave her a nod. The store had tripled in size since she'd first come here. Over the past year and change, Jauld's General Store had earned a reputation for quality, variety, and fair prices. As a result, they'd begun to draw more business than they could handle. She and Jauld solved the problem by buying some of the adjoining property and building on additions. They'd also hired a couple of clerks. Now that Isolda had her hands full with Rory, it was impossible to keep up with the store on her own. "I'm heading home. Got to feed the little one."

"See you in the morning, Miss Isolda."

The walk home was two blocks along the dirt road, and the evening was fine. She inhaled deeply, breathing in the scents of clover and pine. Glancing at the side of the road, she spied a few bees hovering over the white flowers. Honey would be in season soon. She'd have to contact the local beekeepers tomorrow and make sure she got some in stock the moment it was available.

In her arms, Rory squirmed and fussed. He wanted to walk, probably to meander and look at the bees, but Isolda was dead on her feet and eager to get home.

Not that home life was enjoyable. Ever since that day in the shop when Jauld's friends had insulted her, Jauld had become cool and distant. He wasn't the loving husband she'd dreamed of. It was clear now that no matter how hard she tried, her husband was never going to warm to her. He wasn't violent or cruel; just indifferent.

It was as she'd feared—she wasn't pretty enough to be loved. And yet she could not help feeling angry at his scorn. She'd never tricked him. He'd known exactly what she was and made the marriage offer of his own volition. At the time, it seemed he'd liked her. Now, for some reason, he didn't.

He ought to appreciate one thing about her: she was making him wealthy. She'd transformed his business from a dingy junk shop to a clean, modern store that customers traveled miles to visit. Through her efforts—Jauld seldom lifted a finger to help—his fortunes and hers had improved. They'd been able to make renovations to their house. She'd bought a nicer wardrobe and some face paint in hopes of appealing more to Jauld's eye. It wasn't working, as far as she could tell, but he did still come to her bed. She didn't enjoy sleeping with him, but she was glad he did. It was the only way she'd have more children.

Rory was the one bright spot in her life. He wasn't an easy baby—he was insatiably curious, always getting into trouble—but, even so, he was a delight. For years she had envied her sisters their fine marriages and fine children. Now she had a baby of her own, and little Rory had become the center of her world. It didn't matter whether Jauld appreciated her improvements to the store. She wasn't doing it for him. She was doing it for Rory, who would one day inherit the fruits of her labor.

Stepping inside the house, she shut the door behind her and set a squirming Rory on the floor. When she looked up, her eyes met those of a strange woman sitting at the kitchen table. Isolda froze. The stranger was little more than a girl, perhaps sixteen years old, or at the most eighteen. She didn't look dangerous—her wide eyes suggested she was more scared of Isolda than Isolda was of her—but what was she doing here?

Isolda snatched Rory up from the ground. "Who are you, and why are you in my house?" Rory kicked and began to cry in frustration, but Isolda clung to him.

The girl's mouth fell open, but she said nothing.

"Isolda, you're home." Jauld emerged from a back bedroom. "This is Chari. I'm sure you two will be like sisters before long."

Isolda trembled. This could not be happening. Please, let this not be happening. "What is she doing here?"

"She lives here now," said Jauld. "Chari is my new wife."

13

"You're putting far too much effort into this."

Marius ignored his bodyguard's words. Yes, they'd been at it for a while, and his first idea, of going to the Riat City Guard to ask them for information about where the Sardossians hid, had failed. He'd tried to frame his inquiry in terms of public health: there was a fever going around in Sardossian circles, and he wanted to heal it before it got out of hand. A prefect named Caellus had ushered him into a back office and asked him a lot of questions, most of which Marius had to dodge so he wouldn't get Isolda into trouble. And Caellus had given him no information in return.

After leaving the guardhouse empty-handed, he'd come up with a better idea. He knew that Rory worked at a fruit stand.

Isolda had not said which fruit stand, and of course there were many in a city the size of Riat. But the Sardossians were concentrated in the harbor district. That was where the gunpowder factory had blown up. So he began at the site of the old gunpowder factory and worked his way outward with Drusus in tow, checking every fruit stand they came to. No doubt this unaccustomed exercise was the root of Drusus's ill temper—but at the fifth fruit stand, Marius's persistence paid off.

From an observation point across the street, he watched a smiling Sardossian boy with an apple in one hand and an orange in the other dart out of the Chelani Corner Market into the crowd of passersby. He hopped up to potential customers one by one, presenting the fruits. Apparently the prejudice most Kjallans held toward Sardossians didn't apply to children when they were smiling and cute—or perhaps the customers simply mistook Rory for a Riorcan. Either way, Rory managed to lure quite a few customers toward the fruit stand. "Knows what he's doing, doesn't he?"

"A born hustler," growled Drusus.

"He's charming. A good salesman."

"So you've found him," said Drusus. "What now?"

What now, indeed? He couldn't approach Rory. The boy had street smarts. He knew to conceal his and Isolda's whereabouts. "We wait."

"For what?"

"For his work shift to end," said Marius. "Then we follow him to Isolda."

Isolda shoveled more saltpeter into the base of the mill with the other ingredients, handling her all-wooden tools with care. To throw a spark here could be fatal, not just for her but for everyone in the factory. She stirred to spread the materials evenly in the well and took up the lead rope for the mule harnessed to the central shaft. She clucked and stepped forward, but the mule balked. He'd been working all afternoon, and he knew as well as she did that his shift was nearing its end. His mind was on his stall and his feedbox. "Get up," she barked. "We're almost done." The mule gave a desultory toss of his head but leaned into the traces and began to pull. With a rumble, the great stone wheels of the mill began to turn, grinding to dust beneath them the raw materials of gunpowder.

Ten rotations around the mill, step by tedious step, and the grind was nearly finished. Her boss, old Twitchy Fingers, stood two mills away, talking to another worker. He was probably making the rounds to hand out the day's pay. Nonetheless, her stomach knotted at the sight of him.

One or two more times around and she'd be finished. She led the mule slowly around the mill. The groaning of the wheels and the grating of the powder filled her ears. This was the music of gunpowder production. It wasn't a pleasant tune, but by the end of the day, it produced one that she liked much better: the jingle of coins in her pocket.

Nearby, Twitchy Fingers said, "This batch is looking good."

Isolda rounded the bend, and he came into view. The mule, who didn't like Twitchy Fingers, flung up his head, yanking the lead rope. Isolda shook her rope-burned hand and clucked to send the mule forward again. The grind was nearly done, but if she let her mule decide when to stop, she'd never get him to work tomorrow. As they neared Twitchy Fingers, she murmured, "Whoa," and the mule stopped.

Twitchy Fingers held out a few quintetrals. "Today's payment."

She reached for the coins, praying that he would just hand them over this time.

Twitchy Fingers grinned and yanked his hand away. "When you've unhitched that mule, meet me at the tavern next door. It's a good day to unwind, don't you think?"

Gods, not this again. "I can't. My son is waiting for me."

"He goes all day without you. He can manage a little longer."

She shook her head. "He's off work now, and I can't leave him on his own." Not to mention that the last thing she wanted to spend her hard-earned money on was a drink with her grabby boss. Rather than reaching for her coins, which would draw her into a wrestling match, Isolda turned toward the mule, letting his body guard one side of hers as she unbuckled his traces.

"Send young Rory for a pastry," said Twitchy Fingers. "Boys are always hungry."

"Are you offering me extra coin?"

Twitchy Fingers sidled closer. "Maybe I am."

Ugh—that was *not* what she'd meant. "Please, just give me my money. I need to take Rory home." He was standing too close, and she could not run away. She had the mule half unhitched, and she needed her wages. If only her old boss had not been killed in the explosion four years ago. He'd paid her without argument or difficulty every day.

"This job doesn't have to be all work. Give me a smile, won't you?" Twitchy Fingers slipped an arm around her. His fingers touched her breast through her shirt.

She winced and drew away. "Let go. Please." Pinned between Twitchy Fingers and the mule, she couldn't move. Anger welled up. Her arms tensed, and she had an intense desire to elbow him.

Maybe slap his face, too, and kick him in the cods. But she needed this job.

"*Relax*," said Twitchy Fingers.

Her body was stiff as an oak. "Please stop."

"Mom!"

Her son—gods, he'd arrived just in time. She twisted out of Twitchy Fingers' grip. "Rory?" Twitchy Fingers made another grab for her, but she dodged him and circled around the mule, jumping over the traces to look for her son.

She was shocked to see a man behind Rory—a *big* man. He looked angry, and he was running in her direction. Her muscles tensed for flight, but she could not leave without Rory. So she darted toward the man and grabbed her son. The charging man veered around her.

He grabbed Twitchy Fingers by the shirt and threw him against the wall.

The mule flung up his head, brayed, and kicked at the traces.

Clutching Rory's arm so hard it was sure to leave a mark later, Isolda turned to flee and smacked head first into the broad chest of another man. He grabbed her, but not roughly; he only steadied her. "Easy—it's Marius. And you needn't be afraid of Drusus."

That man was Drusus? She turned to see.

Drusus punctuated his words with blows as he held Twitchy Fingers against the wall. "Is that. . .how. . .you treat. . .a woman?"

Isolda shrank against Marius. Much as she might have enjoyed watching her boss take a beating, she knew that what she was really watching was the end of her employment.

"Stop it! Help!" cried Twitchy Fingers.

Several other millworkers gathered around to watch, but nobody intervened.

"She told *you* to stop," said Drusus, hitting him again. "But did you listen?"

His blows were so fast that Isolda could barely see his arm move. Twitchy Fingers was trying to block them, but he couldn't get his arms up in time. Isolda had heard of war mages whose magic granted them preternatural speed and strength. Was Drusus one of them?

"Enough," said Marius.

Drusus released Twitchy Fingers and returned to Marius, Isolda, and Rory, examining his hands and flicking the dirt out from beneath his nails. He brushed a smear of blood from his knuckles. "Not a bad workout, but your factory manager fights like a rabbit."

Twitchy Fingers reeled against the wall, battered and bleeding. "You have no business coming in here. I'll call the city guard!"

Drusus laughed. "Go on and try."

Isolda knew he would call nobody. The gunpowder factory was illegal. Her stomach sank. Where was she going to work from now on? Twitchy Fingers was sure to fire her, and she didn't even have today's wages. Looking around, she saw the coins he'd held back from her. They were scattered across the mill floor.

Now appeared to be as good a time as any to retrieve them. She darted out of Marius's grip and dropped to her knees to pick up the coins, shaking black powder from each. Thank the Vagabond nothing had struck a spark.

Twitchy Fingers aimed an accusing finger at her. "You ungrateful bitch. You're fired! Get out of here, and don't come back!"

Isolda staggered, trembling, to her feet. She grabbed Rory's hand and headed for the door.

She emerged from the factory floor into the waning sunlight of a summer evening.

Marius trotted up behind her. "I'm sorry. I've made a mess of things, haven't I? I didn't mean to cost you your job."

Isolda's eyes welled with tears. "Never mind. It wasn't your fault."

"But it was. Drusus would never have acted if I hadn't told him to. I was furious at the way that man was treating you, and I acted rashly. I didn't think."

Isolda wiped her eyes. It was impossible for her to be angry with Marius. "You meant well."

"That man was mean," said Rory. "I'm glad he got beat up."

Drusus, silent at Marius's side throughout this conversation, chucked Rory on the shoulder.

She took Rory's hand and squeezed it. It was easy for Rory and Drusus, and even Marius, to think strictly in terms of what pleased them. They weren't the ones who had to pay the bill when it came due.

"How long has your boss been acting that way?" asked Marius.

"As long as I've known him." She waited for him to blame her. *Why haven't you done something about it? Why didn't you find another job?*

But all Marius said was, "I'm sorry."

She felt herself flushing as a wave of emotion overcame her—embarrassment that he'd witnessed her humiliation, gratitude that he was so understanding, shame that he saw her as an object of pity. Words bubbled out of her throat. "He thinks that because I'm Sardossian he can do what he likes—that it doesn't matter—"

"Well, he can't," said Marius.

Isolda took a deep breath, trying to steady herself. She wanted nothing more than to throw herself into Marius's arms and cry. He was probably the only man in the whole of Kjall who would let her do it, and for that very reason she restrained herself. He was not the cause of her distress. He did not deserve to be clung to by a worthless woman who had nothing to offer him.

"No man should treat a woman like that under any circumstances," added Marius. "I'm sorry I caused all this trouble, but let me repair the damage. I'd like to offer you a job."

"Is that why you came here?" It occurred to her, suddenly, to wonder why he and Drusus had been at the factory. How had they even found her? "What sort of job?"

"I've been thinking about what you said—all those patients not paying."

"You've got to go after them," said Isolda. "Or else you'll go out of business. Send Drusus after your delinquent payers; he's scary enough."

"I can't send Drusus. That's not his job," said Marius. "But you needn't worry about my going out of business. I have a wealthy benefactor who covers my losses."

Isolda closed her eyes. Of course. Everything fell into place. No wonder Marius was lackadaisical about payments—he didn't need them. It was becoming clear that Marius was a far more important person than she'd initially assumed. Who was the wealthy benefactor? A lover? A family member? Perhaps it was the same person who'd paid for his education. If she'd thought Marius was out of her class before, she saw now that he was far, far beyond her in both status and means. "Drusus is your bodyguard, isn't he?"

Drusus's eyes twinkled. "What'd you think I was?"

She shrugged. "A high-class servant?"

"Not far off the mark," said Drusus. "Some people think I'm his lover."

"*Are* you?"

Drusus looked amused. "No. Although he is a fine-looking man—"

"Stop it," said Marius. "Back to the point I was making—it embarrasses me that the surgery is not turning a profit. I hate having to go to my benefactor when I need money. It makes me feel like a charity case."

Isolda nodded. That was a feeling she understood.

"You've also made me aware that some of my patients are taking advantage of me, and I want to put a stop to that," said Marius. "You have a head for business, so here's my offer. You come to work for me as my business manager. Your job will be to make the surgery profitable, by whatever means necessary. But you must also find a way to allow me to help those who can't afford my services."

Rory grabbed her arm. "Mom, take the job. *Please* take it."

Isolda patted his hand but ignored him; her son was no doubt thinking of fish cakes and apple tarts. "Your offer is generous, but you can't hire me. People will boycott the surgery if you've got a Sardossian working there."

His brows rose. "Is it really that bad for your people in this town?"

"I'm afraid so."

"Well, I don't care," said Marius. "If there's trouble, we'll handle it."

Isolda winced. "There could be violence."

"It would be a security problem," added Drusus.

"That's what we have you for," said Marius to Drusus. He turned to Isolda. "How much was the gunpowder factory paying you?"

"Three quintetrals. But—"

"Per day? I'll triple it," said Marius.

Isolda gritted her teeth. She wanted very much to accept this job, but it seemed wrong to ask Marius to take on all the problems that went along with her being Sardossian. "I really don't think you should."

"Your benefactor would not approve," put in Drusus.

"What's the point of having money and protection if I can't do anything with it?" said Marius. "Isolda, you're hired. I'll expect you at the surgery tomorrow morning at eight."

At the breakfast table, Isolda pored over the broadsheets, looking for a story, a hint, any evidence at all that someone had tried to assassinate the First Heir. The shop carried three different broadsheets, and she'd brought home a copy of each of them: the Cus Chronicle, *the* Tinto Gazette, *and the* Weekly Journal *from the distant but influential city of Issves. But she*

couldn't find a word about any assassination attempt, despite having heard from three separate travelers at the store that it had in fact taken place.

Signs of disorder were on the rise. Several platoons of soldiers had marched through town, moving inland. Guard presence was diminished on the roads. Last week, a band of ruffians had threatened Tiwar and robbed the store. She and Jauld had absorbed the loss, but the event spoke of worrisome change. Was the First Heir losing control of the country?

Rory, sitting in her lap, ran his finger along the words of the broadsheet, making nonsense sounds as he pretended to read. But his charm was no comfort to her today. What sort of future would her son have if the country fell apart? And why did the broadsheets say nothing? "Jauld, have you heard anything about someone trying to assassinate the First Heir?"

"Why, is it in the papers?"

"No, but word's going round."

Jauld shrugged. "I haven't heard anything."

And with that, the subject was dismissed. Her husband was the most incurious of men. A usurper of the throne would have to station a battalion of troops in the middle of their village before Jauld would take notice.

He raised his head. "Chari's up. Move those papers out of the way."

Isolda picked up her broadsheets and scooted to the opposite side of the table, taking Rory with her. Glancing up at the approaching Chari, who was visibly pregnant and still in her robe, Isolda felt that familiar gnawing pain in her stomach. She had trouble eating these days.

Chari slid heavily into her seat. "Gods, I'm so tired."

"Get her some breakfast, Isolda," said Jauld.

Isolda shoved her chair back, set Rory down, and rose from the table. She tried to swallow her resentment as she moved into the kitchen to assemble a plate of bread, cheese, and fruit. For Rory's sake, she could not afford to anger her husband.

When Chari had first joined the household, the girl had been terrified and eager to fit in. For a while, she'd been polite and respectful to everyone. But it had not taken her long to figure out that she was Jauld's favorite and that in his eyes she could do no wrong. Jauld slept exclusively with Chari now. He sat next to Chari at mealtimes, and when he went out to see his friends, he took Chari and left Isolda at home.

When Chari became pregnant, she insisted that Isolda take over her household chores because she was too tired to keep up with them anymore. Since then, she'd only become more brazen in baiting Isolda.

"Not the buckwheat," said Chari. "The soda bread."

Isolda set down the knife, stewing. She'd already sliced the buckwheat. It was normally Chari's favorite.

"I help," said Rory. He toddled toward the soda bread loaf, grabbed it, and started to bring it to Isolda. She gave him a smile—at least someone in the house was willing to pitch in with the chores. But halfway across the kitchen, he tripped and fell. The loaf bounced out of his arms and landed on the floor. Rory began to cry.

"Gods, he's such a brat," said Chari. "Never mind, give me the buckwheat."

Isolda picked her son up off the ground and hugged him, whispering words of comfort in hopes they would ease the sting of Chari's nastiness. Rory sniffled a little and toddled away.

Isolda picked up the bread and returned to her work. She knew what Chari was trying to do, and it terrified her. Chari had already won the battle for their husband's attentions; that one went to her by default because she was prettier. But one obstacle remained in the way of Chari's plans for household domination: Rory. As Jauld's only son, Rory was the heir by default. But what would happen when Chari's baby was born?

If Chari delivered a girl, there would be no conflict. Rory would remain heir by virtue of his sex. But if Chari had a boy, she was sure to want her child declared heir over Rory. Already, she was trying to drive a wedge between Jauld and his son, not difficult to do since Jauld didn't like children.

Isolda could not let Chari's baby dethrone Rory; that would undo everything Isolda had worked toward over the past few years. Their wealth was Isolda's. She was the one who'd produced it, and the least Jauld could do, in gratitude or simply as a matter of fairness, was to retain Rory as his heir. But Isolda feared that Jauld was too weak and too foolish a man to stand up for her or Rory. And if he wouldn't, she would have to find a way out of this marriage.

14

Marius was a better Healer than a businessman, but he'd made an excellent business decision in hiring Isolda. It had been a week now since she'd started working at the surgery, and already she'd made some changes. She'd begun by switching suppliers for some of his herbs and tinctures. He wouldn't have known if she hadn't told him, since the products were the same, and the difference would show up only on the balance sheet. But another change was more noticeable: Lady Fabiola had disappeared from the surgery entirely, as had Antonius and several other chronic nonpayers.

A few paying patients had disappeared too, as Isolda had warned him they would. One had demanded that he fire "that piss-head," and another had expressed concern that Isolda might be touching the medications. Marius had suggested that they find another surgery. He did not miss them.

The day Isolda began work, she sat down with him and asked how he felt about various measures she could employ to persuade his delinquent patients to pay their bills. He'd decided he didn't feel comfortable with anything extreme, such as calling on the city guard to throw the delinquents into debtor's prison. So Isolda suggested something milder. She maintained a list of delinquent patients, and when one of them showed up at the surgery, she or Drusus denied that person entrance until the bill was paid. If Lady Fabiola wanted to see him again, she'd have to pay what she owed him. Apparently she'd decided it wasn't worth it.

Marius had never realized how much his day-to-day testiness at the surgery arose from dealing with difficult or manipulative patients. Now that these patients were being screened out at the front door—or screening themselves out—he could focus on the healing itself, which he loved. He went about his work with a new lightness to his step.

While he was delighted with Isolda's work, her private life remained mysterious. Every evening, when the surgery was about to close, Rory came from his job at the fruit stand to meet her. Then the two of them disappeared into the streets of Riat. Marius had no idea where they went.

He wanted to ask her to supper at the villa some evening, but every time he thought about it, the image of her former boss at the gunpowder factory loomed large. He didn't want to be like that old Sardossian lecher, using a position of power to manipulate her into a personal relationship she might not want. And he didn't want to scare her away. He didn't think of himself as an intimidating man, but he was Kjallan, and she was

Sardossian. He had a full-time bodyguard and the weight of the authorities behind him, while Isolda lived by her wits alone.

He tried to pretend that his relationship with her was strictly business, that he wasn't hoping for more. But try as he might to resist it, he was developing an attachment.

How else could he explain the way his heart lifted whenever she was in the room, and his eyes fixed on her face, or, embarrassingly, a little lower? At the palace, he'd danced with eleven Mosari women in a row, each of them undeniably lovely, and he'd had no response, emotional or physical, to any of them. And then yesterday, his hand had brushed against Isolda's in the dispensary, purely by accident, and he'd sprung a cockstand like some mewling fourteen-year-old.

Tonight he would meet with her after the surgery closed. She had some plan she wanted to discuss. It was business, but all the same he felt light in the chest, a little shaky at the prospect of spending time with her.

When he'd finished with his last patient of the day, he tidied up the dispensary, deactivated the light glows in his office, and headed into the waiting room. Isolda was there with Rory. Isolda had knelt down to speak to him, bringing herself to his level.

He'd never seen a mother and son so closely attached. Rory was the only person privy to Isolda's inner world, and sometimes Marius was a little jealous of that.

He cleared his throat. "You wanted to speak to me?"

Isolda rose. As she met his eyes, she turned that dazzling smile on him, the one that turned his knees to butter. In that smile Marius felt her affection, her burgeoning trust, even her admiration—despite her reserve. That smile was a window to her soul, and for a moment, he felt he was seeing the woman she would be if she didn't have to keep two steps ahead of her enemies.

Isolda sat down and motioned him to the chair across from her. "You asked me to do two things when you hired me as your business manager. One was to make the surgery profitable. I believe the changes I've made so far have accomplished that."

"You've done a wonderful job," said Marius.

"You also asked me to come up with a way for you to help indigent patients who cannot pay their bills," said Isolda. "I have a proposal for you. What if we designate one day per month, or even one per week, as a Free Day? On that day only, patients who come in may be treated at no cost."

An interesting thought. "Do you think we'll get the right patients? We might just get people like Lady Fabiola and Antonius. What if no one comes to the surgery anymore on the regular days, and they all come on the Free Days?"

"The surgery will no doubt be inundated on Free Days, but that works to our ends," said Isolda. "We'll be overcrowded. Patients will have to wait a long time to be treated. Those who can afford to pay for your services will soon realize that it's less trouble to come some other time and pay your fee. Those willing to wait all day for free treatment will be the most desperate patients, the ones who can get treatment no other way."

"Let's try it. Schedule one for three days hence."

"I'll do that," said Isolda.

Marius cleared his throat nervously. "You know, we're not so formal here that you need to wear a hat." Her first day at the surgery, she'd come bare-headed, but since then she'd begun wearing a simple brimless bonnet to work. It looked nice and was certainly modest, but he found he missed the sight of her yellow hair, so different from that of his fellow Kjallans.

"Oh." Her cheeks flushed pink as her hand went up to touch the bonnet. "I thought it might be prudent to cover my hair so that I'm not so easily recognized as Sardossian."

Marius blinked. He hadn't considered that might be the reason.

"Of course, if you feel it's inappropriate for me to wear it—" continued Isolda.

"Not at all," he said quickly. "Wear it by all means, if you feel safer that way."

"It's not much of a disguise," she admitted. "Once I open my mouth, they can tell from my accent. But I find it cuts down on the stares, and I don't want anyone reporting me to the city guard."

"I want you to feel comfortable here," said Marius. "Wear whatever you like. I just want you to know you don't *have* to wear it."

"Thank you, sir." She took Rory's hand, left the surgery, and disappeared down the street.

Where did she go in the evenings? He had some notion of her character by now: she was courageous, hard-working, and absolutely devoted to her son. And yet in some ways he barely knew her at all.

For the first time in years, Isolda felt optimistic about her future and about Rory's. Marius was paying her generously, there was no chance of the surgery exploding in a deadly fireball, and Marius never harassed her. Under her management, the surgery was now turning a profit. And while she'd heard a few ugly comments from the customers about sewer rats, and felt some unfriendly stares, so far there had been no serious trouble from Marius's clients or from the neighbors.

The Free Days were a spectacular success.

The first one drew some unwelcome faces, such as Antonius, who owed the surgery a great deal of money. But it also attracted patients entirely new to Marius. The waiting room filled up, and a line spilled out the door. When she informed Antonius that the wait to see the Healer would be four hours, he left in a huff.

Most of the new patients stayed. They were shabbily dressed, some of them shoeless. Isolda knew she was looking at Kjall's poorest, the unfortunates who didn't have the money to pay a Healer. That such people existed among Kjall's legal citizens did not surprise her; the situation was the same in Sardos. Healers were rare and expensive. The poorer class had always gone to apothecaries instead; her father could not have made a living otherwise.

At the end of the first Free Day, Marius came out of his office, fuming. "I can't believe it. Five cases, *five*, of broken bones that were never healed or even properly set. And why should that be, when a Healer's magic can cure a fresh break so easily?"

"I'm sure it's because they couldn't afford a Healer when it happened."

"I *know* that's why," said Marius. "It's infuriating. I've done what I can for them, but I can't fix a bone that's healed improperly—the body doesn't remember. Some of these people have permanent limps or useless arms, and what good is that to

Kjall? Why do we cripple our able-bodied people for want of a little coin?"

"You're helping," she assured him. "Word will get out about the Free Days. You saw mostly old injuries today, but next time someone breaks an arm and can't afford a Healer, they'll come on your next Free Day."

"I hope so." He smiled. "This was a good idea you had. I feel like I accomplished more good in one day than I do all week."

At Marius's bidding, she scheduled another Free Day for the following week.

Word spread, and the second Free Day was even better attended than the first. A few Sardossians showed up, showing signs of a fever. Marius was delighted to cure it, but at the end of the day, when they were closing up, he told her it wasn't the best solution to the problem.

"I'm glad they came, but they should be warded," he said. "With proper wards, they wouldn't have picked up the evil spirits in the first place. I wonder if we could get Nonian to come and ward people at our next Free Day. Ask him for me, please."

She spoke to Nonian the next day. He said he would come, but only if he was paid.

Marius grumbled but finally said, "Fair enough. Warders aren't as well-off as Healers. It isn't reasonable for me to ask him to work for free. Can the surgery afford to pay him?"

Isolda grimaced. "Not easily. I asked how much he would charge. If we bring him in, we'll have to schedule the Free Days farther apart, or risk losing money."

Marius waved his hand. "Forget it. I want the Free Days no more than a week apart. Today I saw somebody with a broken leg who'd waited four days to come in. Four days! Can you imagine?"

She could.

"I'll speak to my benefactor," said Marius. "Maybe he can help."

The mysterious benefactor again. After a month working here, Isolda still had no idea who that person was.

On the third Free Day, a line formed at the surgery door before they even opened. The surgery was so crowded, and some of the cases so urgent, that Marius kept the surgery open an extra two hours in order to accommodate a few more patients. Isolda stayed late too, which meant that Rory, who'd finished his work at the usual time, ended up waiting for her.

Isolda counted out four more patients, the most Marius could see in his remaining hour, and sent the others home. She locked the front door and sat in the slowly emptying waiting room, making sure the patients were sent to Marius in the correct order. Drusus, who sometimes stayed in the office with Marius and sometimes in the waiting room, had chosen the waiting room today. He was in the corner, reading a book.

Rory fidgeted in a chair for a while. Then he got up and hopped about the room, looking out the windows. Finally he went to Drusus and announced, "I can read."

Isolda tensed as Drusus looked up from his book. Marius's gruff, snobby bodyguard had warmed to them a little bit over the past month. But he was far from approachable, and she had no idea if he liked children.

"You can read? I don't believe it," said Drusus.

"I'll show you." Rory circled around so he could see the words of Drusus's book right side up. He placed his finger on the page and began sounding out words.

Drusus turned to Isolda, raising a brow. "Did you teach him this?"

"He'll need it if he's to become a warder someday."

Drusus chucked Rory on the shoulder. "You're pretty good at reading. I'll tell you what. Let's read this page together. I'll read one sentence, and you read the next."

For a half hour, Drusus and Rory read together. The book was too advanced for Rory. It was written by a naturalist, a book about birds, and much of the vocabulary was beyond Rory's ability. Isolda winced every time her son struggled with a word. But the boy soldiered on gamely, and Drusus was patient.

The last client left Marius's office. Isolda rose to let him out the front door and watched the office door expectantly, knowing that Marius must soon emerge.

After a few minutes, Marius did, yawning. "Thanks for staying late, Isolda." He dropped a handful of coins into her palm.

Her payment was heavier than usual today. She counted coins and saw that he'd given her a few extra quintetrals—a bonus for overtime.

Drusus closed his book. He said to Rory, "Keep practicing at home. Next time we have a late night at the surgery, bring one of your books and you can show me how much you've learned."

"I don't have any books at home," said Rory.

"No books?" Drusus glanced at Isolda.

She shrugged. There were a lot of things they didn't have.

"We're saving money so I can learn magic," said Rory.

"Tell you what," said Drusus. "I've got some books at the villa that I've already read. You can borrow them. But only if you promise you'll practice your reading. What do you say? Clasp wrists on it?"

Rory nodded gravely and clasped the big man's wrist.

Isolda's heart swelled. Never before had she worked with such delightful men, both Marius and Drusus. She was beginning to think there might be a place for her in this once-unwelcoming country.

15

As Marius headed down the dark street from the surgery to his villa, he thought of the one thing he would change about his life, if he could. He was too gods-cursed busy. His work in the surgery kept him tied up all day, and yet Drusus had idle time—time he had used tonight to speak with Isolda and her son. Marius was jealous.

At the villa, he and Drusus sat down for a late supper of partridge stew. There was no conversation, since Drusus rarely spoke unless spoken to, and Marius thought back to that afternoon when Isolda and Rory had taken lunch here at the villa. Rory had been obsessed with helping the cook, and Marius and Isolda had enjoyed a pleasant conversation at this very table. How much livelier the villa was when Isolda and Rory were in it.

He broke the silence. "That was a nice thing you did for Isolda's boy."

Drusus grunted. "That boy won't have a chance at the university if he doesn't start studying at home. He works all day at a fruit stand, earning money to pay his way. Think of his competition—the other boys at the university will be rich men's children who've never had to work a day and who've had full-time tutors since they were six."

Marius knew this was true, and yet he bristled at the idea that an education had to be started in early childhood. "I did all right."

Drusus pointed a spoon at him. "Your cousin is the *emperor*. You were seldom at the university. You had the best tutors the Imperium could buy."

"I think Rory will do well. He's bright and motivated."

"That's why I want to help him," said Drusus. "But it may not be enough. And his race isn't going to do him any favors."

Marius had to agree. Rory might not be readily identifiable as Sardossian—unlike his mother, he had no accent. But his yellow hair made it clear he wasn't Kjallan. He might be mistaken for a Riorcan, but Riorcans weren't much better tolerated in Riat than Sardossians. "I didn't think you liked children."

"Depends on the child," said Drusus. "Rory's all right. But some of those children at the imperial palace I could do without."

"They're a bit spoiled, you think?"

Drusus shrugged.

Marius tried to think of children he knew at the imperial palace, but the only ones he knew were Lucien and Vitala's boys. He'd met Rhianne's children, too, but they were only visiting at the time. They lived in Mosar. Drusus, however, had worked at the palace for years before being assigned to Marius, and had undoubtedly seen a great deal more. "I like Jamien and Maxian."

"I don't know Maxian well," said Drusus. "But Jamien's a terror."

"*Jamien?*"

"Gods help us when he inherits the throne."

Marius could hardly believe what he was hearing. He'd never heard the imperial heir spoken of with anything but effusive praise. "I think Jamien is charming."

"Charming he is," said Drusus. "And intelligent. But he's not the same person in private as he is in public."

"What do you mean? Give me an example."

Drusus shook his head. "It's not my place to speak of such things. Forget what I said—please."

Marius dropped the subject but resolved to watch Jamien more closely from now on. His bodyguard, a lifelong observer of the imperial family, had an astute understanding of people and their motivations. Marius would be a fool not to listen. Perhaps there was some way he could intervene and help set the boy on the right path, although he couldn't imagine how to raise the issue with his cousin. "You seem to be getting on well with Isolda."

"I'm warming to her. She's brave. Did you see that stain on her syrtos this morning?"

"I confess I didn't notice."

"She washed it off as soon as she came in," said Drusus. "Someone threw dog shit at her while she was walking to work."

Marius's hand hit the table with a thud. "They did *what?*"

"I imagine that sort of thing happens to her all the time."

How had Marius not known? He wanted to run out into the street and find whoever had done it. Or perhaps, more sensibly, he could hire someone to escort her to and from work. "She told you about it. Why didn't she tell me?"

"She didn't tell me, either; I saw her washing it off. I'm sure she doesn't want to bother either of us with her problems."

How sad that she thought she would be *bothering* him. "When we first met her, I thought you didn't care for Isolda."

"She improves upon acquaintance."

Marius set down his spoon. "Are you interested in her?"

"Romantically?" Drusus looked up from his food. "You know I'm not allowed to fraternize."

"When your contract ends," said Marius. "It's just a year and a few months away."

"That's a long time," said Drusus. "But it doesn't matter. I haven't a chance with Isolda. She's got eyes only for you."

"You think so?" Marius's stomach lifted. "How can you tell?"

"Gods, man, you must be blind if you can't see it. That woman *worships* you."

"She never says anything."

"What do you expect her to say?" said Drusus. "You're a wealthy, well-connected Kjallan. She's a poor Sardossian refugee with no papers, previously married, and with a child. People throw dog shit at her. She's not in your class, and she knows it. You think she's going to make eyes at you like a fool and risk losing a job that means everything to her?"

He hadn't thought of it that way. "You're saying she'll never make the first move. So I should do it."

Drusus eyed him. "You know you can't marry her. Won't that just make a mess of things?"

Marius was starting to wonder if perhaps he could marry her. Emperor Lucien would surely disapprove of the match, and he hated to disappoint his cousin, who'd done so much for him. But Lucien didn't own him. Marius was self-sufficient now. "I just want to get to know her better."

Drusus frowned. "You're too busy during the workday. You need to get her away. Ask her to supper. Or go out with her on Sage's Day."

Marius sighed. "I don't want to be like her old boss, that horrible man at the factory—"

"Stop it," said Drusus. "Marius, you will never be that man. What are you going to do if she turns you down?"

"Nothing, I suppose. What can I do?"

"That's the difference between you and the factory manager. He didn't respect her. He didn't take no for an answer, but you will if she turns you down. Now, are you going to ask her to see you sometime, outside of the surgery?"

Marius nodded. "I am." The prospect was frightening. Even so, he couldn't wait to ask.

16

"Have a seat, please," Isolda told the bewhiskered man in the wool hat. The smell of alcohol wafted into the surgery with him. "What's your name?"

He sank, loose-limbed, into the chair in front of her desk. "Name's Basilius."

Isolda consulted her list. "Basilius Stefanus?"

The man nodded.

"Sir, if you'll just come back with me to the business office, we need to go over some paperwork."

"Paperwork?" He sniffed, but followed her into the back office.

She closed the door for privacy and took a seat behind her desk. Basilius sat opposite her. "Sir, our records show that you've got an outstanding debt to the surgery of eight tetrals. Once you've arranged payment for the money owed, I can get you on the schedule for today."

Basilius stared. "That's why you called me back here? To hit me up for eight tetrals?"

"It's surgery policy, sir." And much as she disliked being alone with this man, it was also surgery policy not to embarrass clients by mentioning their unpaid debts in a public space.

He leaned back in his chair. "Don't have eight tetrals."

"I'm sorry, but the Healer is treating only paying patients today. If you'd like to come on our next Free Day, it's five days from now—"

"Five days?" Basilius raised his leg, complete with its dirty boot, and plopped it onto her desk. Dried mud sprinkled her paperwork. "I've a broken knee here."

Isolda doubted the knee was broken, given that he'd walked into the surgery on it. She eyed the mud on the desk. "Sir, you can either pay the eight tetrals you owe the surgery, or you can come back in five days."

Basilius removed his foot from her desk and leaned forward.

Catching a whiff of his sour breath, she recoiled. It could have stopped a four-in-hand.

"What do you know about tetrals, rat bitch?" he snarled, raising a hand as if to strike her. "Go back to Sardos where you belong."

Isolda's pulse spiked. In the street, she dealt with hateful men by running away. But here in the surgery, acting as the business manager, she was trapped. "Sir, it's—it's the official policy of the surgery," she stammered. She glanced at the door. Marius was not far away, and neither was Drusus. Should she call for help?

"Oh, fuck you and your piss-head friends." Basilius wheeled around and stomped out of the office.

Isolda sat motionless in her chair for what seemed an eternity, terrified to return to the waiting room lest she find him still there. After a while, she rose and quietly peeked out. He seemed to be gone. The only other person in the waiting room—a matronly woman with an unspecified complaint she wouldn't disclose to anyone but Marius—eyed her in an unfriendly way.

Marius's office door opened, and Marius emerged with his patient, a man with sunken cheeks and thinning hair.

Marius clasped the man's wrist. "The tincture tonight, and again tomorrow night. And tell your brother you need to rest— Healer's orders."

"Thank you," the man rasped.

Marius glanced at Isolda and frowned a little. "Everything all right?"

Perhaps he could see the stiffness in her posture. But the incident was over; no need to bother him when he had other things on his mind. She nodded and indicated the matronly woman. "Flavia is next."

Marius invited Flavia into his office.

Back at her waiting-room desk, Isolda made a notation on the book for Gracilis, the man who'd just left, and for Flavia, who was in Marius's office now. The bell rang over the surgery door, and she glanced up.

Basilius was back—and in the company of a large, bearded man.

She scrambled up from her chair.

The bearded man stomped toward her. "My friend says some piss-head's shaking him down for scurry."

She backed away. "It's not for me; it's for the Healer. Basilius owes the surgery eight tetrals for previous visits."

"You want eight dibs? I'll give you eight dibs." He grabbed for her.

She jumped out of reach just in time, feeling the scrape of his fingernails on her sleeve.

He circled around the desk toward her, and a knife flashed into his hand.

"Marius! Drusus!" she cried.

Basilius came at her from the other side. Pinned between the two of them, she retreated, and her back hit the wall. She glanced quickly from one man to the other. Basilius seemed the less scary of the two, so she ran at him, hoping to slip by. He grabbed her as she passed. She lashed out reflexively and felt her open hand connect with clothed flesh, but then something struck her shins, knocking her off balance. She hit the floor, and someone's weight landed on top of her. The breath flew out of her lungs with a whoosh.

She lay stunned, awaiting the blow or knife cut that must follow.

Instead, she heard screaming, and the weight rolled off her.

She staggered to her feet. What she saw defied the imagination. Basilius and the bearded man were writhing on the floor, clutching at themselves all over as if they were being eaten alive by ants. But she saw no blood or any sign of injury.

Marius stood nearby, his teeth bared in fury. Drusus picked up the bearded man as if he were a bag of laundry and tossed him across the room into a chair, which toppled over. Then he tossed Basilius after him.

Isolda could hardly believe Drusus's strength; it seemed inhuman.

She coughed and pounded her chest, and brushed off her clothes. Had the knife bitten her anywhere? She didn't think so.

"What in the Sage's name happened?" cried Marius. "Are you all right?"

"I think so." She'd taken a crack to her elbow, and her back was sore. Not bad—certainly she could have been hurt a lot worse. She pointed at Basilius. "That man is one of your patients. He didn't want to pay his bill—"

"And he attacked you?" Marius looked aghast.

"He left and brought a friend to do it."

Marius stared at the pair on the floor. "How much does he owe?"

"Eight tetrals."

"Why would anyone make such a fuss over eight tetrals? Three gods."

"Because she's Sardossian," said Drusus.

Marius growled deep in his throat.

"He called me a rat bitch and said I should go home to Sardos," said Isolda.

"Not much of a naturalist, is he?" observed Drusus. "A female rat is called a doe."

"We'll have to call the city guard," said Marius. "I can't have people coming in here and attacking my employees."

"If you do that, they'll arrest Isolda," said Drusus.

"Three gods," groaned Marius. "You're right. We'll send her to the villa and *then* call the guards—"

"But she's the one who witnessed the crime," said Drusus.

"I saw enough," said Marius.

"Come outside for a moment," said Drusus, glancing at the two groaning men. "We can leave them there for the time being."

Isolda and Marius followed Drusus outside onto the street.

Drusus spoke in a low voice. "If you bring the guards here, those men will tell them about Isolda, and then it won't matter whether you hide her at the villa. They'll find her."

"We can't just ignore what they did."

"Of course we can't. We deal with it as a private matter," said Drusus.

"Are you sure?"

While the men argued amongst themselves, Isolda puzzled over why Basilius and his friend had stopped fighting. Drusus had picked them up and thrown them, yes, but by the time he did that, they'd already been subdued. She'd never seen a man scream and twitch the way they had. And afterward, they'd lain docile on the floor, like mice in shock after being tormented by a cat. And yet neither Marius nor Drusus had even drawn a weapon.

"It's the only way, given the circumstances," said Drusus. "I'll handle it."

"All right," said Marius. "I'll escort Isolda to the villa."

"What are you going to do?" Isolda asked Drusus. She wasn't sure what they meant when they said they would deal with it as a private matter.

"Never mind." Marius took her arm. "They won't trouble you any further. Can you walk?"

Isolda nodded and let him lead her down the street. She felt jittery and strange. Everything looked foreign, as if she was seeing the neighborhood with different, sharper eyes.

Inside, Marius helped her to a chair in the sitting room. She collapsed in it.

"Are you all right?" asked Marius.

"Just tired." She wasn't sure why, since it was the middle of the day, but she could barely keep her eyes open.

"Sleep, then," said Marius, and she obeyed.

She awoke to someone's hand on her arm, and started.

"Be easy," said Marius. "Everything's all right."

Isolda yawned. She wasn't sure why she'd slept so long, except she remembered being shaky and tired after the ordeal at the surgery. She glanced at the window and saw that it was dark out. "Have you seen Rory?"

"He's in the kitchen," said Marius. "He came by the surgery about an hour ago, and Drusus collected him."

"What happened to Basilius and the other man?"

"They won't be a problem anymore," said Marius.

Isolda sat up in her chair. "Drusus didn't kill them, I hope."

"No, he just made it clear they're not welcome at the surgery anymore."

Isolda had a feeling the conversation between Drusus and the two men had involved more fists than words. But never mind. She couldn't go to the city guard, and if rough justice was all that was available to her, she'd take it. It was a good thing she had friends like Marius and Drusus to look after her.

Marius moved his hand down her arm, searching for painful spots.

When he reached her elbow, she winced.

"A bit of trouble there?" He took her arm in the crook of his own to immobilize it. Moments later, pain stirred deep within her elbow joint. She hissed and stiffened, but after a moment, the pain eased, and she felt a sensation of heat in its place. Marius was using his healing magic on her. As strange as it felt, she forced herself to relax. "It's warm."

"Everybody says that," said Marius. "And we don't know why that happens. I think it's the energy involved. You know how you get hot when you run, because your body is working hard? I'm asking your flesh to work hard right now."

"Work hard at what?"

"Repairing itself."

Isolda's body eased back into the chair. The sensation of warmth was growing while the pain faded. Marius moved on to her shoulders, searching for other bruised areas. She directed him to her back, and sighed deeply as his magic diminished the pain there.

"Have I got all of it?" asked Marius.

She nodded. "Your magic is miraculous."

"Praise the gods that they give us such gifts," said Marius.

"Why did those two men fall down screaming when you came over to us?" she asked. "It was as if you did something to them—or Drusus did—but I never saw it happen."

"You might as well know, now that you work with a Healer, that healing magic has an ugly side," said Marius.

"What do you mean?"

"I mean that just as I can knit the shards of a broken bone together, I could split that bone apart, creating a fracture with the touch of my hand. And that's not all." He leaned in and touched his hand to her chest. She tensed but did not protest—she knew she could trust Marius. "Do you feel your heart beating?"

She nodded.

"I could stop it," said Marius. "It would take me only an instant. You would die, and there would be no mark on you. No one would ever know what had happened."

Isolda shivered.

Marius removed his hand. "But don't worry. There's a profusion of laws forbidding that sort of thing. And most Healers can't do it because it requires special training."

"Which you've had?"

"My family insisted on it," said Marius.

"The men fell down screaming because you. . .broke their bones?"

"No. I used a torture spell. It's temporary and doesn't cause any damage, but it puts the victim in so much pain that they can't do anything. It will stop the strongest man in his tracks."

She blinked. "How is it possible that someone can be in excruciating pain yet suffer no harm?"

"Nobody knows the mechanism by which it works," said Marius.

Isolda was impressed but a little alarmed. Marius's magic was more frightening than she'd realized. "It's as if you have almost total control over another person's body."

"Not really. I can't make people do things, as mind mages can." He hesitated. "People ask me, sometimes, if healing magic can make a body move, make it act, as if it were an automaton. But it cannot. On rare occasions, someone will come into the surgery and ask me to. . .make someone attracted to them, you know, in a. . ." His cheeks flushed, and he cleared his throat. "In a romantic way. They go away disappointed because my magic can't do that either. We Healers don't traffic in love-philters or any other manipulations of will; that's beyond our ability."

"Oh." She was glad Marius couldn't use his magic to force someone to be sexually attracted to him. But he didn't need magic for that. Not with her.

"It's too late for you to be out in the streets," said Marius, "so I'm going to insist that you and Rory stay at the villa overnight. I'll have the servants draw you a bath so you can wash, and we'll set you and Rory up in a guest room. Once you're out of this syrtos, Arrod can launder and mend it."

"Thank you." It made sense that she should stay; she didn't like the idea of walking the Riat streets at night, just herself and Rory. But it wasn't going to be easy staying the night here either. She struggled enough working alongside Marius at the surgery, loving him and wanting him when she knew he was destined for someone else—someone prettier and more sophisticated, not to mention more Kjallan. Was it right for her to keep this job at all, given that she had no long-term future here? Certainly her presence was causing Marius and Drusus a great deal of trouble. It felt wrong to impose on them.

Yet she needed the money, and she loved the work. Gods curse her, she did not have the strength to leave.

17

The day dawned gray and muggy, and the house was still quiet when Marius rose. He knocked on Drusus's door to wake him and headed to the kitchen to see what was left over from yesterday. Half a melon, two rolls, and a bit of cheese—slim pickings. Drusus might eat all that on his own and ask for the main course.

Marius went to the cellar and selected cornmeal, honey, salt, and a jar of bacon fat. Corn cakes weren't fancy, but he doubted Isolda or Rory would turn their noses up at them, and he knew Drusus wouldn't.

He'd just heated up the pan and was about to drop some batter into it when Drusus completed his perimeter check and strolled in. "There's something you need to see."

"Can it wait?" said Marius, eyeing his hot pan.

"No."

Marius took the pan off the fire and followed Drusus, who led him out the front door. It was a typical Sage's Day morning, if a bit cloudy. Almost nobody was out on the street. "What am I looking for?"

"Behind you."

He turned and saw something hanging from his front door. "What in the Sage's name?" He leaned in for a closer look. It was a rat, tied by its grotesquely broken neck. "A child's prank?"

"Hardly," said Drusus.

"You're saying it's because of Isolda."

Drusus slid the string off the door lever and stepped away to toss the rat into the alley. "This has become a security concern, one I have to tell the emperor about."

Marius was less than enthusiastic about bringing the emperor into this. He hadn't been looking forward to telling Lucien that he'd hired an illegal Sardossian refugee. And yet he could hardly prevent Drusus from performing his job as a Legaciattus. "Do what you must." He went back inside and put his pan on the fire.

Drusus followed him into the kitchen. "They hung the rat here, not at the surgery, which means they've been watching us. They know Isolda's at the villa."

"Such courage they have, killing a rat," said Marius.

"Doesn't mean they won't do worse next time," said Drusus. "Are you going to tell her?"

"About the rat?" He sighed. "I suppose I'll have to." He would need to offer her some kind of protection, such as an escort to and from work, until this blew over. But he'd rather it wasn't their first topic of conversation when she got up this morning. He had so few chances to talk to her outside of a business setting, and he wished that for once they could just enjoy their time together instead of having it ruined by a couple of bigots.

"I'd be remiss in my duties if I didn't report it," said Drusus.

Marius dropped three spoonfuls of batter into the pan and watched them sizzle in the bacon fat. "I said you should do what you must. But I don't care what the emperor says; I'm not firing Isolda."

"You could pay her off," said Drusus. "She needs money, after all. Then you can find someone else to be your business manager."

"Pay her off, as if she were a mistress I'd become ashamed of?" Marius gave his bodyguard a look. "What sort of man would I be to cower in fear over two drunken oafs?"

"It's not just your safety at stake. It's hers."

"Those two might leave her alone if I send her away, but she'll still be in danger from the thousands of other men who hate Sardossians." Marius flipped the first batch of corn cakes. "When she's with us, at least she has some protection."

"My job is to protect *you*," said Drusus. "I can't look after her."

"Then I will," said Marius.

Isolda lay in Marius's guest bed, watching the windows lighten in a gray, indistinct sunrise. She'd tossed and turned last night, thinking of Marius, but her unrequited longing could not keep her up indefinitely. The bed was more comfortable than the one she slept in normally, and exhaustion had overtaken her. Now she just wanted to lie here forever.

Today was Sage's Day, the one day of the week the surgery was closed. There had been no days off at the gunpowder factory, nor at Jauld's store. But gods, it made a difference to have a day of rest.

She put on a spare syrtos the servants had left for her. It was a man's syrtos, probably belonging to Marius, and huge on her. She doubled up the fabric and tied it firmly with the belts. The garment smelled of him.

She went in to breakfast. Rory, who'd shared the guest room with her, had risen an hour earlier. He was sitting at the table with Drusus and Marius, scraping up the last bits from his breakfast plate. Rory greeted her with a cheerful, "Good Sage's Day." Drusus's plate was clean too, but Marius had no plate at all.

"Ah, you're up," said Marius. "I didn't want you to eat alone, so I waited."

"I ought to have been up earlier." She hadn't considered that Marius would go hungry waiting for her.

"You needed your sleep," said Marius.

"Hey, kid," said Drusus to Rory. "You ever groomed a horse?"

Rory shook his head. "We've never had a horse."

They'd had two at one time, when they'd lived with Jauld in Sardos, but Rory must not remember; he'd been too young.

"Marius keeps a couple of them in the attached stable. I'll introduce you, and Rufus will teach you how to groom."

Rory banged the table with his knees in his haste to get up. He and Drusus left.

Isolda hadn't known Marius kept horses. She kept adjusting her estimation of his wealth higher, but his money couldn't come from his business, which hadn't been profitable until recently. So it had to be family wealth. And then there was that strange bit about his receiving training in the darker forms of healing magic, when most Healers-in-training did not.

It occurred to her that she and Marius were now completely alone. For all the time she'd spent with him at the surgery, she had seldom been alone with him longer than a minute or two. Drusus was always around, and sometimes Rory. She felt suddenly shy, but forced herself to make conversation. "I'm glad you fed Rory straightaway—the boy is insatiable."

"Because he's so sturdy and healthy. Do you like corn cakes?" asked Marius. "The cook's off duty today, so you'll have to put up with a bachelor's efforts."

"I'm not sure I've ever had them," said Isolda. "But I'm willing to try."

He left the dining table and returned carrying two plates. He set one of them in front of her.

Two corn cakes were stacked on her plate, along with some sliced fruit. She cut into the first corn cake, and it flaked beautifully. "This bachelor's effort doesn't look so amateurish to me."

He shrugged. "For years, I cooked all my own meals. I'm a bit repetitive in my tastes, though. Corn cakes most mornings, soup most evenings."

"I can see why you'd eat these most mornings. They're delicious."

"They're simple, I know—not a lot of flavor—"

Isolda raised another bite to her mouth. "They've got a lovely, delicate flavor, and if you added anything stronger you'd overpower it."

He grinned. "Thank you. Is that my syrtos you're wearing?"

"It must be," she said. "Arrod loaned it to me."

"I like it on you."

Isolda's cheeks warmed, and she looked down at her plate. That sounded a little bit flirtatious. But Marius wouldn't flirt with someone like her. She was letting her imagination run away with her.

"Do you enjoy working at the surgery?" asked Marius.

"It's the best job I've ever had."

"You're marvelous at it," said Marius. "Hiring you was the best business decision I ever made. I like you, Isolda. I mean, I like your work. I mean—" He cleared his throat. "There's so much about you I don't know."

Isolda was wary. "Such as?"

"What do you want out of your life here?" asked Marius. "I know you'd like Rory to go to the university and become a warder, but what do you want for yourself?"

"I'm happy doing what I am now."

"I'm glad, but that's not what I meant," said Marius. "You seem to be directing your energy toward Rory and his future, but do you plan to marry again? Go back to Sardos at some point?"

She shook her head. Perhaps Marius was worried she'd find a better situation and leave the surgery, but that wasn't going to happen. Opportunities for her were thin; she was lucky to have any job, let alone one this perfect. "I'm never going back to Sardos. As for remarrying. . ." She winced. "I was fortunate to marry once. It won't happen again."

"Why?"

Her stomach clenched, and she put down her spoon. "I'm twenty-six. I have an eight-year-old child. I'm Sardossian. And

I'm. . ." She couldn't choke out the words *not pretty enough.* "I'm not the sort of woman men are looking for." She couldn't believe she was confessing to Marius her great shame, that for all her skills and talents she was worthless as a wife. She was focusing her efforts on Rory because he still had a future. She, at age twenty-six, was washed up.

"I think you underestimate yourself."

She shook her head. "One can dream, but what's the use if the dreams can't come true? I'll always be an outcast in Kjall. As for remarrying, if I were prettier I might think differently about my chances of finding someone—"

"Oh, but you're beautiful," said Marius.

Isolda fell silent. It was kind of Marius to say, but she knew better.

"I mean it," said Marius.

"I've accepted what I am," she said finally. "You don't need to pretend, to say things that aren't true in order to spare my feelings—"

"I'm not sparing your feelings," said Marius. "I didn't see your beauty when I first met you, but now I wonder how I ever missed it."

Tears filled her eyes.

A lump bobbed in Marius's throat, and he took a shaky breath. "I was thinking we should go out for dinner sometime. Away from the surgery, just you and me."

Isolda could not answer; her mind was a whirl of confusion and questions. Was he trying to seduce her, and to what end? As much as she wanted him, sleeping with her boss could only hurt her. It was like walking blindfolded into a busy street—even if she managed not to get hit by a wagon, she was sure to step in horseshit.

He wasn't going to marry a woman like her, so any affair they might have must be short lived. Could she bear it when he let her go in favor of someone else, perhaps his future marriage partner, a woman sure to be prettier and more sophisticated? It had happened to her once before, and she had barely survived it. And that was with Jauld, a man she'd never cared for. If Marius, this man that she admired and loved so deeply, found his marriage partner and set her aside, she would be devastated. Better to be alone in life than to risk that.

She was, perhaps, being unfair; Marius was not Jauld and would never be cruel or thoughtless. But one didn't extend a marriage proposal out of kindness or pity. Marius would never marry someone as beneath him as she was.

"I'm sorry," said Marius. "I've made you uncomfortable. It's all right to say no. I don't want to be like that man you worked for at the gunpowder factory—"

"Oh," said Isolda. "You are nothing like him."

"But I'm making you uncomfortable?"

She looked down at her hands. "It's complicated. I'd like to go to dinner with you sometime, but I don't know if I can do this again. Not after. . ." She trailed off, choking on the painful truth.

"You mean after your husband died? I'm so sorry."

Marius had it wrong. That wasn't the reason, and as far as she knew, Jauld was still alive. She'd entered the marriage in good faith and given him everything. And then he had betrayed her in every possible way. Her throat caught as the pain of the last ten years rose up like bile, and she choked out a sob.

Marius was out of his seat in an instant, gathering her into his arms. "Gods, Isolda, I should never have mentioned—you must miss him terribly."

She shook her head violently and buried her face in his shoulder. "I don't miss him at all." Poor, dear Marius. He had everything backward, and it was her own gods-cursed fault for not telling him the truth. She was still married! If she slept with Marius or any other man, she'd be committing adultery, a capital crime in Sardos. Divorce, too, was illegal there. Sardossian law had her tethered to Jauld for the rest of her life.

Marius stroked her back as he held her. "Is that what's upsetting you? If he didn't treat you well, then it's perfectly natural you wouldn't miss him. You shouldn't feel guilty about that."

He still had it wrong, and no wonder, when she was giving him lies upon lies. But she couldn't tell him she was married. What if that changed his opinion of her? What if he believed she was wrong to abandon her husband, and especially to take Rory away from his father? She'd violated half a dozen laws in coming to Kjall. Marius was a respected, well-connected Kjallan, and a deeply moral man. He also had a supportive family, and he might not comprehend what it was like to be alone in the world.

In her situation, there had been no good answers. Backed into a corner, she'd done what she had to do. But with a single visit to the authorities, he could erase everything she'd accomplished and have her sent back to the hell that was her old home.

"*Did* he treat you badly?" asked Marius.

"Yes." That seemed safe to say, and it was true.

Marius tilted her chin up so that he was looking her in the eye. "I would never treat you badly."

Isolda opened her mouth to reply—*I know you wouldn't*—but she could not stop staring at Marius's lips, so close and inviting. They were mostly dry and soft, but a shiny spot of moisture had formed in the middle of his bottom lip. She wanted to lick it. A shiver of desire snaked from her core up through her spine. She wanted nothing more than to go to bed with this man, and to Soldier's Hell with the consequences.

Marius leaned down and kissed her. She found her lips moving to meet his.

With Jauld, she'd always hesitated a bit, knowing the kiss was obligatory. Jauld had chosen her—perhaps because she was all he could afford, but still, he'd done the choosing—and she had never chosen him. Marius, on the other hand, was a man she'd wanted since the day she'd laid eyes on him, and her adoration had only grown since then.

His kiss was gentle and chaste. It left her wanting more.

Marius pulled back. "I'm sorry. I should have asked first."

"Kiss me again," she said. "And don't ask." If he asked, she might say no, and she didn't want to say no. She wanted to hold this man, to take him deep into her body and never let him go. It would destroy her in the end, but gods, she couldn't resist. He'd asked her what she wanted for herself, and she'd avoided the question, because she couldn't tell him the truth: she wanted *him*.

His mouth descended on hers again, and her heart sang. He was gentle at first, but when an involuntary moan escaped her, he pressed harder, tightening his arms around her. Her troubles faded away, and her world became Marius, his hard body surrounding her, his lips plundering hers. Her body turned to jelly in his grasp.

Then the floor beneath them gave a jolt, and every window in the villa exploded.

Isolda raised her head. Chari's cries from the back bedroom were growing more agonized—perhaps the baby was crowning. It was customary in polygamous marriages for the senior wife to act as midwife to the junior, but Chari had seemed horrified at that idea and whispered in Jauld's ear, "What if she hurts the baby?" Thus Isolda had been banished from the birthing room, and Chari's sister had come to attend her instead.

Isolda sat at the kitchen table with Rory in her lap. The household was tumultuous these days, as was the entire nation of Sardos. Last month, the First Heir had been assassinated. It was said he'd named an heir beforehand by writing the name on a piece of paper and sealing it in a strongbox. But after his death, five separate men claimed that the name on the paper was theirs, and no conclusive evidence had arisen to prove one claim over the others.

Armies were massing, and violence seemed inevitable. A recruiter had swept through their village already, gathering the unmarried men as well as any boys over the age of ten—anyone who wasn't an heir—and hauling them off in a wagon to gods knew where. They would end up fighting on behalf of one of the brothers; Isolda didn't even know which one. Both of her clerks had been taken by the recruiters, leaving her to manage the store alone. She'd had to reduce the store's hours, but unfortunately it made little difference. Sales had dropped below half of what they had been before.

Rory had been spared by the recruiters on account of his youth. But youth didn't last forever, and while Isolda hoped the battle for the succession would be resolved quickly, the previous succession had dragged on for ten bloody years.

She'd told Jauld they needed to cut back on their household spending to survive the hard times ahead, but he wouldn't listen. He'd recently bought a new phaeton and a pair of fancy carriage horses that he liked to drive to town and show off. But those horses were eating up their savings. She'd started fixing the books at the store a little and setting money aside—literally hiding it behind a brick in the storeroom—so that when Jauld ran through all their savings, they might still have something to survive on.

A tinny wail rose through the closed door of the birthing room.

Rory clutched her arm. "What's that?"

"It's a baby," said Isolda.

"Oh." He heaved a sigh. "It sounds like a monster."

"Do you think you have a baby brother or a baby sister?"

"A baby brother." That was Rory's hope, because he liked the idea of having another boy to play with.

Isolda prayed for a sister.

Jauld emerged from the birthing room, smiling and misty-eyed, carrying a cloth-wrapped bundle. Isolda's stomach clenched. She rose from her seat, and as he brought the bundle near, she peered at the squirming, naked infant. It was a boy.

Jauld stroked the baby's face with a fingertip and beamed. "Isn't he the most beautiful child you've ever seen?"

The baby's face was squashed, and his head was cone-shaped, and he was red all over. Rory was the handsomer child by far, but she knew better than to be rude at a time like this. The baby would improve with age. "He's lovely."

"His name is Troi," said Jauld. "And I'm making him my heir."

Isolda's gut went hollow. Her eyes snapped to his. "You can't do that. He's just a baby."

"But I can," he said. "It's a father's prerogative to select his heir."

Her world was crashing down around her. Jauld knew nothing about this child, nothing at all. Only that he was a boy, and the son of himself and Chari. Isolda's pulse throbbed hot in her ears. If Rory was no longer the heir, he could be taken by the army recruiters. She could spend the next eight years raising him only to see him die in a war which benefited nobody except some spoiled prince. "The store, the money that we have—I earned it! The wealth came from me. It should pass to my son, not to Chari's."

Jauld's eyes narrowed. "The store has always been mine. I knew you were going to be difficult about this, but the decision is made. Troi is my heir." He turned away.

Isolda set Rory on the ground—how horrifying that he was hearing this!—and trotted after Jauld. "You betrayed me once when you took the money I earned and used it to buy a second wife. But you will not betray me a second time. I won't have it."

He snorted. "You know perfectly well no one else would have offered for you. You should be happy to have a place here."

"I wish you'd never offered for me. Better no husband at all than a worthless one."

Jauld's face contracted, and he delivered an open-handed slap across her face.

Isolda retreated a step. Her face stung where he'd struck her.

"You're the one who's worthless," said Jauld. "And that's why your brat will inherit nothing." He turned and went into the birthing room, slamming the door behind him.

Someone was crying. As her panicking mind climbed down from the shock of Jauld's assault, she realized it was Rory, back in the kitchen. She hurried to her child and scooped him up. "It's all right, love, it's all right," she soothed.

But it wasn't all right.

She had no choice. She must leave this place. If it killed her, she would leave—and she would take Rory with her.

18

Glass glittered on the street. Marius stepped around it and stretched upward as if that might help him see beyond the three-story buildings that blocked his view of the harbor district. A roiling ball of black smoke took up half the visible sky.

"That'll be at the harbor," said Drusus.

Marius turned to Isolda. "It may have been your gunpowder factory."

The moment the windows had blown, Isolda had run to the stable to fetch Rory. He was unharmed, and now she stood clutching him to her body and staring ashen-faced at the black cloud.

Marius didn't know what to say. This was personal for Isolda. If the explosion was indeed the gunpowder factory where she used to work, many of her friends could have been injured or killed. He took her hand and squeezed.

Isolda took a step toward the smoke, pulling him with her. "I have to go there. Can Rory stay here with you?"

Glass crunched under Marius's boots. "It's not safe for you to go."

"My friends are there. They may need help."

He admired her determination, but what could she realistically accomplish?

"There is nothing you can do for them," said Drusus, voicing Marius's thoughts.

Isolda continued to move forward. "People might be trapped inside the building. I know my way around. I know where the passages lead—"

"Within minutes, the whole site will be swarming with guards," said Drusus.

"I could go through the alley and in by the southern door—"

"The guards will surround the place," said Marius. "If by some miracle they don't find you, someone else will." If anti-Sardossian sentiment had been bad before, it was only going to get worse in the wake of this explosion. The smartest thing Isolda could do right now was stay out of public view. "Of course you want to help, but somebody has to stay with Rory, and it can't be me or Drusus. I'm a licensed Healer. I have to go to the site right away."

His maid, exhibiting perfect timing, trotted out of the villa, carrying his formal syrtos, the green one with the double white belts that marked him as one of the city's Healers. Marius took it and shrugged it on over his tunic.

Isolda's eyes barely focused as she watched him dress. "You're right. You have to go. You'll do more good there than I would."

"I'll bring back news as soon as I can. And Isolda—I don't think the neighborhood is entirely safe for you and Rory." Now was not the time to talk about the dead rat they'd found hanging on the door. "I want you to lock the place up tight." He turned to his maid. "You hear? Lock up. Nobody goes in or out."

The maid nodded.

Marius headed off in the direction of the harbor, trailed by Drusus.

The scene at the disaster site was as chaotic as it had been the last time. One building was a blown-out husk that belched black smoke. Nothing was left of that one to salvage, but fire mages were working to put out the flames that had jumped to neighboring buildings.

Thick smoke settled over the harbor, cutting visibility to no farther than ten feet. The air smelled of sulfur and charred wood. People flickered like shadows through the gray. On his right, in the distance, someone screamed for help. Marius turned to move in that direction and spotted a red coat shining through the haze—a city guardsman.

Five minutes later, the guards had cordoned off a bit of street space for him and assigned him a fourteen-year-old boy to act as his assistant.

"Bring me whoever needs help," Marius instructed the boy. "Kjallan, Sardossian—I don't care who they are or where they're from."

The first patient delivered to him was a Sardossian woman with burnt yellow hair and blackened skin on her arm. Her jaw clenched in a rictus of pain. *She could have been Isolda*, thought Marius.

Burns, though grievously painful and horrifying to behold, were easier to heal than most injuries. Laying hands on her, he called to his magic.

Half an hour later, he heaved a sigh, fatigued from continuous healing. In a short space of time, the scene had changed utterly. He'd gone from a single patient to having dozens stack up outside the cordoned-off space. He'd healed his burn patient only halfway because someone more critical had turned up, and he'd had to switch. He hadn't had the chance to get back to her yet. Drusus was playing both triage and defense, pushing away the onlookers who cried out to Marius and grabbed at his clothes, wanting help. Apparently there were a lot more wounded than there were Healers.

His burn patient was trying to tell him something in Sardossian. Isolda could have translated, but she was back at the villa.

"I'll get back to you, I promise," said Marius. He might be here all night—or longer.

Her gaze darted over his shoulder. Distractedly, Marius wondered why. Then a red-coated city guardsman stepped up and took the woman by the arm.

"Hey," said Marius. "She's my patient. Leave her alone."

"Aren't you finished with her?" asked the guardsman.

"No. Can't you see I'm busy?" He'd removed a spike that was impaled in a man's chest, and now he had to control the bleeding.

The guardsman let her go. "Orders have come down from the palace. All Sardossians in the area are to be taken into custody. You can heal them first, but they can't go free."

"Orders from the *palace*?" said Marius. His own cousin had ordered the Sardossians to be detained? He supposed the political pressure on Lucien must be enormous—and now he really wasn't looking forward to telling the emperor about Isolda. At least she was home at the villa and safe from this detainment order. "You're saying I'm supposed to heal these people and then hand them over to you to be deported?"

"That's what I'm saying," said the guardsman.

Marius growled under his breath and shook the blood from his hands. He couldn't countermand his cousin's orders. He could decline to heal the Sardossians under these ridiculous conditions, but what good would that do? Then they might be thrown on the boat still injured and in pain.

His assistant arrived with a helper, bearing a groaning Sardossian man on a makeshift stretcher. The ghastly tip of a broken femur poked out of the man's leg.

"We'll do that one next," Marius said to his assistant.

All he could think to do right now was to keep working.

It was late when Marius finally headed home, so late that he half expected the sun to rise before he reached the villa. Riat's harbor district, normally quiet after the pubs and bawdy-houses closed their doors for the night, had never gone to sleep. The fires had been doused, the smoke had blown away, and most of the injured had been treated, but the city guards were still at work rounding up Sardossians for deportation.

He'd heard there was rioting on the east side of the harbor, and he'd treated several people—two Sardossians and a Kjallan—who'd been injured in the violence.

As he and Drusus crossed from the harbor district into the south hills district, the disorder quieted, and he began to feel reassured that Isolda had avoided the worst of the trouble.

Inside the villa, Marius found her asleep in a chair.

She awoke with a start at his touch. "Marius!" she cried, pressing her hand to her chest. "Gods—I don't know when I dropped off. For the longest time I couldn't sleep at all—"

He knelt beside her chair, laying his hand over hers. "I'm glad you finally did."

"What time is it? Look at you, absolutely covered in soot. Was it very bad? Were there many killed?"

"There were a lot of survivors," he said, trying to focus on the positive.

She rose from the chair. "I should go. It's over now—I can talk to my friends at home, find out who got away and who didn't—"

"Isolda," he said, rising with her, "you can't go, not just yet. The city guards are rounding up Sardossians for deportation."

She stared at him. "The survivors are being deported?"

"I'm afraid so," he said. "It was the emperor's direct order. Nothing I could do to stop it." At least she didn't know the emperor was his own cousin.

She let out a shaky breath. "I'm sorry. It's not your fault."

"I know this is hard—" he began.

"I have to go home."

Marius shook his head. "Eventually, yes, but not now. There's rioting in the harbor district, and the guards are still rounding up your people. You want to be sent back to Sardos? You and Rory?"

"No." Her body drooped.

He wrapped an arm around her waist and led her toward the guest bedroom. "Stay here tonight. Stay as long as you need, until Riat loses interest in this and moves on to something else. You need sleep."

"You're the one who needs sleep," she said. "You look pale. Healing takes a lot out of you, and this was supposed to be your day to rest."

"I'll sleep easier knowing you're safe in the guest room next door," said Marius.

"Then I'll be there," said Isolda.

19

Isolda felt strange walking to the surgery the next morning, as if it were just another day, when only yesterday the gunpowder factory had exploded and any number of people she knew could have been killed. Of course there was nothing she could do to stop a tragedy that had already happened. She'd only be putting herself and Rory at risk if she rushed home right now, and yet she could hardly stand not knowing who had survived and who hadn't.

Luck alone had spared her, her luck in being noticed by Marius. If he hadn't hired her to work in his surgery last month, she'd have been in that factory when it blew. She felt guilty somehow, as if she'd betrayed her own people.

But life had a way of soldiering on. She had work to attend to, a living to make.

Rory had already left for the fruit stand. She worried about him being on his own in a city so crazed with anti-Sardossian sentiment, but it would be suspicious for him to miss work right after the explosion. Rory had no accent, and his boss took him for Riorcan. That was an illusion worth maintaining.

Marius, walking ahead of her, halted just short of the surgery.

"Is something wrong?" She peered around him, looking for a patrolling guardsman, but her eyes fell instead on crude black lettering painted across the surgery door: "PISS HEAD GO HOME."

Her scalp prickled, and her hand went to her head, checking for the bonnet that covered her yellow hair. Marius and Drusus were looking at the door, not at her, and yet she felt stared at, naked and exposed. Certainly they were both thinking about her right now.

Drusus swept a finger across the writing. "Paint's still wet."

"Not giving up, are they?" said Marius.

"You think it's Basilius?" asked Isolda.

"Him or his friends," said Drusus.

Isolda swallowed. Marius had told her the problem was taken care of, that Drusus had carried out some sort of rough justice on the two men. Apparently it hadn't worked. But she couldn't blame Marius or Drusus for that.

"I meant to tell you yesterday, but then the gunpowder factory blew, and I got sidetracked," said Marius. "This is not the first incident. Someone hung a dead rat on the door to the villa yesterday morning."

"Oh gods, I'm sorry." Isolda blinked rapidly. Once again, she was causing trouble for Marius, who didn't deserve to be exposed to this sort of ugliness. "I'll leave."

"Whatever for?" asked Marius.

Such an adorable man, and brave, too. Isolda forced her words past the lump in her throat. "I don't want this to happen to your wonderful surgery. I'll find work elsewhere." Forcing her leaden feet to move, she turned to go.

"Don't be silly." Marius took her by the arm. "You can't let those sapskulls win."

"But they're going to keep at it—"

"The paint on the door is nothing," said Marius. "I'll hire someone to wash it off or paint over it. From this point forward, Drusus can handle the patients who owe the surgery money. What a sapskull I was not to set it up that way in the first place! It doesn't make sense to put you in that role when you're so vulnerable, both as a woman and as a Sardossian. Nobody's going to pull a knife on Drusus—"

"I really don't like causing you all this trouble."

"You're not causing trouble." Marius led her firmly back to the surgery door. "Basilius is. You are wanted here, and he is not."

Isolda wiped her eyes. She loved this job and she loved Marius; she wanted to stay. Still, her conscience nagged at her.

"I think Drusus and I should escort you to and from work for a while," added Marius. "Until the trouble blows over."

"Oh—thank you, but you can't do that." It wasn't just a matter of inconveniencing him. She couldn't let him escort her home because if she led a Kjallan to where she and her fellow Sardossians hid, her people would be furious, and they might not let her stay anymore. If there were any of them left to *be* furious, after what had happened yesterday.

"I don't mind," said Marius. "You know I need the exercise."

Isolda smiled. While it was true Marius didn't exercise much, he was young, and he looked perfectly fit. "It's not a matter of putting you out, it's just that my people are in hiding, and I can't give away their hiding places."

"Oh." Marius's brows rose. "Well, perhaps if we escorted you part of the way, just far enough to discourage men like Basilius."

That would solve the problem, but Marius was missing the bigger issue. "I don't think you understand. This isn't something that's going to blow over. I deal with this sort of harassment *all the time*. It's not going to be a couple of incidents and then we're done with it. It's likely to be over and over again, not just Basilius but other people, and it will keep happening as long as I'm working here. That's why I'm saying I have to leave. Do you see? It's not going to go away!"

Marius's smile faded. "I admit, that's. . .sobering. Is it really that bad?"

Isolda nodded.

"Then we'll deal with it for years on end if we have to," said Marius. "Come, let's open the surgery. We can put a canvas over the door until it's fixed."

She let Marius lead her through the door, astonished that he could so easily commit to taking on a problem of this magnitude, one that had never been his to begin with.

Drusus took the ruined door off its hinges, and they opened for business with the surgery exposed to the open air. Drusus took Isolda's place in the waiting room, screening patients, and she removed to the back office to catch up on bookkeeping.

With relief, she dove into the world of numbers. Numbers were objective and safe. They didn't care about your accent or the color of your hair. And this week, the numbers were uncommonly good. An hour's work turned up the happy news that despite the negative effect of the Free Days and the distraction of Basilius, business was up and so were the surgery's profits. Marius would be pleased with her report at the end of the day.

Isolda cocked her head. Something was going on in the waiting room. An argument? She stopped scratching her quill against the paper. Drusus was using his low voice, the dangerous one that meant business. Did someone else owe the surgery money? She heard another male voice besides Drusus's, one that was unfamiliar.

Then a third voice joined in: Marius. He sounded upset. She raised her head.

Footsteps sounded, moving in her direction. As the men neared, she began to make out what they were saying.

"You have no authority to do this, none at all," said Marius.

"Our orders come from the emperor," said the man she didn't know.

Three gods. Was this the city guard, come for her? She scrambled up from her chair, looking around the windowless room. Nowhere she could run to.

"I'll wager you were sent here by Basilius," said Marius. "He's a common thug who's vandalized my property and harassed my workers. It's him you should be taking, not her."

"By imperial writ, all Sardossians are to be taken into custody."

"Not this one," said Marius. "She works for me and had nothing to do with the explosion. She was with me when it happened, far from the harbor district."

"If you have a grievance with my carrying out this order, you can take it up with the emperor," said the guardsman.

"He will," said Drusus. "You can count on that."

The door to the back room opened to reveal two uniformed men from the Riat City Guard. Without preamble, one of them stepped inside and grabbed Isolda by the arm.

"You saw my bodyguard's insignia," Marius was saying.

"An insignia doesn't countermand my orders," said the guardsman.

Marius turned to Isolda. "Please don't be frightened. I can't stop him from taking you, but I'm going to get you out, I promise."

"How long before the Sardossians are deported?" asked Drusus.

The guardsman shrugged. "Don't know."

Isolda, looking at the open door, wrenched her arm, hoping to take the guardsman by surprise and dart away. She had every confidence that Marius would try to help her, but none whatsoever that he had the power to do so. Better to escape if she could. For a moment she felt the guard's grip slipping, but then he tightened it and twisted her arm.

"You want me to put you in shackles, piss-head?" snarled the guardsman.

"Don't you hurt her," said Marius. "It will be your head if you do."

"Remember the insignia," added Drusus.

The guardsman's hand loosened on her arm just enough to ease the pain.

"Go quietly, Isolda, for your own sake," said Marius. "I'll get you out."

Gods, if she was in custody, what was going to happen to Rory? She couldn't say anything to Marius about him directly, lest she tip off the guards, but perhaps she could drop a hint. "I didn't get to the fruit market today. I hope that's all right."

Marius blinked. Message received. "Perfectly all right."

Gritting her teeth, she let the guardsman lead her out the surgery door.

"Shove over," called the guard into the crowded holding cell as he pushed Isolda into it. The cell looked like it was built to hold five to eight people, but nearly thirty Sardossians were crammed inside. Most of them sat on the floor, wedged together like ill-fitting puzzle pieces, while a few around the edges stood, trading tired legs for breathing room.

As the door clanged shut behind her, Isolda looked over her cell-mates. She recognized several, all of them people she'd seen around the factory or in the underground and knew vaguely.

Then her eyes lit on someone she knew well. "Emari."

The young woman looked up, and her soot-stained face crinkled into a smile. "Isolda."

Emari was at the far end of the holding cell, and while the sea of humanity between them seemed impassable, Isolda was determined to get there. She waded her way across, ignoring the grumbling, and apologizing for stepped-on fingers. When she arrived, Emari persuaded the others to clear a little space for her.

"Were you in the factory when it blew?" asked Isolda.

Emari nodded. "It was the storeroom that went. The millers nearest that direction—I don't think they made it."

Isolda mentally catalogued the millers she knew and their usual stations. "Did Rill get out?"

"I didn't see her. Doesn't mean she's dead, though. The scene was chaos."

"This isn't the only holding cell for Sardossians, is it?"

"I saw Taia taken by the guard—you remember Taia?—and she's not here. So there must be at least one more."

"I don't think Rill made it," said a neighboring cellmate. "She was one mill down from Poller and the others, who were one mill down from me, and when we got out the door there was nobody behind us."

Isolda's stomach tightened. One by one, she ran through the list of people she knew and asked Emari and her neighbors about each one. It turned out that three people she knew besides Emari were known to have survived, and of those, two had been picked up by the guards. Emari wasn't certain about the third. But the list of people whose fates Emari did not know was long. Isolda feared most of them were dead. There was no word on Caz, her Sardossian friend who worked at the docks rather than the gunpowder factory, but she assumed he'd survived since he would have no reason to be near the disaster site. Nobody knew whether he'd been swept up by the guards, and he wasn't in the holding cell.

"I didn't think they'd get you," said Emari. "Doesn't that new job of yours keep you out of the harbor district?"

"The guards came for me at the surgery," said Isolda. "I think someone tipped them off. How long have you been here?"

"Since yesterday afternoon."

"Is there any word about what's going to happen?"

"We're being deported," said Emari. "I heard they're outfitting two ships."

"When?"

"No idea."

Isolda hugged her knees. Marius had promised to help her, but he had no authority to break her out of a guardhouse's holding cell. If she wound up back in Sardos, what would she do? Rory, left behind in Riat, would be effectively orphaned. Where in Sardos would the ship drop them off? She couldn't stand the thought of going back to Jauld, but single women couldn't hold jobs in Sardos.

There was no life for her in Sardos, none at all. If Marius couldn't break her out, she'd find a way back to Kjall or die trying.

20

"He's in a meeting." The Legaciattus pointed Marius toward a chair. "If you'll wait over there, he can see you for five minutes when he's done."

Marius eyed the chair and thought of Isolda in the hands of the Riat City Guard. They could be interrogating her right now. Or hurting her. Or loading her onto a ship. "How long will the meeting be?"

"A couple hours."

Long enough for a great deal of mischief to take place. Isolda could be beaten; she could be raped. Nobody talked about that sort of thing, but everybody knew it happened in guardhouses. What if the deportation ship was being loaded this very minute, and by the end of the day, she'd be gone? "Do you know when the deportation ships are scheduled to leave?"

"I don't."

"This is too urgent a matter to wait," said Marius. "Tell the emperor I must see him right away. I won't require much of his time."

"Sir, it's an important meeting. . ."

The Legaciattus sounded uncomfortable, almost wheedling. Marius had put him in a tight spot. On the one hand, Lucien would be annoyed at Marius's interruption. On the other hand, Lucien would be angrier still if his guards *didn't* interrupt him for a truly urgent matter.

But Marius's sympathies did not lie with the guard; that man's discomfort was nothing to what Isolda could be experiencing. "I need to see him right now."

"Can you tell me what it's about?" asked the guard.

"It's for his ears only."

"Have a seat," said the guard. "I'll tell him what you've said."

"Thank you." Marius retired to the chair he'd been pointed to, and Drusus took a seat beside him. The waiting room was an august one. Dignitaries from all over the empire had perched in these chairs while anticipating their audience with the emperor. Marius could not relax. He sat on the edge of his chair, tapping his heel against the polished marble floor.

"It takes a long time to outfit a ship for a journey of that distance," offered Drusus.

"I hope you're right," said Marius.

They lapsed again into silence. A clock chimed, and Marius's gaze darted toward it. The clock sat on a carved wooden table against the wall. Now that he'd noticed it, he could hear its ticking. He counted the seconds as they passed.

Finally the great double doors opened, spilling out the emperor and his guards.

Marius stood and inclined his head in a gesture of respect.

Lucien looked strained. "You've inconvenienced me greatly, so make this fast."

Marius skipped the remaining social niceties. "One of my employees at the surgery has been taken into custody by the Riat City Guard, and I need her back."

Lucien took a seat across from him. "Did she commit a crime?"

Marius sat. "No, she was taken because she's Sardossian."

"Then it was on my order," said Lucien. "We've tolerated these refugees and their illegal factories long enough. I'm having the guards round all of them up and send them home. You may be assured that we're being humane about it. My order specifies no interrogations and no abuse. Just gather them up and put them on the ship."

"Sir, this woman is a valued employee. As you know, my surgery used to lose money, but since she started as my business manager, we've been turning a profit. I can assure you she had nothing to do with the gunpowder factory explosion, because she was with me when it happened."

"She was with you on a Sage's Day?" asked Lucien.

Marius's cheeks warmed. Lucien knew he did not open the surgery on Sage's Day. "Yes, sir. An innocent situation." Mostly.

"Yet she's an illegal refugee."

"Sir, I need her for my business. She works hard, and she's not a trouble-maker."

Lucien frowned and tugged at his ear. "How do your patients react to seeing a Sardossian at work in the surgery?"

"Reasonably enough," said Marius.

Lucien raised his eyebrows at Drusus.

Drusus unfolded his arms and said, "I have some security concerns that I've been meaning to talk to you about. But they're not the woman's fault."

Lucien appeared torn, his eyes moving from Marius to Drusus and then back to Marius. Finally he gestured to one of his guards, who spun on his heel and left. "I'll have my clerk give you a writ authorizing you to take this woman back from the City Guard, but only because I don't have time to discuss this at length." The guard returned in the company of a second man, who bore a tray with writing utensils and the imperial seal. "And next Sage's Day, you will have lunch with me—both of you—and we'll have a longer conversation about this Sardossian employee and the security concerns."

"Yes, sir," said Marius, relieved at getting his writ but dreading next Sage's Day. "Er—could I also have a writ that says you've authorized her to work at the surgery and the guards can't pick her up again?"

Lucien gave Marius an exasperated look. "Very well, but it will be temporary, lasting one month."

"Her name is Isolda," Marius offered. "Oh, could you write that second one not just for her, but for her family? She's got a son. He's Jamien's age."

"A son." Lucien sounded annoyed.

"And how long before the deportation ships sail?"

"Three days, last I heard," said Lucien.

"Thank you, sir," said Marius. He'd pushed the emperor as far as he dared.

Since it was getting on toward evening, Marius dropped by the fruit stand, hoping to find Rory before he got off work. Otherwise the boy would run to the surgery, find it closed, perhaps learn that his mother had been picked up by the guards, and panic. Luck was with Marius, and he was able to collect the boy and explain the situation as they rode from guardhouse to guardhouse in search of Isolda.

He found her in the third guardhouse he visited, crammed into a holding cell filled with other Sardossians. She was easy to pick out of the crowd; hers was the face that lit up on seeing him and Rory. She looked tired and frightened but unharmed. As she waded through the mass of humanity toward him, she clutched the hand of a younger woman, bringing her along.

Marius's heart sank. His writ permitted only Isolda's release.

"This is Emari," said Isolda. "Can you get her out too?"

Marius turned to the guard. "It's just one more woman. What's the harm?"

The guard shook his head. "Writ says Isolda and nobody else. You know these Sardossians breed like rats."

Marius had seen few Sardossian children in Riat besides Rory. But it was clear the guard wasn't going to be flexible. "I'm sorry, Isolda. I haven't the authority to help your friend."

Isolda nodded, sniffled, and hugged Emari.

The guard took Isolda's arm and yanked her away. "You're free, piss-head, so get out of here."

"Watch your mouth, soldier," said Marius, bumping against him to take Isolda. As his flesh and the guard's briefly touched, Marius wordlessly inflicted on the man an itchy rash that would have him scratching under his armor all afternoon.

Outside the guardhouse, Drusus took Rory onto his horse, while Marius helped Isolda onto Gambler and swung up behind her on the saddle. He pulled her close to make the best use of the limited space, and she laid her head on his shoulder. "Are you hurt at all?"

"Just tired and hungry."

Thank the gods for that. "I want you to take this." He handed her the second writ. "Fold it up and keep it on your person at all times. It authorizes you and your family—that's Rory—to be here in Riat without being arrested or deported. It's only good for a month, but at least that's one month you won't have to worry."

She stared at the paper in awe. He wondered if she recognized the imperial seal on it. Probably not; the seal was known only to those in positions of authority.

"Such a gift," she murmured.

He had no reply. He didn't think of it as a gift at all, but as her just due for the good she'd done the surgery. And of course, for selfish reasons he wanted her to stay here in Riat. As they rode, he kept the pace slow, letting her rest and enjoying the feel of her warm body against his.

At the villa, Marius told Isolda they'd both be taking tomorrow off—after their various ordeals, they needed rest. His villa had a private bath in the basement, not as large or as fancy as the ones at the public baths or the imperial palace, but nice enough, with hot-water and cold-water pools, and they had the great advantage of privacy. He authorized her to use the bath and had dinner sent to her guest room. As for himself, he'd be eating a light meal and collapsing before the sun set, having been up most of the previous night.

He slept until mid-morning, and when he woke, he could tell Aurora had been busy: the house smelled of freshly baked bread. He strolled into the kitchen and fetched the loaf that was drying on the rack. Back at the dining table, he sliced off a hunk, drizzled oil and honey over it, and stuffed the soft deliciousness into his mouth. He'd gorged himself on half the loaf when Isolda emerged, refreshed and wearing one of his old tunics. Gods, there was something about her wearing his clothes that made his blood rush south. But he wouldn't pester her, not now at least. He pushed the remaining half of the loaf toward her. "Eat."

She took it and sliced off a wedge.

He passed her the oil and honey. She was more willing to eat at his table than she used to be, perhaps because she felt more established here. She was an employee of the surgery and thus contributing, at least indirectly, to his household. As he understood it, she wasn't averse to eating, only to taking charity. He hoped she didn't perceive the rescue as charity.

She ate the first wedge of bread in silence, picking up all the crumbs so that she missed nothing, and then spoke. "I can't thank you enough for getting me out of there."

"It was no trouble," said Marius.

"I think you must have gone to a great deal of trouble," said Isolda. "Was it your benefactor who authorized my release?"

"Yes."

"He must be well connected. Did your request for help strain your relationship with him in any way?"

"No," said Marius.

Isolda eyed the remainder of the loaf.

"Have more," he urged. "Eat all of it, if you like—there are two more loaves in the kitchen. Where's Rory?"

"He's off to work already." She reached for the loaf eagerly and cut another wedge. "I've done some thinking. I've always known about the gunpowder factory and its dangers. If I'd said something earlier. . ." She shook her head. "I don't know who I'd have said it *to*, but maybe I could have prevented those deaths, and maybe your emperor wouldn't be deporting Emari and the others." She put the bread down and clasped her hands in her lap.

"You take too much on yourself," said Marius. "Anyone in that factory could have reported it. *I* could have reported it. But none of us did, for various reasons."

"I used to think it was enough," said Isolda, "that we could live here and hide from the authorities and just survive. But what kind of future are we building for ourselves? For our children? We need to be accepted here, not just grudgingly tolerated—or *not* tolerated, by some—and that means finding legitimate work."

"How many legal job opportunities do your people have?" said Marius.

"Almost none," said Isolda. "But Rory and I have managed to find legal jobs, and so did a man I know. We can't keep endangering the lives of innocents. I know the man who ran that gunpowder factory, and he's not a Sardossian at all. He's Kjallan." She picked up the wedge of bread she'd abandoned and began to eat.

Marius blinked. He had never considered that the factory owner might be Kjallan. But now that he thought about it, the owner *had* to be. How could a Sardossian acquire the raw materials as they came into the harbor? How could a Sardossian sell the finished product?

"If he's not stopped, he'll start another factory," continued Isolda. "Why wouldn't he? Cheap Sardossian labor means profits for Kjallans."

"What do you propose to do?" Even though he now had a writ to protect her and Rory—lasting one month—he wasn't enthusiastic about her having anything to do with the Riat City Guard.

"Does my information about the Kjallan owner have any value?" she asked. "Your benefactor must have political connections, and I owe him a favor. What if I told him what I know?"

"I think he'd be interested."

"Then I'll tell him, provided he won't ask me to betray any of my Sardossian friends."

"I'll be speaking with him in a few days. I can present your offer to him then." It might make his Sage's Day conversation with Lucien less awkward.

"Thank you." Isolda let out her breath.

Marius observed that she'd finished her bread. "How do you feel? Do you need to rest some more?"

Isolda shook her head. "I'm not tired at all. I'm fact, I'm feeling. . ." She licked her lips and bit them nervously. "Yesterday we were in the middle of something. Do you think we might continue?"

That took him by surprise. But it was a good surprise. After everything she'd been through yesterday, she was thinking about yesterday's interrupted kiss? That bolstered his confidence. "I don't know," he said, feigning gravity. "Do you think we might blow out all the windows again?"

She grinned and rose from her seat. "Let's find out."

He took her into his arms, folding her into the crook of his body. What a delicious fit she was. Isolda was a medium sort of woman, average height and average build, with breasts neither large nor small. She was the sort of woman men tended to overlook, since nothing out of the ordinary struck the eye.

But for the man who took notice, she was perfect. The curve of her hip, outlined by the belt of the simple tunic she wore, struck him as the very picture of womanhood. How he wanted to run his hand down that curve and over the lovely roundness of her bottom and thighs. He'd love to see those curves unclothed, especially those breasts that looked like they would fit perfectly into each of his hands.

He settled for kissing her.

She tasted of honey from the late breakfast they'd shared. Her lips were warm and yielding, and her cheeks flushed pink with arousal. He stood, bringing her up with him, and tightened his grip around her, even though she was sure to feel his half-mast cockstand through their clothes. No reason she shouldn't know.

She seemed to want him as well. Her questing fingers explored the contours of his body, running over his clothes. She found bare skin where his syrtos ended on his leg. One touch, flesh to flesh, and he was hard.

If her hands were roaming, so could his. Still clutching her to him with one hand, he let the other hand explore the outline of her neck and shoulders, the curve of her breast and hip. He found the roundness of her pert bottom, which he stroked, aware of how close he was to her pleasure center.

"Marius," she said through the kisses.

"Hmm?" he said, barely able to articulate.

"We need to stop—just for a little while."

He took his hand away. "Is something amiss?"

"No," she said. "Well. . .yes. I want all this and more, but I have to take care of a little detail first."

Now he understood. "You need wards. We can go to Nonian's—"

"It's not wards," she said. "But it's important. Do you trust me?"

He nodded, though he wished she would trust *him* and be more direct about what she wanted. "You can't tell me about it?"

"I'd rather not. It's. . ." She shook her head. "This may take me a few hours, but I'll be back. Will you be here?"

"Yes." Perhaps, in time, she would have more faith in him.

She pulled away, and he released her. Her hair was mussed and her tunic wrinkled.

"I'll be back," said Isolda.

He nodded again and watched, perplexed, as she went out the door.

21

Based on the number of faces Isolda saw in the city's underground, she estimated that about half of her people had survived the explosion and escaped the deportation roundup. It was a relief to see that she and Rory would not be the only Sardossians in the city henceforth—but that was not why she had come here.

At Marius's villa, she'd let her desires carry her away, but her conscience had intervened. She wanted Marius in a way she'd never wanted a man before, and it was clear that he wanted her too, but she was not a free woman. She was married, and until she got herself unmarried, she couldn't sleep with him.

Telling him the truth about Jauld wouldn't be enough. Marius would forgive her for having lied before, she was certain, but that wouldn't salvage the romantic side of their relationship; he would put an end to it at once. He was forgiving, but he was also principled. Marius would not sleep with a married woman.

Ahead, a sign hung drunkenly on a door: *The Pilgrim*. In its distant past, this building had been an inn. Now sunk below ground, it moldered away in the dark. How it had come to be here was a mystery even to her people, but Riat's sewers weren't just underground passages for wastewater. There were structures down here, shops and storefronts from a previous age. Though old and rotten, they made excellent shelters for refugees in hiding.

The door was wedged open by a sunken ceiling and warped girders. She crept through the doorway, circling around the standing water on the floor. "Caz?"

"Isolda?"

She followed his voice to the farthest bedroom, which was also the highest and driest.

The room's original furnishings had been looted long ago. Now bags and blankets hid almost every inch of floor space.

Caz, a tall, strong, yellow-haired Sardossian, hovered possessively over one such pile of blankets. "Good for you, dodging the reds. Is your boy all right?"

She nodded as she picked her way across the floor. "He's at work."

"Good for him."

Caz was unusual among Sardossian refugees in that he spoke the Kjallan language and had a legitimate job working alongside Kjallan laborers, and from what she understood, that job paid well. She hadn't met him until she came to Riat. Before he'd emigrated from Sardos, he'd been one of the strays, a disinherited third son of a second wife. Abhorring violence, he'd declined to join the army and had eked out a living as a farm laborer. His size, strength, and amiable nature had made him a valued employee. Now instead of slinging hay bales, he slung crates and casks at the Riat shipyard.

He had remained staunchly single, and for a while she'd wondered why. In Sardos, marriage would have been out of the question for a stray such as himself, but here in Kjall marriage was a possibility, and casual affairs were common among the refugees. He did not lack for female admirers, but he'd encouraged none of them. Isolda suspected his tastes lay in another direction.

Isolda valued him as a friend because he was more knowledgeable about Kjallans and their ways than any other Sardossian she knew. "I've a question. How does one get a divorce in Kjall?"

"First, one has to be Kjallan," said Caz.

"Are you sure?"

"If you go to the authorities, they're going to arrest you. Unless you've got plenty of bribe money."

"They won't arrest me. Look." She pulled the writ from her pocket and unfolded it for him, feeling as giddy as a child showing off a new toy.

Caz's brow lowered. "You know I can't read."

She'd forgotten. Caz spoke beautiful Kjallan, and with only a slight accent, but he couldn't read or write in any language. "Right, I'm sorry. It says I'm authorized to stay here in Riat, with my family, for one month, and the guards can't arrest me."

"Really?" Caz whistled. "That's worth more than *gold*. Don't let anyone here see it."

"It has my name on it. And it works! A guard stopped me on the way here. I almost wet myself, but I pulled this out and showed it to him, and he read it and kind of sniffed at me, and then he walked away."

"Oh, I believe that," said Caz. "Kjallans love their papers."

Isolda smiled. "It's not *papers* they love—"

"Oh, but they do! More than wine, more than women. It's a good thing they worship the Three, because otherwise I think they'd erect a statue of a writing desk and worship that. Where'd you get it?"

"From my boss at the surgery."

"He's more than just your boss, I'll wager," said Caz.

"Perhaps." Isolda's cheeks warmed. "And that's why I need a divorce, because legally I'm still married to Jauld, and I don't want to be. How do I get one?"

"At the apparitor's office. But I think your husband has to go too."

Oh, gods. Jauld was an ocean away, and even if he were here in Riat, he would never grant her permission to divorce him. "Do you think I could maybe forge a document saying—"

"I've a better idea," said Caz. "I'll go with you and pretend to be your husband."

What a perfect notion that was! But so very risky for Caz. "I can't ask you to do that. What if the guardsmen see you?"

"That's the beauty of it." He grinned. "They can't arrest me. I'm family, so your holy writ protects me."

"But after we're divorced, you won't be family anymore."

"If you don't tell them, I won't," said Caz. "But just in case—you got five tetrals on you?"

Isolda reached into her pocket. "Why?"

"Give it here."

"What for?"

"Bribe money."

Isolda blinked. "Who takes bribes in Kjall?"

Caz folded his arms. "*Everybody*. How do you think I've survived here for so long, working in the open with this hair and this accent?"

Isolda handed him the five tetrals. "Why have I never known this?"

"Because you're good-natured and you think everyone else is the same way."

"I do *not* think that," said Isolda, with indignance.

"And you were too poor, working at that gunpowder factory."

"Your bribes may have worked before, but now that the imperial order's come down—"

"Makes no difference," said Caz. "Since the explosion, I've bribed two guardsmen already."

"It's different for you. Everyone likes you." It amazed Isolda how Caz seemed to skate through life, relying on his personal charm to get him out of trouble. He seemed to be able to draw a smile out of anybody, even a city guardsman.

Caz shrugged. "Why do you want a divorce? This man you want to be with will never know about your old husband, and who cares what the Kjallans write in their moldy books? As far as I'm concerned, you were unmarried the moment you stepped off the boat."

"The law doesn't see it that way," said Isolda. "Marius won't want to sleep with a married woman."

"So he's a self-righteous ass. Who cares what he thinks?" said Caz. "He's just using you."

"He's not. And he's not a self-righteous ass."

"Is he going to marry you?"

"No."

"Then he's using you."

Isolda shook her head. "His feelings for me are genuine, as are mine for him."

"And when it's time for him to get married to somebody else, he'll toss you out the door like yesterday's old straw."

"Probably," said Isolda.

"You're making a mistake, getting involved with a Kjallan. Even if he does give you a writ worth its weight in gold."

Perhaps she was. For all that she'd meant to keep her distance, she was in love with Marius. When he showed her the door someday, as he ultimately must, he would break her heart. And yet every fiber of her being pushed her toward this inevitable anguish. She could no more stop herself from loving Marius than the sun could stop its march through the sky—and its inevitable sinking beneath the horizon.

"You're not going to listen, are you?" Caz rose to his feet. "I knew you wouldn't. Let's go to the apparitor and play husband and wife."

Isolda looked at the sign on the building with trepidation: *Imperial Apparitor*. Never before had she sought out someone as potentially hostile to her people and to her interests as an official clerk of the Kjallan Empire. But Caz said this was the man they had to see, and the writ in her pocket gave her the power to be here.

A bell rang over the door as they stepped inside.

The office was small and dusty. A gray-haired man with a Kjallan hawk nose peered at her from behind a desk in the corner. A closed door led to some sort of back room.

"Are you the apparitor?" she asked.

He stared at them. "You're Sardossians. You can't be here. There's—"

"We're here legally. Look." She took the writ from her pocket, unfolded it, and laid it on the desk for him to read, keeping her finger on it because it was too precious to entrust to a stranger.

The apparitor studied it. "Have friends in high places, do you?"

Isolda supposed he meant Marius's benefactor. She nodded.

"This expires in a month."

"But it's good for now." She picked up the writ and pocketed it.

Caz slid into one of the chairs on the other side of the desk. "I'm here to divorce my bitch of a wife."

Isolda glared at him as she took the seat beside him. Embellishment was not necessary.

"Your name?" asked the apparitor.

"Jauld Morbel."

"Spell it."

Caz gave Isolda a blank look, and she spelled it for him. The apparitor wrote it down and turned to Isolda. "Your name?"

"Isolda."

"Isolda Morbel?"

She shook her head. "Just Isolda. Sardossian women do not have surnames."

The apparitor's brow furrowed. He hesitated, and a drop of ink fell from his quill to the paper. "Women in Kjall do have surnames, so I'm going to put down Isolda Morbel." He blotted the ink spot and began to write. "Reason for the divorce?"

"Um. . .adultery," said Caz.

"Yours or hers?" asked the apparitor.

Isolda said, "His."

At the same time, Caz said, "Hers."

They glanced at each other. Isolda had rehearsed some of the questions with Caz before coming in, but she had not expected that one, given that men in Kjall seemed to be able to divorce without a reason.

"We were both getting the bull's feather on the side," said Caz. "Also, she snores."

Isolda gave him a discreet kick.

"Adultery," recited the apparitor as he wrote. "Both parties. Any children in the marriage?"

"A boy, Rory, eight years old," said Isolda.

"Custody to you?" the apparitor asked Caz.

"No, to her," said Caz. "I don't want that brat. Who knows if he's even mine?"

"He's legitimate," put in Isolda quickly, worried that Caz's embroidery of the facts might somehow end up in the apparitor's official record.

"Custody of the son to the mother," said the apparitor dubiously. He wrote some more and looked up at Isolda. "What was your name before your marriage?"

"Just Isolda."

"I can't put down just Isolda," said the apparitor. "In this country, a legal name has at least two parts, more often three. It should be your name, followed by your father's name, followed by your grandfather's name. If you didn't have a surname before, you're going to have one from now on, so come up with something."

Her father's surname had been Tanem. It seemed silly to take her father's name, given that she would probably never see him again, and it wasn't Sardossian custom anyway. "I can choose any name I want?"

"I don't care what you put down."

She thought for a moment, and combined two Sardossian words: *ang*, meaning *woman*, and *helm*, meaning *free*. "Isolda Anghelm," she told the apparitor.

Caz, sitting next to her, raised a brow. He knew the meaning, even if the apparitor didn't. *Isolda, woman who is free.*

The apparitor's quill scratched on the paper.

22

When Isolda knocked at the door to Marius's villa, there was no immediate answer. She waited a little while, wondering if Marius might have gone to the surgery after all. She'd walked right by the surgery on her way here, but hadn't given it much of a glance. Her mind was so full: Caz and the clerk, her divorce that was all of thirty minutes old, her newfound freedom that would allow her to indulge in an affair with the man she'd admired for years.

She knocked again, in case no one had heard her the first time, and the door opened.

Marius stood before her, clad in a light silk robe.

Isolda swallowed. His hair was wet, suggesting he'd just come out of a bath, and the robe clinging to his damp body left nothing to the imagination, with the silk outlining every muscle on his shoulders and torso. She forgot sometimes that Marius was a big man, in part because he was always in the company of the slightly larger Drusus, but also because Marius never used his size and strength to intimidate. Looking at him now reminded her that his gentleness was a choice.

She realized, suddenly, that they were alone. Marius seldom answered the door himself; usually Drusus or a servant did it. "Where's Drusus?"

"He's around, but making himself scarce." Marius smiled. "Did you take care of the detail you spoke of?"

"Yes, it's done." Thank the gods.

Marius held out his arm. "I don't suppose you'd like to tell me about it?"

"I'd really rather not." She took his arm, and he led her inside.

"Are you hungry at all?" he asked. "Tired?"

"No, I. . ." She swallowed. He'd arranged privacy for them, so he knew perfectly well what she was after. "I'd like to see your bedroom."

"Then I'll show you."

Marius's bedroom was the only room in the villa she hadn't yet seen. It was much as she'd expected: a utilitarian space, neat and tidy, lacking in pretension. His furnishings included two chests, a table and chairs, and a bed in the center of the room, the mere presence of which caused her cheeks to flush. The pieces appeared to be a matched set, carved from the same red-brown wood and upholstered in blue. While they lacked showy damask, silk, or gold accents, their quality was evident in the artistic swoop of their lines and the heaviness of the wood.

Marius followed her gaze to the furnishings. "My father made those."

She looked up in surprise. "Your father?" Given Marius's wealth, she'd thought his father would be military, or a business owner, or an imperial official; not somebody who worked with his hands.

"I was thinking we should talk a little," said Marius. "Before we take things much further."

"Talk," she repeated, uncertain about this.

"There's a lot you don't know about me. And much I'd like to know about you."

She nodded. What could she safely tell him? Now that she was officially divorced, she saw no reason she couldn't share with him most of her history with Jauld, if Marius wanted to hear that awful story. But the crimes she'd committed in order to emigrate to Kjall—stealing the store's money and her son, running away in violation of half a dozen laws—those were acts that shamed her. Could this wealthy Kjallan who'd always had family sheltering and protecting him understand the desperation that had driven her here?

"I come from a noble family," said Marius. "But I wasn't raised in one. My mother, as a young woman, was promised to a legatus in an arranged marriage. She didn't want to marry him, so she fled Riat and eloped with my father, a craftsman named Anton."

Isolda ran her hand along the curve of a chair arm. "His work is exquisite."

Marius nodded. "He's meticulous. On some of the jobs he had when I was growing up, the people who hired him would complain that he was slow. But that was only because he cared enough to do things right."

Isolda felt a twinge of jealousy. Her father, too, had been a conscientious, meticulous man, and she had always admired him. But she hadn't seen him, or her mother, since her marriage to Jauld. In Sardos it was customary for fathers to make a clean cut from their daughters when they married so that there would be no conflict between the husband and his father-in-law. Marius's father, it seemed, had remained part of his adult son's life. "He must love you very much."

Marius sat on the bed. "He and my mother live in Riat now. They're across town, so I just have to saddle up Gambler when I want to see them."

Isolda's throat tightened. What a luxury that must be, to see one's parents whenever one desired. Even if she had a horse to saddle up and cross town with, she had nobody to visit. Her family was just herself and Rory now.

"Will you sit with me?" asked Marius.

She was feeling shy despite having come here with the express aim of sleeping with him. Nonetheless, she crossed the room and sat by his side, sinking into the goosefeathers.

Marius slipped an arm around her. "After my mother eloped, she concealed everything that might give away her identity. She dressed humbly and adopted the local accent. Despite her efforts at blending in, she was discovered by my uncle. He left her where she was, with my father, but took away her firstborn daughter—"

"Wait, why would he leave her and take the daughter?"

"He was concerned about heirs and preserving the bloodline for future generations. Because my parents were afraid to have more children after that, I didn't come along for another ten years. They let me believe I was the eldest—my missing sister, a decade my senior, was never mentioned. My parents had gone deeper into hiding by then, living in obscure rural towns. My father was originally an upholsterer, but he feared his profession might identify him, so he worked as a carpenter instead. When we were discovered again, this time by my cousin, I was twenty-two years old and a journeyman apothecary. Until that moment, I'd had no idea my family was anything out of the ordinary."

"Did you ever find your missing sister?"

"Oh, yes," said Marius. "I see her once in a while, but she lives far away."

Now that Isolda had heard Marius's story, she better understood his duality: his humble nature and preference for peasant clothes and simple foods, paired with exceptional wealth and the influence of a powerful benefactor. He was an intriguing man, but his life story made it all too clear that he could never marry her. If Marius's family had been upset when his mother had married a Kjallan commoner, Isolda could only imagine the pyrotechnics that would ensue if Marius married a Sardossian refugee.

However, that was nothing she hadn't assumed already. "This benefactor you've spoken of—he must be part of your mother's family."

"He's my cousin," said Marius. "The one who found us."

"I take it he would not approve of my being with you."

"It's none of his business."

As involved as this cousin was in Marius's life—going to all that trouble to find his missing family members—she had a feeling he would *make* it his business, especially if her relationship with Marius became serious. She'd have to make sure it didn't become serious. In freewheeling cities like Riat, it was acceptable, even expected, for single men and women to have affairs before marriage. If her relationship with Marius was nothing more than a casual affair, the cousin should have no reason for concern.

Marius took her hand and clasped her fingers. His touch, innocent as it was, tingled against her flesh. "I should have told you about my family a long time ago. I'm sure you must have wondered about my clothes and the fact that I prefer parsnip soup to broiled swan."

"I did mistake you for a servant at first, when I saw you in your tunic and breeches," said Isolda. "That was four years ago, when I woke up in your guest room. But within minutes I'd learned otherwise. After that I didn't think twice about what you wore or what you ate, other than to be curious about your habits—but only because you fascinated me, and I wanted to know everything about you."

"I've always felt comfortable around you, and I think it's because I never felt judged," said Marius. "I sensed that you wanted to know me as I was rather than wanting me to be someone different."

"Why would anyone want you to be different?"

He gave a self-deprecating laugh. "Lots of reasons."

His family must have expectations of him that he was unable or unwilling to fulfill. It was natural enough, now that she thought about it. The wealthy side of his family would have possessed one set of scruples and ideals, and the poor side of his family another set, and he'd been raised with the latter. "I understand that your family situation is complicated. And I sympathize with not being able to meet someone's expectations, because that was my life story in Sardos. But. . .I tell you this honestly, Marius. I have never known a better man than you, and it would never occur to me to judge you based on something as silly as what you eat or what you wear."

Marius wrapped an arm around her and hugged her. "I think that's the nicest thing anyone has said to me."

"It's the truth."

"Will you tell me more about what you just mentioned—your experiences in Sardos?"

She swallowed. "The story's involved, like yours, but not nearly so happy. Are you certain you want to hear it?"

"Absolutely certain."

"My father was an apothecary," she began.

"Ah," said Marius. "I thought that might be the case when I first met you."

"I'm the third of three sisters, and I'm. . .well, I'm the plain one."

"Never say that about yourself, because it's not true." He kissed her on the lips.

Isolda flushed. She was starting to believe that Marius genuinely found her attractive despite her lack of traditional beauty. He had his choice of women, and he'd chosen her. He was not like Jauld, buying a wife he wasn't attracted to because he couldn't afford a prettier one. Marius was with her because he wanted her, not because he had no better alternatives.

She continued her story. "My parents believed I would never marry, so they prepared me to act as my father's assistant in the apothecary shop. He taught me the names of the herbs, how to measure them, how to dry and store them, how to haggle with suppliers for good prices."

"Now I understand why you're so good at running the surgery," said Marius.

"But then someone arrived with a marriage offer," she said. "A shopkeeper named Jauld, who'd seen me in the apothecary. We married, and I had a look at the general store he owned. The building was in disrepair, and sales were poor, but the location was promising. I cleaned it up and found better suppliers—"

"Like what you did for me," said Marius.

"Not at all," said Isolda. "Before I turned up at your door, you already ran a clean, high-quality surgery. You had a problem with patients not paying. But in the case of Jauld's store, I replaced almost everything. I built it practically from the ground up, and through my efforts, we became wealthy. Not like your family, perhaps, but comfortable enough for some luxuries."

Marius's hand stroked her forearm. "I hope he was grateful."

Isolda sighed. "He was not. His friends mocked him for having a plain wife, and I think my success with the store didn't mean much to him, for all that he enjoyed the extra money. I didn't know it when I married him, and it wouldn't have mattered since I didn't have a choice, but Jauld was a shallow sort of man. He wanted nothing in the world but for his friends to envy him. And they did! His friends envied him because he had a wife and they didn't. That was why they abused me—they wanted to take him down a notch. Jauld was such a fool that he took their mockery to heart."

"The simpleton," growled Marius.

"Our marriage had always been fragile—I tried to love him, but it was hard. His friends' insults embarrassed Jauld and destroyed what little connection we had. First he stopped being kind. Then he used the money I'd earned him to buy a second wife."

Marius's hand froze. "He *what?*"

Isolda's throat went thick, and her eyes swam. At least one person other than herself was shocked by what Jauld had done. "Her name was Chari. She was younger and. . .and prettier—"

"He was a sapskull, Isolda, to be fooled by his friends' ploys and, even more so, to fail to see your beauty." Marius sighed. "I hope you will not think me crass and provincial for saying this, but I don't believe in multiple marriages."

"Nor do all Sardossians," said Isolda. "Multiple marriage is not every family's experience in my country. My father took only one wife. My experience with Jauld was my first in a two-wife household, and it was not a happy one. Perhaps Jauld imagined that Chari and I would be friends, but that didn't happen. We might, perhaps, have reached an uneasy harmony if Jauld had treated us equally, but he favored Chari and allowed her to harass Rory and me. He ousted me from his bed and slept exclusively with her, while allotting me the role of household servant."

Marius snorted. "No wonder you do not miss him. If he were not already dead, I would wring that simpleton's neck."

"Before Chari, the home I shared with Jauld had been a refuge from the pressures of the shop, a place where Rory and I could relax and be ourselves. But after Chari joined, there was no safe place for me anywhere. The two of us were locked into a grueling competition for Jauld's affections, one I had no chance of winning. I didn't even really *like* Jauld, and I don't think Chari did either. Can you imagine? We were fighting over a man neither of us wanted."

"Well, if he was all you had—"

"In all honesty, I'd have preferred nobody," said Isolda. "But we *had* to compete for him. In Sardos, there can be only one heir within a family. The heir gets everything, and the other children get nothing. Boys who are not their father's chosen heirs are called *makari*—in the Kjallan language, *strays*. Strays must make their own way in the world with no help from their parents. Usually they join the army or work as laborers. Most of them receive no education and never earn enough money to purchase a license to marry. They are dead ends, the throwaway children of Sardos. Rory was the eldest, and I wanted him to be the heir. But Chari had a son, too."

"He chose Chari's son over Rory?"

"He did. That's why I had to leave."

"Of course," said Marius. "When Jauld died, Chari's son must have inherited the store and all your assets, wiping out everything you'd worked for. Or were they killed in the war, too?"

"No, they still live," said Isolda, hating that she was omitting the most relevant detail, that Jauld was still alive too.

"So you left. I'm glad we had this talk," said Marius. "I see now why you've been so reluctant to talk about your time in Sardos. It sounds like it was a terrible time for you, and I won't bring it up again unless you desire it."

She nodded, wondering if she could tell him the rest of the story. He'd been understanding so far. Should she confess the truth about Jauld? That she had stolen from him and Chari in order to come here?

"I'm sorry to say that what happened to you isn't unknown even here in Riat," added Marius. "I've seen it happen many times. Our laws do not permit a man to take a second wife, so what men like Jauld do here is divorce the old wife so they can marry the new. I told you I don't believe in multiple marriages. But in Kjall we have divorce instead, which is nearly as contemptible."

Isolda felt a sudden chill. "You are opposed to divorce?"

"When you make a promise to love somebody, I think you should keep it," said Marius. "In Osler, where I grew up, men never abandoned their wives. I have a low opinion of a husband who discards his wife the way he would a lame horse. My parents have been married for over thirty years."

"So have mine," Isolda said in a small voice. She, on the other hand, had abandoned her husband and, just today, finally divorced him. Would he have a low opinion of her if he knew?

Never mind. He didn't need to know. She was unmarried and not committing adultery, and any affair she had with Marius would be short-lived.

Marius took her face in his hands, angled her lips toward him, and kissed her. A shiver ran through her, and her body went soft. She liked letting him hold her, move her, position her where he wanted. *Do things to me*, she thought, not knowing exactly what she wanted him to do, just something.

"I have another confession to make," said Marius. "I'm not terribly experienced in the bedroom. It's not that I have no experience at all; it's just that the affairs I've had previously didn't last."

Affairs. Multiple. Isolda's stomach clenched.

"I imagine you're curious, so I'll just tell you," said Marius. "I courted a few women at the university while I was learning to be a Healer, and they were all pleasant at first, but when they discovered some of my less sophisticated habits, they either lost interest or tried to change me. These were fashionable women seeking a fashionable lover, and I didn't suit. Eventually I got tired of trying to be what they wanted. It hurt that they didn't actually like me; they only liked the idea of what I *could* be. I became bitter and stopped courting entirely."

Isolda shook her head. She couldn't imagine why any woman who had the opportunity to be with Marius would turn it down. Thank the gods these other women had failed to appreciate his "unfashionable" self, or else she might not be here in his bedroom right now. "I imagine you think I'm more experienced than you because I was once married, but I'm not sure that's the case. All I had was the same experience over and over again."

"A good one?"

"Not particularly."

"I know a few things," said Marius. "But mostly from the Potter's Daughter books."

She blinked. "What?"

"Perhaps you don't have them in Sardos. They're a series of. . .well, erotic novels." His cheeks colored. "No one knows who writes them. There's First Life of the Potter's Daughter, then Second Life of the Potter's Daughter, and so on."

"I don't wonder we don't have them in Sardos," said Isolda. "Even if someone translated them, they'd probably be illegal."

"I only read the first two, but I picked up a few tips."

She smiled. Marius was adorable when he was blushing.

"The books say that different women enjoy different things." He slipped an arm behind her back to support her and eased her backward onto the bed.

Uncertain what to do, she let him mold her like putty.

He unbelted her syrtos. "So perhaps I could try some of those things, and you could tell me what you like and what you don't like."

Isolda stiffened. "I don't think I have any idea what I like."

"So we find out." As he drew the fabric away from her breasts, his breath hitched, and he stared.

She felt a little shy under the scrutiny, remembering the scene with Lady Fabiola. Her breasts were only of moderate size compared to that woman's.

"Gods, Isolda, I think your former husband must have been blind." He leaned over and kissed her.

She liked the kissing—should she tell him?—but her body felt tingly, and she wanted more. She yearned for his touch. Not wanting to speak while her mouth was occupied, she reached for his hand and guided it to her shoulder.

He stroked her bare skin, and she arched like a cat. Her favorite part of Marius's body was his hands. Broad and callused, they were rough against her skin in a way that sensitized all her nerves, much like the stubble of his shaven face when he kissed her. She was all smoothness and curves, while he was power and rough edges.

He left her mouth and moved downward, trailing kisses along her neck.

It tickled.

"Not something you like?" he asked.

"It tickles, that's all."

He did it again, more firmly.

This time it didn't tickle. Instead it felt like nothing she'd ever experienced. Her insides went molten, and a small moan escaped her lips. When his hand found her breast, she was nearly overcome.

"Reading those novels was embarrassing at the time, but I'm glad I did it," said Marius. He ran his hands over her breasts, stroking and sometimes squeezing gently. She didn't care for the squeezing, but when his hand traveled over her nipples, *gods*. He was still working his way downward, and then he put his mouth on her breast.

She shuddered.

He licked one breast while stroking the other. Each time his tongue crossed her nipple, her whole body quaked. She had never had a lover like this. When Jauld had taken her to bed, he hadn't spoken but two words to her. He'd kissed her a bit, stroked her breasts, and did his business. It hadn't been unpleasant, just boring.

This was something entirely different.

"What do *you* like?" she asked.

"You could help me out of this." He indicated the silk robe.

She pulled the loose belt free and peeled the garment off his shoulders. His bare chest was as lovely as its outline had suggested, firm and muscled with a smattering of dark hairs. Though she felt a little shy, she wanted to touch him. As he leaned over her, his body presented itself like a canvas, inviting her exploring fingers. She stroked his sides lightly, and his skin twitched. "Not there?"

"Touch harder," he said.

She returned to the spot with a firmer touch, stroking and rubbing.

Marius groaned. "Yes—oh, yes, like that."

Gaining confidence, she ran her hands over the landscape of Marius's back and shoulders. What a wonder he was, and so different from Jauld. While she'd seen Jauld's body on many an occasion, she'd rarely touched him like this. If Jauld had been a poor lover, she had to admit that she was equally at sea when it came to lovemaking, possessing neither experience nor any form of guidance, such as the erotic novels that had helped Marius. Her relationship with Jauld had been too fraught and uncertain for frank discussion about sex, and they'd muddled through without much satisfaction for either of them.

Marius groaned—she must have found a good spot. She stroked him there a while longer, and when she felt braver, she moved to his chest, which felt more intimate. She ran her hand through the sparse hair, felt the outlines of his pectorals, touched his nipples. Marius had used his mouth and tongue as well as his hands. Should she do that as well? She wondered what he tasted like.

Before she could find out, Marius moved downward.

She tried to rise, but he said, "Stay there. I'm going to try something I think you'll like."

She lay back, trusting him. He eased her legs apart. Then he lowered his head and made a tentative lick.

"Marius." The sensation was intensely pleasurable, like nothing she'd ever felt. But it didn't satisfy—it left her craving more. "Do that again. Please."

"This one is from the Potter's Daughter." He licked her again, and then again.

Gods. All that burning sensation, that tingling in her body—it all came down to this, to his mouth and tongue on her sex, wringing the most delicious sensations out of her. She pressed herself closer to him, thinking, *stronger, harder, faster*, and he wrapped his arms around her legs, imprisoning them so she had no choice but to accept the rhythm he'd chosen.

She relaxed, submitting utterly as his tongue-strokes drove her into a frenzy of pleasure and increasing need.

"Something's happening," she said as the sensations built within her body, a growing tension that hinted at pyrotechnics to come.

"It certainly is," he said, and drove her on.

"I can't—I can't—" Her words turned into a groan as all that tension transformed into intense and delirious pleasure. Her body shuddered in time with Marius's tongue strokes. Her core turned to jelly, and the sensation spread, melting her from her insides to her toes and fingers. She lay back, panting.

As Marius returned, bringing his great body atop her again, she rubbed him in all the places he loved and showered him with kisses, grateful for that lovely feeling he'd given her.

"Has that not happened to you before?" he asked.

"No." If she'd felt anything like that before, she'd have remembered. She felt sorry for Chari, stuck with Jauld, who lacked the knowledge or perhaps even the desire to give his partner such an experience.

His cock nudged her sex, and she parted her legs in invitation. Marius entered her slowly. She was tight.

She'd had no lover since Jauld. It had been years since she'd done this, and her body had reverted to a state similar to the one on her wedding night, as if she were a virgin all over again. But this time she was wet and ready for her lover. There was no pain, only a delicious sense of fullness as he slid all the way in. She wrapped her arms around Marius. This was as close to him as she could ever get, with his body sunk to the hilt inside hers.

"Has it been a while?" Marius asked.

"Over seven years," she admitted.

"Then I'll be gentle." He moved inside her. "You feel amazing."

He felt amazing. She didn't think she'd have another climax like the one before—her body seemed spent, like it wasn't ready to do that again—but the sensations were lovely, and more than anything she loved the closeness and the intimacy. She stroked him all over, wanting his skin against her skin. Anything to increase his pleasure.

He was panting now, moving faster. She bent her legs, spreading them, urging him deeper.

His hand found her breast, and she moaned as he thumbed her nipple. She no longer felt that sensation of tightness. He'd become forceful, almost fierce in his movements, and it felt wonderful. His power, his beauty, his strength—he was spending it all on her body, spending it on loving her.

"Gods," he said, and shuddered. She recognized it, the same body motions she'd gone through, or nearly so, that wondrous peak of pleasure. She stroked him through it as he had done with her.

When it was over, he gave a great sigh and collapsed beside her.

I love you, she wanted to say. But she didn't want to ruin the moment by suggesting that this affair could be more than a casual dalliance. He knew better, and so did she.

23

Marius was worried about his cousin, the emperor.

He never imagined he'd one day be concerned about the well-being of someone so wealthy and powerful. During his days in Osler, far from the imperial seat, he'd envisioned an emperor's life as one of comfort and ease. Not once in Lucien's life as emperor did he have to work a shift, cook his own food, or wash his own clothes. When he wanted something done, he simply expressed his wishes to his underlings, and they made it happen.

Even so, Lucien looked harried and pale where he sat across the desk from Marius in the imperial office, and there were dark circles under his eyes.

"Rough night?" Marius asked carefully.

Lucien rubbed a hand across his face and did not answer. He turned to a servant who waited by the door. "Tea. Make it strong."

The servant disappeared.

"Is the empress well?" asked Marius.

"Perfectly so," said Lucien.

Marius nodded, relieved that the problem didn't appear to be with Vitala.

"It's this harbor business," said Lucien. "Funding it, you know, and then there are the land issues in the east, and this business with the Sardossians."

"Should I come at another time?" asked Marius, not enthusiastic to discuss "this business with the Sardossians."

"Oh, no," said the emperor. "You and Drusus promised to tell me about this Sardossian you've been employing." He turned to Drusus, who was leaning against the wall, pretending to be invisible. "Come and have a seat."

Wordlessly, Drusus sat next to Marius.

"Well—" Marius began hesitantly, but the servant returned with a tea tray, and he paused.

Lucien accepted the tea tray, waved the man away, and poured, filling Marius's and Drusus's cups before his own. He blew the steam from his cup, sipped, and sighed. "There's nothing like good Dahatrian. What were you saying?"

"The good news is that I'm turning a profit at the surgery now."

"Excellent. Does this have something to do with the Sardossian woman?"

"Yes. I hired her as my business manager."

Lucien wrapped his hands around his teacup as if to warm them and leaned back in his chair. "Tell me about her. What's her history?"

"Her name is Isolda. She spent her early years in Sardos helping her father run his apothecary shop. Later, after she married, she ran her husband's general store and apparently grew the business to several times its original size. But then the blood wars started, and her husband was killed, so she came here with her young son."

"Illegally."

"I assume so."

"Sardossians often have fascinating histories," said Lucien. "Some are just army deserters with no skills beyond carrying a musket. But you do find some like this Isolda with education and talent. Did you serve the writ I gave you? Were you able to get her out of custody?"

"Yes, she's back at work now. Thank you, sir."

"If she was working for you and not at the gunpowder factory, how did she happen to be picked up by the city guard?"

Marius hesitated, and Drusus jumped in. "She's made enemies at the surgery, sir, through no fault of her own," he said. "A man who owed Marius money took out his frustration by bringing a friend and attacking Isolda—"

"He attacked her physically?" asked Lucien.

"There was a knife involved," said Marius.

Lucien rubbed a hand across his forehead. "Why did he bring a friend?"

"One can only imagine he found Isolda too intimidating to tackle on his own," growled Drusus.

"Go on," said Lucien.

"Marius and I subdued them, and I administered a little rough justice—"

"You didn't call the city guard?" asked Lucien. "Oh— because she's illegal. Continue."

"I thought that would take care of the problem, but the next day, they started leaving angry messages. A dead rat on the door of the villa, something about 'piss-heads' painted on the door of the surgery."

"You should have told me about the attack the day it happened," said Lucien.

"It was going to be in my report," said Drusus, looking chagrined. "I figured since the target of their aggression was Isolda rather than Marius—"

"Are you arguing with me?"

"No, sir." Drusus swallowed.

"Continue," said Lucien. "What happened next?"

"The city guards came and arrested Isolda. We're pretty sure it was because those men tipped them off."

"Drusus, I want you to find Octavius," said Lucien. "Get three men and go to Riat. Arrest the men who attacked Isolda and bring them back to the palace for interrogation. These are not petty crimes, especially when the emperor's cousin is involved."

"Yes, sir," said Drusus.

"What are you waiting for?"

Drusus scrambled up from the table and left.

Marius stared after him.

"Bit of a lone wolf, that one," said Lucien, when Drusus had gone. "Are you satisfied with him?"

"Completely," said Marius.

"Good," said Lucien. "Now that I've scolded him, I'm going to scold you. I'd like you to reflect on how much danger you put yourself in by bringing Isolda into your service."

"It's not her fault," said Marius.

"Of course not. It's yours," said Lucien. "My people are going to have to interrogate those men to make sure they're not a threat to the imperium—"

"They're ordinary thugs, sir."

"Probably, but we have to make sure. If we don't end up executing them, we'll have to blank their minds and relocate them, at the very least. So it's a great deal of trouble, both for us and for them."

Marius said nothing. Lucien spoke as if that were a bad thing, but all he felt was relief. Basilius and his friend would trouble Isolda no longer. And they deserved to be punished for what they'd done.

Lucien sighed and poured himself a second cup of tea.

Marius needed to take control of this conversation. He needed to persuade the emperor to make Isolda's one-month writ permanent, but it was clear that wasn't going to happen today. Lucien was going to need a lot of softening up first. "I imagine that gunpowder explosion caused you a great deal of trouble."

"Gods," groaned Lucien. "One of my investors almost pulled out yesterday. 'Why pay for a new harbor,' he said, 'when you can't keep order at the old one?'"

"Would it help if I could give you the name of the man responsible for the explosion?"

Lucien blinked. "What do you mean?"

"I mean the name of the man who ran the gunpowder factories," said Marius. "Isolda wasn't involved in the explosion, but before I hired her, she worked at that factory. She knows who runs it, and it's a Kjallan."

Lucien set down his teacup. "Who is it?"

"She didn't say. But she said she'd tell *you*."

"I just deported her people. Why would she talk to me?"

"She doesn't know who you are. She knows I have a wealthy benefactor, and that the benefactor ordered her release from the guardhouse. As a gesture of thanks and goodwill, she said she would give the information to the benefactor."

"Wonderful," said Lucien. "She likes me as long as she doesn't know who I am. Why does she want the factories shut down?"

"Because her people die in those explosions, too. And she wants her people to obey the laws here and become legitimate citizens."

"They're never going to be legitimate citizens."

"Well, she's hoping," said Marius.

Lucien grunted. "I'll take the information if she's willing to share it. Will she speak under truth spell?"

"I think so," said Marius. "She asked, as a condition of her volunteering this information, that she not be questioned about the whereabouts of her fellow Sardossians."

"Fair enough. Vitala may be the one to actually speak to her, since she's been looking into the explosions, and she's got a covert identity in Kolta. I've got my hands full with this harbor funding business anyway. We'll come by some evening. Your relationship with Isolda—is it strictly business?"

"Er—not strictly." His cheeks warmed.

"I had a suspicion. Are you being careful?"

"In what respect, sir?"

"Given this 'benefactor' business, I take it you haven't told her who you are," said Lucien.

"She knows I grew up in Osler, that my mother eloped, that I'm half commoner and also part of a noble family. I didn't tell her *which* family."

"Keep it that way," said Lucien. "My enemies would like nothing better than to get at me through you. Your single bodyguard is an absolute minimum of security for a big city like Riat, and the only reason it's working—if indeed it *is* working—is that nobody knows who you are. If word gets out, I won't be able to protect you in the city. I'd have to recall you to the palace to keep you safe. You understand?"

Marius nodded, wondering how long he could realistically keep the secret from Isolda. He'd planned to tell her eventually, working up to it in stages, since he knew she was afraid of the Kjallan authorities and would particularly resent Lucien after the deportation order. But Lucien was suggesting that he could *never* tell her. It felt wrong, even duplicitous, to be intimate physically while concealing something so fundamental about himself. And yet he could hardly argue with the need for imperial security.

Lucien gestured to the guards, and to Marius's surprise, they left the office and closed the door behind them, leaving him alone with the emperor.

"If that's settled, there's a matter I'd like your guidance on," said Lucien.

"Mine?" blurted Marius. He was hardly in a position to advise the emperor.

"It's a sensitive subject, and I believe you're uniquely qualified to help."

"What, sir?"

"It's about my younger son, Maxian," said Lucien. "He keeps turning up with bruises. He always has some explanation: he got it in tumbling practice; he fell off his pony. But I've never known a child to be so prone to injury."

For once in a discussion with the Kjallan emperor, Marius felt within his element. "Are you looking for a medical cause? Some people are more prone to bruising than others, and it's related to the action of their blood. I could have a look at him."

"I'm hoping you'll find a medical cause because I don't like the alternative. And I'd appreciate your discretion in this matter."

"Of course," said Marius.

Ten minutes later, Marius was with Lucien in the imperial nursery, looking over the emperor's five-year-old son. The guards and nurse had been sent out of the room, leaving the three of them alone. With Lucien's help, Marius coaxed the boy into stripping down to his smallclothes, and sure enough, the boy had a number of bruises on his body. It was normal for small children to have bruises on their arms and legs, particularly their shins and sometimes even their foreheads, because they were active and not very coordinated at that age. Maxian's bruises, however, were mostly on his chest and neck.

"Has he ever cut himself and bled more than seemed normal?" Marius asked Lucien.

"Not that I'm aware of," said Lucien.

Marius addressed Maxian. "Do you remember ever having a cut that wouldn't stop bleeding?"

Maxian shook his head.

It was hard to get much out of Maxian when he didn't feel like talking. Marius indicated the largest and freshest bruise, the one just above his stomach. "How did you get that one?"

Maxian shrugged.

"You said it was from falling off your pony," prompted Lucien.

Maxian nodded.

"How did you land?" asked Marius.

Maxian shrugged again.

"Did his bodyguards see it happen?" Marius asked Lucien.

"Supposedly," said Lucien. "But one of the difficulties of being a man in my position is that people can be afraid to tell you the truth."

"I'd like to test his blood to see if it's too thin. The test will hurt for a moment, but it won't do him any harm. Do I have your permission to administer it?"

"What do you think, Maxian?" asked Lucien. "Is it all right if your uncle Marius tests your blood?"

After a moment, Maxian nodded.

Marius gently took the boy's arm. "I'm going to move my finger across this spot and open a little cut on your skin. It's going to bleed. You don't have to look at it if you'd rather not. After I see what your blood looks like, I'm going to seal it right back up and you'll be good as new. All right?"

Maxian nodded.

"Here we go." Using one hand to shield what he was doing, Marius slid his finger across the boy's wrist and opened a shallow cut.

The boy didn't cry out, but he turned his head away. Blood dripped from the wound onto the floor.

Lucien's mouth was a thin line as he watched. "Well?"

"Wait a moment," said Marius. The drops slowed and then stopped entirely. Marius slid his finger over the wound again and sealed it. "There you go, Maxian. All done."

The boy let out a sigh of relief and examined his wrist. The wound was gone, and the only evidence of its prior existence was a bit of smeared blood.

"What did you learn?" asked Lucien.

"I don't have an answer yet. Let me heal these bruises while I'm here." The simple exercise of touching each bruise and calling upon his healing magic gave him time to think. Sometimes excessive bruising was caused by a bleeding disorder, but Maxian's blood was normal. Therefore his bruises must have been caused by something else. Either there was a medical cause Marius hadn't the experience to identify, or the bruises had been inflicted through trauma. Were they accidental, or was someone hitting the boy? If the latter, who was doing it? Certainly not Lucien, since he'd been the one to bring the problem to Marius's attention. One of the nurses? One of the guards? Jamien? The *empress*? The last thing Marius wanted to do was suggest to the emperor that one of his family members could be doing this to his son. And if Marius accused a nurse or guard, he could only imagine the severity of the consequences that might result.

Lucien bit his lip. "Is it the bleeding disorder you mentioned?"

"No," said Marius. "But it might be something else." He was not in a position to make accusations when he had no evidence, only guesses. For all he knew, there might be another medical condition that caused bruising, one so rare that his training had not covered it. There were people he could talk to, more experienced Healers who might know the answer. As the last bruise faded beneath his fingertips, he stood. "I'm going to talk to some colleagues. I'll get back to you when I know more."

Lucien nodded. "Thank you, cousin."

24

Against all odds, Isolda's formerly chaotic life began to settle into a routine. The writ she carried with her at all times protected her from the city guards. And while the deportation of so many of her friends had left a hole in her heart, the reduction of the Sardossian population did ease tensions between her people and the Kjallans. Harassment became less frequent, and Basilius disappeared entirely—Marius said he'd spoken to the guards and had him and his friend arrested.

Marius and Drusus escorted her to and from the harbor district when she wanted to go home, but now that she shared Marius's bed, she usually preferred to stay at the villa and save the trip. Rory returned from his job at the fruit stand at around the time the surgery closed, and the three of them had dinner. Afterward, Rory headed out to play stick ball with the other children in Marius's neighborhood.

It warmed her heart to see her Sardossian child mingling freely with these wealthy Kjallan children. Children this age didn't seem to be as conscious of class and race as adults. None of the boys cared that Rory had yellow hair or that he worked for a living while they spent the day with their tutors. They cared only whether Rory could throw and hit and run, and as it happened, he could do all three rather well. He was so eager to join his friends in the evening that he bolted his dinner, and he'd be out until long after the sun had set, playing by the light of the street glows.

Rory's engagement elsewhere had a side benefit: it allowed Isolda to spend most evenings alone with Marius.

But on this particular evening she wasn't sure if she'd be going to the villa. Just as the surgery had closed, two carriages had pulled up alongside the building, their silver trim gleaming in the setting sun. Could this be a visit from Marius's cousin and benefactor? The conveyances were fancy enough—understated, yet solid and well made. Footmen riding on the back stepped down to open the doors, and the carriages disgorged an intimidating crowd of people.

Isolda backed away, instinctively seeking the shadows as Marius emerged from the surgery to greet these visitors. As she was looking down the street for Rory, preparing to collect him and leave for the harbor district, Marius headed toward her in the company of two of the well-dressed women.

"Isolda, this is Kolta." Marius indicated the taller of the two black-haired women. "And Shona." He indicated the other. "Kolta is an imperial representative investigating the gunpowder factory explosions, and Shona is a mind mage in her service."

Isolda swallowed. So that's what this was about: the benefactor had taken her up on her offer to provide information about the gunpowder factories.

"I trust them completely," added Marius. "You'll be in good hands."

"Isolda, I'm so pleased to meet you." Kolta held out her hand.

After a moment's hesitation, Isolda clasped her wrist.

"My understanding is that you're sharing information voluntarily, as a service to the empire," said Kolta. "We'll be using a truth spell to ascertain the veracity of what you tell us, but if there's a question you prefer not to answer, you're under no obligation to say anything at all. You may end the interview at any time. Are these terms acceptable to you?"

"Yes, ma'am," said Isolda.

"Let's use the surgery building for privacy." Kolta brandished the key, which Marius must have given her.

"One moment, please. I have to find my son." Looking around, Isolda spotted Rory trotting up the sidewalk toward the villa. He hadn't seen her yet. His eyes found Marius first. Marius waved him over and headed for the villa in the company of several other people from the carriages.

Good enough; Marius would look after him. She nodded at Kolta, who opened the door to the surgery and motioned her through.

The surgery was empty and dimly lit by the setting sun. Isolda stepped from one light glow to another, touching to activate them. When she turned back, two of the servants or bodyguards had stepped inside the surgery. Kolta seemed to expect this, so Isolda decided it was all right.

Kolta set up a group of chairs in the waiting room and directed Isolda to sit next to Shona. "I don't know if you've had a truth spell cast on you before—"

"I haven't," said Isolda.

"It's absolutely painless," said Kolta. "But Shona needs to put her hand on you."

Isolda nodded.

"She won't say anything unless she detects a falsehood." Kolta opened her carrying pouch and pulled out a writing tablet, a quill, and an ink pot. "Remember, if there's a question you don't want to answer, just tell us you don't want to answer it, and we'll move on."

"I understand," said Isolda.

Shona reached out and gently took Isolda's arm.

Isolda forced herself to breathe. She'd never been in the presence of a mind mage before.

"What can you tell us about the gunpowder factory explosion?" asked Kolta.

"Both of the factories that exploded were run by the same man," said Isolda. She waited a moment to see if the mind mage would say anything, but she didn't, and a gentle nod from Kolta encouraged her to continue. "His name is Antonius Galbus. I believe he runs a legitimate business as well, something to do with shipping—"

"Did you say Galbus?" Kolta's eyes went to those of the mind mage. Shona gave a slight nod, and Kolta turned back to Isolda.

"Yes," said Isolda.

Kolta dipped her quill and began to write.

"I know the blame for the explosions has been placed on my people," continued Isolda, "and it's true that my people staffed the factories, but it was Galbus who provided the raw materials and the equipment. He also sold the finished product. I believe he will start another factory soon, once he finds a suitable location."

"Did you see any other Kjallans at the factory besides Galbus?"

"Occasionally I would see another Kjallan man there, but I don't know his name."

"What did he look like?" asked Kolta.

Isolda thought for a moment. "Short and thin. Dark hair. A prominent chin."

Kolta nodded. "Let's talk about how the factory was run. How did you get your raw materials?"

Isolda leaned back in her chair, feeling more relaxed. She'd worked at the factory for years, and knew every detail of its operation. "The cycle began on Sage's Day, when the barrels arrived. Always the wagonloads were covered in raw wool to conceal the contents. The factory had a loading zone, fully enclosed, which was separate from the other facilities. Once the wagon was fully inside, the men would unload it, throwing off the wool and rolling the barrels out from underneath. . ."

As she spoke, Kolta wrote furiously.

As Marius escorted his guests into the villa, he wished fervently that his cousin would have informed him in advance of this visit, especially if he was going to bring an unfamiliar noblewoman along. Perhaps this was the emperor's revenge for Marius's dropping in at the palace unexpectedly to ask for Isolda's writ. But if he'd had time to prepare, he could have informed his cook in advance to buy meat or fish. As it was, Aurora had spent the day baking bread and simmering his favorite meal, parsnip soup. A perfectly good supper for himself and Isolda and Rory, but it was not going to appeal to this well-dressed noblewoman. Lucien had introduced her as the unmarried daughter of the Tullians, a wealthy family from the north the emperor had been courting as potential investors for his harbor project.

Marius suspected another sort of courtship was in the works.

He felt the young woman's displeasure as she looked him over. He wasn't wearing a syrtos today—he never wore one on workdays—but was instead clad in his customary tunic, belt, and breeches. By chance, he'd chosen his least threadbare tunic, the one of soft blue linen, but his breeches were an old pair, selected for comfort, and they were frayed at the bottom. He knew he was making a poor impression.

He was also annoyed at having to give up the evening comforts that had become customary for him after a day's work: a hearty meal, Rory's enthusiastic chatter about stick ball, a more intimate conversation with Isolda after the boy had run off to join his friends. And later, the pleasures of the bedroom.

Instead, this evening he would have to play the role of Highly Marriageable Imperial Cousin.

"I understand you're a Healer?" asked the young noblewoman, seating herself at his dining table.

"Yes." He tried to recall her name. Gratiana?

"What an unusual choice," she purred with a smile. "What made you choose healing magic instead of some other variety?"

"I've been drawn to the healing arts since I was a boy," said Marius. "In my youth, I served as an apprentice to an apothecary, so it seemed only natural that when I began my magical education, I should continue in the same line of study."

"You may not be aware of this," said Lucien, taking the seat next to Gratiana, "but Marius's parents raised him in a small town far from the imperial seat. It's only recently that he came here to Riat."

"How fascinating," said Gratiana. "Your parents must have wanted you to know how the common people lived."

Marius didn't know how to answer that.

Aurora entered, bearing a tray of freshly baked bread. She set it on the table, disappeared into the kitchen, and returned with the pot of parsnip soup. The room was crowded, with all the plainclothes Legaciatti standing around, but she weaved her way through them and ladled some soup into each guest's bowl. Marius cut the bread into slices.

Gratiana eyed the bread. "How rustic. I believe it's important to know how the common folk live. We lose sight of it, shut away in our villas and surrounded by servants."

"You're quite right," said Lucien. "Now that the wars are over, Kjall's greatest challenge to overcome is poverty. Since I started giving the land grants to unemployed veterans, production has improved. But the next step is to increase imports and exports, and that means building a world-class harbor."

Marius caught the hint of an eye roll from Gratiana, and gathered that she'd heard this speech before.

"You must treat commoners at your surgery," Gratiana said to Marius.

"Of course," said Marius. "I treat anyone who walks in the door."

"What sort of things do they talk about?"

Marius had no idea how to respond to this. "Mostly they tell me about their symptoms. The reason they came in."

Gratiana stirred her soup. She dipped her spoon and brought it to her lips, tasting the broth. She concealed her displeasure well, but he could tell she didn't like it. She set her spoon down and reached for the bread.

Everybody liked bread, regardless of their social class, and Aurora was a master baker.

Marius picked up his bread, dipped it in the soup, and chewed happily.

When he looked up, Gratiana was staring at him.

Had he made some sort of social error, dipping his bread in the soup? He'd always eaten it that way, as had his parents and his sister, not to mention everyone he'd known in Osler. This was the delight of parsnip soup, dipping one's bread into it to absorb the flavors.

Lucien, who'd been sipping his soup in the polite manner of an aristocrat, picked up his own bread, dipped it in his soup, and took a bite without saying a word.

The gesture did not go unnoticed. Dipping one's bread might not have been fashionable among the Kjallan upper crust until now, but if the emperor did it, it became the new fashion.

Gratiana dipped her bread in the soup.

Marius let out his breath. Crisis averted.

Gratiana smiled. "That blue is certainly your color—it brings out your eyes. If it were just a shade or two darker, it would be perfect. I know the most excellent tailor in Riat, and he just received a shipment of dark blue fabrics. Shall I give you his name?"

Marius stiffened. However well-intentioned her words, they were veiled criticism. Gratiana seemed a decent enough woman for what she was, but she represented everything he couldn't stand about the Kjallan nobility. She possessed an almost fetishistic curiosity about the "common people" while simultaneously looking down on them. Like so many powerful Kjallan women, her interest had nothing to do with Marius himself but in his relationship to the imperial throne. If he married her, she would lose no time in asking him to change all his personal habits and perhaps even his profession.

Still, it was clear that Lucien had brought her here because he needed this family's help with the harbor. Marius wasn't going to go so far as to marry or even court this woman, but he owed it to his cousin at least to be polite, and perhaps to steer the conversation in a more productive direction.

He forced himself to sound enthusiastic. "I'd love the name of your tailor. Did he design the dress you're wearing now?"

"Oh, no." She laughed. "He only makes men's clothes."

"Well, if I were a woman, I'd want the name of your dressmaker." This was the first he'd looked closely at her dress. It was a shimmering mixture of purple and yellow, quite lovely now that he noticed. "Is that Mosari silk?"

Her face lit, and Marius realized this was the first genuine smile he'd seen on her. "Oh, yes. So few people realize how superior Mosari silk is to other varieties."

Good thing Rhianne had taught him how to identify it. "It's a lovely fabric."

"And so rare. I've been asking for a red dress of Mosari silk for ages, but we just can't get the material."

"The emperor was telling me the other day that when we build this new harbor, we'll be able to triple imports from Mosar into Riat." He hoped that would prove tempting to her. She might want the silk to remain rare, so that only the most privileged families could possess it, but it sounded like she was having trouble acquiring it herself.

"Really?" Her eyes went to Lucien. "Would that mean more Mosari silk?"

Lucien nodded. "Yes, and many other luxury goods besides."

Marius allowed himself to relax. It appeared she did want imports to increase.

"What about lemons?" she asked. "Up north, we always run out of lemons in the cooler months."

"The harbor should improve lemon imports as well."

Marius smiled. He might not be able to fulfill the role Lucien hoped for, that of marrying into this influential family and assuring him of their political and financial support for the harbor project, but he could at least show his support in other ways.

Isolda's meeting with Kolta took nearly two hours. Isolda had thought she would just hand over the name and a few details and be done with it, but Kolta wanted to know absolutely everything: when and where the materials were delivered, the quality of the materials, how they were handled, what safety precautions were employed, how the finished product was handled, when it left the factory and in what manner.

What Kolta intended to do with all this information, Isolda had no idea, but it was clear the dark-haired woman took the situation seriously. Isolda felt honor-bound to remember as much as she could in hopes that it would prove helpful.

Suppertime came and went. By the time the interview was over, it was dark out, and the Sage was up.

"You've been enormously helpful," said Kolta, stacking several pages of her hand-written notes. "I hope we've made the process as painless as possible."

Shona, the mind mage, rose from her chair. She hadn't said a word throughout the entire questioning process. No need, since Isolda had told the truth. Isolda had declined to answer a couple of questions that she felt might implicate some of her Sardossian friends who hadn't been deported, and Kolta, as promised, had moved on to other subjects without pressing her.

As they headed out of the surgery, Isolda saw that Marius's meeting in the villa had broken up as well. Marius was on the front step of the villa in the company of a nobleman who appeared to be in his thirties—was this man the benefactor?— and a young woman barely out of her teens.

Kolta and Shona walked over to the group, apparently certain of their welcome, but Isolda hung back. The young woman smiled at Marius, and Marius smiled back. She offered him her wrist. He picked it up and kissed it.

Isolda's chest went tight. That was what this visit was really about—her sharing of information about the gunpowder factories was only a sideshow. Marius's cousin was introducing this woman to Marius as a potential marriage partner. Why else would he have brought her to Marius's villa?

AMY RABY

"Mom!" Rory dashed up to her and hugged her around the waist. He was flushed and sweating. "I scored six marks today."

"Wonderful," she said, her eyes still on Marius and the young woman. "Have you had supper yet?"

"No."

She hadn't either. "Let's go and do that."

"Marius said we can eat at the villa when the people leave."

"Not tonight," said Isolda.

"Why not?"

She detected a touch of a whine in her son's voice. Rory preferred the food at Marius's to what they could scrounge up elsewhere, and the pickings in the harbor district would be slim this late in the evening. Still, she couldn't bear to go to the villa now. She blinked away tears. Why was she letting herself get upset about this? From the beginning, she'd known it would happen. Marius was miles out of her social class and also highly marriageable. At his age, his family would be putting pressure on him to marry. If he didn't choose this woman, he would choose another one, soon enough.

She'd known it would happen, but she couldn't bear it.

Marius handed Gratiana into the front carriage with Vitala. The street emptied as the imperial party packed themselves into their carriages, but Lucien hung back on the doorstep. When only the two of them remained, the emperor pulled Marius aside for a whispered conversation.

"Did you learn anything about Maxian's problem?" Lucien asked.

"Not yet," said Marius. "I talked to some people at the university, but I didn't get a clear answer. There's a disorder I didn't know about that causes bruising, but it also has some other symptoms, such as swelling in the neck. I didn't observe that when I saw Maxian."

Lucien nodded. "I'll check for swelling when I get back."

"I'd like to talk to a few more people," said Marius. "I don't think I've explored every possibility." He desperately hoped to find a medical cause, because the alternative was that the child was being abused, and that was a conversation he didn't want to have with Lucien. Yet for Maxian's protection, it would have to be done once he'd eliminated everything else. He knew at least one more Healer at the university he could speak to on the matter before he started making accusations that were sure to throw someone's life into turmoil.

"Thank you," said Lucien, as they clasped wrists. "And I appreciate your discretion." He climbed into the front carriage and closed the door behind him. The drivers slapped the reins, and both vehicles rolled away.

Marius sighed and rolled his shoulders, letting out the tension of having to be "on" for an extended period of time, and in his own home at that. Finally, he could just be himself. He looked around, searching for Isolda.

She was walking away down the street, clutching Rory's hand.

He ran after them.

When he caught up, Isolda turned and said, "I need to go home."

"I don't believe you've had supper yet," said Marius. "I know it's late, and the food's cold, but I can put the soup over the fire again. You should stay here tonight, both of you."

Isolda clasped his wrist, a formal gesture that chilled him. Why not a hug or a kiss, given how intimate they'd been?

"Thank you," she said. "You've been very kind. But I shouldn't stay."

"You're not leaving, are you?" He had a terrifying sense that she was ending the relationship, or at least backing away from it.

"I'll be at the surgery tomorrow morning," she said.

He swallowed. That didn't answer the whole of his question. "If you must go back, at least allow me and Drusus to escort you. I don't know what you saw, but that woman—" He let out a breath, and paused to collect himself. "She's just someone I have to be nice to for my cousin's sake. I'm not interested in her. I swear I'm not."

Isolda turned away, as if to hide tears.

"You're the one I want," he said softly. "Not her. Not anyone else."

She spoke in a trembling voice. "But you will marry someone else, eventually."

"I haven't thought that far ahead," said Marius.

That seemed to be the wrong answer, because she turned and walked away, taking Rory with her.

He trotted after her. "At least let me escort you to the harbor district." He gestured to Drusus, who caught up with them. But Isolda broke into a run, and Marius, feeling it was not proper to chase a woman, stopped and stood shivering, with his hand outstretched in the night air.

25

Three days had passed, and Marius didn't know what to do about Isolda. Each day, she showed up for work on time, well-dressed and smiling. She did her work with courtesy and efficiency, and in the evening, when Marius invited her back to the villa, she politely declined to join him. Every time. Neither would she let him and Drusus escort her back to the harbor district.

His affair with her had ended almost as soon as it had begun, and all because of his affectionate farewell to Gratiana, which hadn't meant a thing. It was for Lucien's benefit that he'd attempted to be charming. And while Lucien might have hoped a romance could blossom between him and Gratiana, it hadn't. He had not seen the woman since.

Yet when Isolda gave him that tight smile, he saw the pain in her eyes. The problem wasn't Gratiana or the fact that he'd kissed her hand. It was something more substantial.

At supper an hour later with Drusus, he blurted, "Why can't I marry Isolda?"

His bodyguard answered without looking up. "Because you're the emperor's cousin, and she's an illegal refugee." They were eating pan-fried venison tonight. Marius didn't care much for venison, but Drusus was on his second helping.

"I have no obligation to Lucien—"

"Of course you have an obligation," said Drusus. "He's your emperor and patron. He's given you everything."

"But I never asked for anything," said Marius. "What he gave, he gave for his own reasons."

"You accepted."

"There was never an agreement that in exchange for his financial support, I would allow him to choose my marriage partner," said Marius. "I'm not going to marry someone just because it nets him one more investor for the harbor. His need for investors is a short-term problem. Marriage is forever."

Drusus snorted. "Not necessarily."

"It ought to be."

"Lucien never said you had to marry someone who would further his harbor project," said Drusus. "Just someone appropriate to your station."

"I know." The emperor, who had been generally supportive and had legitimate reasons for being upset with the Sardossian refugees, did not deserve Marius's pique. Marius was lashing out because he couldn't figure out whom to be angry with. He didn't want to disappoint his cousin, but neither did he want to marry a noblewoman appropriate to his station. He wanted to marry Isolda.

"Talk to him," said Drusus. "He'll hear you out."

"I should." The gunpowder explosion was a fading memory now. Tensions with the refugees had receded somewhat, and Lucien might be more receptive to the idea of offering Isolda long-term citizenship. But he'd likely resist the idea of Marius marrying her. Marius dreaded the conversation, all the more so because he had an additional sensitive subject to discuss with the emperor: Maxian's bruises. He'd talked to every Healer he could find at the university, and none of them knew of a bruising disorder that would explain Maxian's injuries. He was going to have to tell the emperor that the bruises had been inflicted by blows. But who would have the audacity to hit the emperor's son?

"So, there you go," said Drusus. "Next Sage's Day when you have your lunch with him, tell him you want to marry Isolda and see what he says."

Marius blew out his breath. "Maybe I should ask Isolda first."

"I wouldn't blindside the emperor," said Drusus. "Don't you think she'll say yes?"

"I hope." It was hard to be certain, given how much she'd pulled away from him of late, but his impression was that she was keeping her distance not because she wasn't interested, but because she believed he was going to marry someone else and didn't want a casual affair. "Speaking of the emperor, there's something I want to ask you."

Drusus loaded a third helping of venison onto his plate. "Go ahead."

"The subject is a sensitive one—"

His bodyguard looked up with brows raised.

"It's nothing you've done," said Marius. "It's just that I can't tell you the reason I'm asking. Do you remember that time you told me Jamien wasn't the same person in private as he was in public?"

Drusus's face became guarded. "I don't recall saying such a thing."

"You said he was a terror."

Drusus looked down at his plate. "I'm sure I didn't."

Marius felt profoundly sad. For all they'd been through together, did Drusus not trust him? "This is important. The emperor specifically asked me to investigate a situation I think might be related. So if you know something—"

"Sir, I do not know anything," said Drusus. "If I did, it would not be my place to speak of it."

Marius sighed and fell silent.

Isolda tugged Rory closer to her in the crowded tavern, and stirred the contents of her bowl. The potato soup was thin, almost translucent. She brought her spoon to her lips, sampling the tasteless broth, and eyed the tavern crowd. It consisted mainly of Sardossian men who'd finished their workday. For now, they were jovial and throwing back cheap gin, but in an hour or two, this place would get rough. By then, she hoped to be safe underground with Rory.

Caz slid onto the seat next to her, setting his gin mug on the table. "Haven't seen you here in a while. Is that Kjallan dandy treating you all right?"

"Marius is no dandy." Caz's mere presence relaxed her. He was a big man, and sufficiently respected that no one would give her or Rory any trouble in his presence.

"Did you two have a scrap?"

Isolda glanced at her son's soup bowl. He'd already finished. "Rory, run home so I can have a talk with Caz."

"I want to hear what you say about Marius," he complained.

"Go," she said softly.

Rory left the table, stiff-backed.

"I've stopped seeing him because he won't marry me," said Isolda.

Caz blinked. "Didn't you just meet this man?"

"I've known him for a couple of months," said Isolda. "I don't mean he won't marry me *now*; I mean he won't marry me *ever*. His family is wealthy. They would never stand for me, and I think they pay most of his expenses."

"You mean if he marries you, the flow of money stops."

"Probably," said Isolda. "They bring young noblewomen to his house in hopes he'll fall in love with one of them."

"But you're the one who warms his bed at night," said Caz.

"Not anymore."

"Why throw yourself out prematurely? If the fun is going to be temporary, might as well enjoy it while you've got it." He tipped back his mug, taking a swallow. Then he wrinkled his nose. "Tastes like raw pine needles."

"You should know better than to buy gin here," said Isolda.

Caz shrugged. "Answer my question."

"I left because I can't bear it," said Isolda. "This was never just a bit of fun for me. Marius might see it that way, but I don't. I'm in love with the man."

"Ah," said Caz. "Don't you know you should never fall in love with a Kjallan?"

"I think about him day and night," said Isolda. "I've never known such a man as Marius. He's so *good*. He's the standard by which I judge other people, by which I judge myself—"

"Come on," said Caz. "Is he a man, or is he a god?"

"I mean it," said Isolda.

"Nobody is that perfect."

She shook her head. "I'm not saying he's perfect, only that he's the best man I've ever known. And so few people appreciate him! He lives simply and dresses unfashionably, and most women can't see past that. It's not that he doesn't have female admirers," she added, thinking of Lady Fabiola. "But either they've got some selfish agenda, or they see him as raw material to be molded into the man they really want. I want him just how he is."

"And you've broken things off with him," said Caz, "because you're afraid he'll marry someone else. Though no one else seems to appreciate him."

"They appreciate his money and connections. It hurts me inside, seeing him every day and knowing that the day must come when he chooses another. If I put some distance between us now, maybe it won't hurt so much when that happens. Maybe I'll be able to clasp his wrist and congratulate him on his good fortune."

"Would it be better if you didn't work at the surgery at all?" asked Caz.

"I'll never find a job that pays as well."

"You're a bookkeeper, aren't you?"

She nodded.

"The shipping company I work for is looking for a bookkeeper. They don't employ a lot of Sardossians, but your

Kjallan is fluent now, and you've got the experience they're looking for. Want me to inquire?"

"How much does it pay?"

"I can find out. Enough to keep you in bribe money, probably."

"Thank you. I'm interested." It made her heart ache to think of leaving the surgery. It was the best job she'd ever had, but one of the reasons she loved it was that Marius was there. Now that his presence brought her more pain than joy, it was time to get out.

26

On Sage's Day, Marius rode up to the palace with Drusus in tow. When he arrived at the gates, the guards, instead of taking his horse and escorting him inside, instructed him to stay where he was and wait. Knowing that Lucien was a busy man and sometimes late to his meetings, Marius dismounted and loosened Gambler's girth.

When Lucien appeared half an hour later in the company of half a dozen Legaciatti, he was not on foot but mounted on a magnificent black horse with a long, flowing mane and tail.

Marius made the customary show of obeisance. When this was accepted, he asked, "Are we going somewhere?"

"Just out of the palace," said Lucien. "If I have to spend one more hour among all that marble, I'll go mad."

Gambler was fresh enough after his breather, as was Drusus's horse, and Marius didn't mind a ride through the imperial grounds. The grounds were extensive, but he'd never seen more than a tiny piece of them. And considering that he had two topics of a sensitive nature to speak to Lucien about today, it would be good to leave the palace gossips behind.

Lucien led the way, setting a faster pace than Marius would have chosen. Gambler, who usually jogged placidly, lengthened his stride to keep up. Marius had not realized his horse was capable of speed. Though he knew the animal came from the imperial stables, he'd always thought of Gambler as a quiet plug.

Drusus and the other Legaciatti rode alongside.

Gambler arched his neck as if to show off, and Marius cast an admiring glance at the emperor's horse, which Lucien rode easily despite his missing leg. The animal's tail dragged along the ground. "Does he ever step on his tail?" Marius asked.

"The trick is not to go backward," said Lucien.

For a while, they stayed on the main road. When they rounded a corner and a lake glistened in the lowlands, Lucien led them on a side path down to the water. There, they slowed their horses to walk along the bank. At a gesture from Lucien, the Legaciatti peeled away, giving them privacy.

Lucien spoke in a low voice. "What have you learned about Maxian's condition?"

Here it was, the first of the conversations he'd been dreading. "I've spoken to several Healers at the university, and I don't think Maxian's bruises have a medical cause."

"Then how did he acquire them?"

"I cannot know, Your Imperial Majesty," said Marius.

"Were they the result of accidents, or did someone hit him?"

"I may be a village hayseed," said Marius, "but I recognize that in a situation such as this, the stakes are high for everyone involved. I don't want to make an accusation when I have no conclusive evidence."

"I understand," said Lucien. "But give me your best guess."

Marius bit his lip. "This is what I know about bruises. Accidental ones are common in children, but they are usually found on the arms and legs, especially the shins. If on the face, the most common location is the forehead. Since Maxian's are on his torso, it may be that someone is hitting him."

"That's what I feared," said Lucien.

"What do you plan to do?" asked Marius, concerned now for the fates of the guards and nurses who cared for Maxian.

"I'm not sure," said Lucien. "Vitala and I will discuss it this afternoon."

Marius sent him a worried glance. What if Vitala was the one hitting the boy? He couldn't say such a thing aloud, not to her loving husband, but it was a possibility.

"If you're wondering whether Vitala might be the one hitting him, allow me to ease your mind," said Lucien. "It's not her."

Marius nodded, letting his shoulders relax.

"I think I know who it is," said Lucien. "But I won't say anything more until I can confirm it."

They rode in silence for a while, and Marius allowed himself to breathe more easily. His duty was done. He'd passed on everything he knew except the bit about Jamien that Drusus now denied he'd ever said. Lucien would work things out from here.

He watched the water as they rode. A breeze was kicking up ripples on the lake. The wind was changeable, and the ripples flowed in different directions. As one set collided with another, they formed little whitecaps.

He longed to bring Isolda here. He wanted to bring her lots of places, to be with her out in the open and stop hiding her in the villa—or away from the villa. His exclusion of her when Lucien had come with Gratiana now felt terribly wrong. There'd been a reason for it at the time: Vitala, acting as her alter ego Kolta, had wanted to talk to Isolda about the gunpowder factories. But he knew, and certainly Isolda knew, that even if Vitala had not needed her, Isolda would have been left out of that dinner party.

He was living two separate lives, one with Isolda and Rory, and another one with the imperial family. This was untenable. He understood why she had pulled away from him. She was no Lady Fabiola, seeking an affair in the shadows. Isolda wanted him, but only if she could have him in the light of day.

He cleared his throat. "Cousin, I'd like your permission to marry."

Lucien turned and looked at him with brows raised. "This is a surprise."

"I've been. . .keeping things quiet. Until now."

"I hope it's not the Sardossian."

Marius suppressed a cough. For all he'd tried to keep things quiet, he was apparently rather obvious. "It is. Isolda."

Lucien's expression remained unreadable as he turned away. "You do not need my permission to marry."

From a legal standpoint, he didn't, but there was more at stake here. He didn't just want Isolda to be his wife; he wanted her to be accepted by the imperial family. And he wanted her to be safe from the city guards. "I think what I mean is that I'm seeking your blessing."

"Ah," said Lucien.

"You told me recently that I couldn't tell her who I was. But if we marry, I must tell her."

"Have you proposed?"

"I thought I should talk to you first."

Lucien visibly relaxed. "There's a problem. You can't legally marry an illegal citizen."

Marius had feared that was a possibility. However, he saw an obvious solution. "You could confer citizenship upon her."

Silence hung between them, and Marius knew Lucien was wrestling with competing interests, not to mention his uneasiness with Marius's choice of partner.

Finally, Lucien said, "It sets a bad precedent."

"What are your objections to the marriage?" asked Marius.

Lucien halted his horse.

Marius turned Gambler side-on so that he and the emperor could look each other in the eye.

"My objections are many," said Lucien. "First, she's breaking the law, and I don't reward lawbreakers. Second, she's far beneath your social class. Did you say she's the daughter of an apothecary?"

Marius nodded.

"And you are from the imperial family," said Lucien.

"*You* married a peasant woman from Riorca," said Marius.

Lucien snorted. "Vitala is an extraordinary woman, one of a kind. How many peasant women, from anywhere, can beat me at Caturanga? How many noblewomen can do it? None. And Caturanga is just one of her many talents."

"Isolda is extraordinary too."

Lucien sighed. "How long have you known her?"

"Two months. I also met her briefly a few years ago."

"I know this is not something you want to hear," said Lucien. "But what if she's interested in you only for your wealth and influence, and especially for the possibility that you could, through your influence, make her a legal citizen?"

"She has no idea that I'm connected to the imperial family," said Marius.

"She knows you're connected to wealth," said Lucien.

"She doesn't care," said Marius. "I'm sure of it."

"Love can make a man blind."

"Would it help if you met her?"

Lucien frowned. "If she meets me, she learns your secret. What if the marriage falls apart and she tells her Sardossian friends who you are? If she wags her tongue, she could jeopardize everything you've built for yourself in Riat."

"Isolda never wags her tongue," said Marius.

"You haven't known her long enough to be sure," said Lucien.

Marius set his jaw. "I want to tell her."

"What if I meet her and don't like her?"

"You'll like her," said Marius. *He'd better.*

Lucien clucked to his horse, sending him into a walk alongside the lake.

Marius steered his horse next to the emperor's.

"Your mother did this, you know," said Lucien.

"My mother eloped and ran away," said Marius. "I'm having a conversation."

"And do you think a conversation didn't happen between your mother and Nigellus before everything fell apart? I'm not Nigellus. I'm not going to scare you back to Osler. I don't like what you're doing, but you're right: I married a peasant woman and a bastard besides, and I thank the gods every day that she found me. If you want to marry this woman, and you're willing to take the risks, talk to her, and then bring her here so I can meet her. All right?"

"Thank you, cousin." It wasn't a promise, but it gave him hope. He and Lucien clasped wrists.

27

The workday was over, but Isolda couldn't go home yet. Marius had asked her to wait while he put a few things away in the dispensary. He'd said he needed to talk to her before she left the surgery. Whether it was about business or something personal, she didn't know.

She ought never to have fallen in love with her boss, and this was why. Her work life and her love life were all muddled up. Being around Marius was shredding her heart one piece at a time, and the only solution she could see was to get out of this situation. Yesterday, she'd spoken with a man at the shipping company where Caz worked, and the fellow had seemed pleased with her. If he offered her the job and it paid well enough to keep her in "bribe money," as Caz said, she'd take it.

Marius emerged from the dispensary. Her heart leapt at the sight of him, an automatic response, but her momentary joy turned to pain as she reminded herself that he was meant for someone else.

"Isolda, thanks for waiting." Marius looked tense. "Can we go somewhere and talk?"

"Your office?" she suggested.

"I was thinking the villa."

Not a business conversation then, but a personal one. "I can't keep coming to the villa. We've no future together, and much as I enjoyed those nights we shared—"

"That's what I want to talk to you about," said Marius. "Our future together."

"I think all that can be said on that subject has already been said."

Marius shook his head. "What I have to say, you've not heard yet. If you're not interested in what I have to offer this evening, I'll never ask you back to the villa again."

He'd piqued her curiosity. "What should I do with Rory?"

"Does he want to play stick ball? I can have Aurora pack a dinner for him."

"He'd like that." Rory had complained about missing his stick ball games.

They left the surgery together. While Marius turned to lock up the building, she collected Rory from where he waited at the corner. "I need to speak with Marius at the villa. You can go straight out to play stick ball. Aurora's going to bring you dinner."

With a whoop of joy, Rory ran for the cross street.

Marius took her arm. "He sounds happy."

Watching Rory pelt down the alleyway, she felt wistful. "He's always liked it here."

"I like his being here," said Marius, leading her to the villa.

Delicious aromas enveloped her as she walked inside. "What's for dinner?"

"I asked Aurora to make something special," said Marius. "Roast pella—it's a Sardossian fish, isn't it?"

She nodded. "Pella is delicious. And bread?"

"Herbed bread, peas with onions, figs, and lemonade."

It sounded heavenly. Far better than the mystery meat stew she and Rory would have had at some dingy tavern in the harbor district.

At the table, Aurora served all the courses at once and left them alone. It occurred to Isolda that even Drusus wasn't about. At least, she didn't see him. But he had to be somewhere.

Marius looked nervous. He sipped his lemonade but did not touch his food. "I've thought a lot about that evening when my cousin came by the villa and you spoke to Kolta in the surgery."

Isolda nodded. The memory of that evening still stung. It had driven home the reality that she did not really belong with Marius.

"I'm not going to insult your intelligence," said Marius. "You read the situation exactly as it was. My cousin brought a young woman along—her name was Gratiana—because he hoped I would court her. If I married her, it would have helped him politically. But I declined."

She refused to be distracted by the fact that he had not liked this particular woman. It changed nothing on the grander scale. "Someday he'll bring a woman you'll be more interested in."

Marius shook his head. "He could bring a hundred women and it would make no difference. He and my sister have been trying this for years now, presenting me with marriageable women and hoping I'll fall in love with one of them. It hasn't worked, and now I understand why. It's because none of those women were you."

Isolda swallowed.

"Every time I visit my family, I count the minutes until I can come back home to you. You're the one I want, Isolda. There is no other woman. There *will* be no other woman. Will you marry me?"

A sob erupted from her throat.

Marius's brows shot up. "Three gods. Please tell me those are happy tears."

"Marius," she choked. Then she leapt from her chair and flung herself into his arms. "Yes. Of course, yes."

He wrapped his arms around her, stroking her back and hair. "Yes to what? Happy tears, or you'll marry me?"

"Both." She buried her face in his chest, trying to stop crying. Her face felt hot and swollen—what an awful state to be in! This wasn't how she'd meant to respond to such a proposal, but then she had never expected to receive one. All the emotion inside of her, pent up not just from the months she'd spent desiring Marius but from the years of her terrible loveless marriage with Jauld, spilled out of her like poison flushed from a wound.

"I brought you a gift," said Marius.

She hiccupped, laughing through her tears. "You don't need to buy me gifts. Do you think I want anything besides you?"

"You'll like this. Sit down."

She took her place at the table, wiping her eyes.

He held out a tiny box.

A box that size couldn't hold anything large. Jewelry, perhaps? A ring or necklace? She didn't think of Marius as the sort to buy jewelry, but perhaps for a special occasion, it made sense. She took the box and opened it. Inside was an unmounted stone about the size of her thumbnail, round and polished and black. Bits of bright color winked through its inky surface: reds and yellows and blues. "How extraordinary. What is it?"

"A riftstone," said Marius.

She gasped.

"Black opal," he said. "It's a pyrotechnic's riftstone. I know you wanted a wardstone for Rory, but since the university fees are the same regardless of the quality of the stone, I thought I'd get you a nicer one. If Rory desires a different type of magic than pyrotechnics, we can exchange it for whatever he prefers."

Isolda's hands shook. She could barely breathe. A riftstone for Rory! Not a common jasper, either, but a rare and beautiful black opal. Rory could be a pyrotechnic if they kept this stone, or, if they traded it for another, a Healer, a war mage, a fire mage. A mind mage? No, Kjall limited that form of magic to women. But he could be anything else, anything at all! She pressed a hand over her mouth. She was going to cry all over again.

"I realize it's more a gift for your son than for you, but—"

Isolda shook her head. "There is nothing in the world I wanted more."

"I thought that might be the case," said Marius.

"How is this happening?" asked Isolda. "I thought you couldn't marry me because of your wealthy cousin. Have you spoken to him yet?"

"I have, and we need to talk about that."

She set the stone in its box on the table and folded her hands in her lap.

"There are a few obstacles we have to overcome before we can do this." Marius glanced at her plate. "You've barely touched your food. Why don't you start eating while I explain the family situation?"

How could she eat? Her stomach was in knots. But to satisfy him, she raised a bite of pella to her mouth.

"There's a secret I've kept from you," said Marius. "It's a big one, and I hope you'll forgive me for the longstanding lie of omission. All I can say in my defense is that I've been under direct orders not to tell anybody, but if we're to marry, I must make an exception. My cousin is the emperor of Kjall."

Isolda choked on the pella. "*What?*"

"It sounds hard to believe, I know, but I'm Emperor Lucien's cousin. His father and my mother were brother and sister."

"You're the emperor's *blood relative?*"

Marius nodded.

"The same emperor who deported my people?"

"Yes."

Gods, he was probably in the line of succession. What a thought, her Marius a candidate for the imperial throne! It seemed unreal. She'd seen his family the night they'd come to the villa, all those people in the two carriages. "You said your cousin came to the villa that night. Are you saying that the man I saw with you was the emperor?"

"Yes, and the woman you met with, who called herself Kolta, was Empress Vitala."

Isolda's spoon clattered to the floor, and she collapsed against the back of her chair. All this seemed impossible, and yet it made perfect sense. It explained everything: Marius's full-time bodyguard, his villa full of servants, his total lack of anxiety about money. Why had she not questioned his ability to walk into the guardhouse with a writ and free her from the Riat City Guard? No ordinary Kjallan citizen had that authority. The clues had been there all along, and she'd ignored them. Perhaps she hadn't wanted to know. "Gods. It's true, isn't it?"

"It's true," said Marius softly.

She wiped the back of her hand across her eyes. "Your emperor hates my people. You really think he'll let you marry me?"

"Let me be clear: I plan to marry you regardless of what he says. But I'd like his blessing for our union, and he's asked to meet you."

"*Meet me?*" The prospect filled her with terror. An illegal Sardossian refugee, meeting with the emperor of Kjall so that he could judge whether she was good enough for his cousin? Of course she wasn't good enough. She wasn't wealthy or connected. She wasn't a legal citizen. She wasn't even *pretty*. "He won't like me."

"He will once he gets to know you," said Marius.

Such confidence, from a man who'd never had to struggle in life. She had a feeling it was not going to be so easy. "What if he hates me? Can he forbid you to marry me?"

"No, but he can deny you citizenship," said Marius. "That's the real issue. It's why we need his blessing for this union."

"His blessing," she repeated numbly. Marius had dangled before her everything she wanted: marriage to the man she loved, a riftstone for her son, and Kjallan citizenship. But all of it was contingent upon the emperor approving her as a match for Marius. She could not imagine that happening. This was the man who had deported Emari, along with hundreds of other

Sardossians. And speaking of fraudulent, there was a problem with her marital status.

"I need to ask something of you," said Marius.

"Yes?" Her mind was racing as she thought through all the angles.

"The fact that I'm part of the imperial family is a closely guarded secret. Lucien has enemies who might do me harm if they knew I was here in Riat, so accessible to the public and with only one bodyguard. For safety's sake, Isolda, you must tell no one who I am."

"Not even Rory?"

"Rory can know once we've got the details sorted out, but nobody else. The emperor is concerned that you might spread this information to the Sardossian underground—"

"I would never do that," said Isolda. "Your secret is safe."

"That's what I thought," said Marius.

Isolda licked dry lips. Marius had probably told the emperor that she was a Sardossian war widow, but if the emperor looked into her background, he would discover the lie. She had a recent divorce recorded in the Kjallan public records. Anyone could look it up. She turned to Marius. He'd told her his big secret. Now it was time to tell him hers. "Marius, I've something to confess to you as well. But mine, unlike yours, is an ugly secret."

A line appeared in the middle of his forehead. "What is it?"

She dropped her gaze, unable to meet his eyes. "I told you that my husband in Sardos was dead. But he's not. He's still alive. At least, he was when I last saw him."

Marius gaped. "So you're still married?"

"No," she said quickly. "I got a divorce here in Riat." But even that was tainted. As long as she was confessing, she might as well tell him everything. "The truth is that it may not be entirely legal. The apparitor wouldn't grant me the divorce without Jauld's permission. Of course I couldn't get that with Jauld so far away, so I had a friend stand in and pretend to be him."

Marius was silent for a moment, as if putting all the pieces together in his head. Then he let out a shaky breath. "I wish you'd told me earlier. This complicates matters."

"I was afraid you'd hate me if you knew the truth."

He reached across the table to squeeze her hand. "I'd never hate you."

"The marriage isn't going to work, is it?" said Isolda. "I stole from my husband—"

"You stole from him?"

"Yes—the money I'd earned at the store. It was the only way I could buy passage to Kjall. So I stole the money, abandoned my husband, and emigrated illegally to Kjall with his child. There I obtained a fraudulent divorce from an imperial apparitor. I don't think your cousin the emperor is going to think highly of me."

Marius swallowed. "None of this changes my opinion of you, or my desire to marry. We may have to work a little bit harder on Lucien, but—"

"The emperor wants better for you." Isolda took a deep breath. "I would want better for you, too. Marius, I can't accept your marriage proposal."

Marius shot up from his chair. "Now hold on a moment, you already *said*—"

"I wasn't thinking." She stood and backed away, shaking her head. "I got caught up in the fantasy and believed in what I wanted to be true. I thought I could escape who I used to be, but I'll never escape that, not even by running away to another continent. You needn't worry about your secret; it will never escape my lips. But I cannot meet with your emperor."

She didn't want to put down the box with its black opal. If her life was tainted, Rory's didn't need to be; a child should not be punished for the sins of his mother. But the riftstone was a betrothal gift—at least it had been intended as one—and if she could not accept the marriage proposal, she could not keep the stone.

She laid the box on the table and walked out.

28

A full week had passed since Marius had proposed to Isolda, and not only had she avoided the villa, she hadn't even shown up for work. He had to conclude that she'd quit her job as his business manager. But where could she have gone? He hoped it wasn't to another gunpowder factory

Back at the villa, with only Drusus for company, he'd had ample time to think about their conversation and where it had gone wrong. Her confession that her husband was still alive had shocked him at first, but on reflection he saw her actions as admirable. Rather than sit and suffer in a miserable situation and allow her child to suffer as well, she'd risked everything to seek a better life for both of them. As for stealing money that was supposedly Jauld's, Isolda had earned the money. Why shouldn't she benefit from it?

Her divorce and its questionable legality were more troublesome. He understood why she had seen fit to deceive the

AMY RABY

apparitor. Jauld was not physically present in Kjall to grant her the divorce, so it could not be accomplished any other way. And *of course* she should divorce Jauld. What justice would there be in her remaining married to a man who'd betrayed and mistreated her, and whom she would never see again? He recalled the "little detail" she'd insisted on taking care of before they slept together. That must have been the divorce. Isolda, despite her checkered past, was a principled woman. She would not sleep with another man while still married.

From an ethical standpoint, he had no quarrel with anything she'd done, but legally it was a mess. Lucien might straighten it out, if he could be persuaded to do so. But first she had to agree to meet with Lucien, which she'd refused to do.

On the second day of her disappearance, he'd tried to track her down again by locating Rory at the fruit stand and following him. But Rory no longer worked at the Chelani Corner Market, nor did he seem to work at any other fruit stand in the harbor district. On a whim, Marius took a gander at the gutted-out buildings that had once been the gunpowder factory. Carpenters were rebuilding them, but there was no factory there now.

He'd heard the Sardossians hid underground. Was that really true?

On his next Sage's Day visit, he confessed to Emperor Lucien the sad tale and asked for help. He'd worried that Lucien might be unsympathetic—after all, the emperor had never wanted this particular marriage to take place. Furthermore, Isolda's confession of fraud with the apparitor and her disappearance afterward seemed to confirm every worst stereotype about Sardossians. But the emperor seemed genuinely sorry that Marius's proposal had met with disappointment.

"I don't know where the Sardossians hide," said Lucien from across his desk in the imperial office. "We deported most of them. But you might ask Vitala. She's got her ear to the ground on such matters."

Marius scheduled a meeting with the empress. She'd been out all morning and then had to meet with someone over lunch, but she agreed to see him later that afternoon.

He found her in the gymnasium, watching over a training session. Three pairs of combatants clashed with rapiers, dancing back and forth across the polished marble floor. Marius looked around for his younger sister, but did not see her.

Vitala waved him over, and he joined her by the wall.

"Where's Laelia?" he asked.

"She fought this morning," said Vitala.

"How'd she do?"

"I wasn't there," said Vitala. "You could ask Horatius." She nodded toward the trainer who was following the action of one pair, calling out corrections. At one point, he stuck out his training stick, and a trainee tripped over it, landing in a heap on the ground. "Stance," murmured Vitala. When Marius didn't leave, she asked, "Is there something else I can do for you?"

"I was wondering if you know where the Sardossian refugees hide."

She turned to him with a raised brow. "Why?"

"Did Lucien tell you I was going to propose marriage to a Sardossian woman?"

"He mentioned it. Are congratulations in order?"

"No," said Marius. "At first, she accepted. But when I told her I was Lucien's cousin, and that she'd have to meet him, she panicked and fled back to wherever her people hide. And now I can't find her."

"Why would she do that?"

"She's afraid of Lucien—after all, he deported most of her people. And there are legal complications having to do with her citizenship and a prior marriage."

Vitala nodded.

"I need to find her," said Marius. "Do you know where she might be hiding?"

"I might have a lead for you," said Vitala. "Riat's history is rather interesting; have you studied it?"

Marius dug back in his mind to those sessions, years ago, with his history tutor. "It's always been the seat of the empire," he offered. "Kjall was originally a small province, which conquered its neighbors to the north and east—"

"I'm talking about the city itself," said Vitala. "Its structure. The harbor district is the oldest district of Riat. It was built on filled-in tidelands, and it often flooded, leading to sanitation problems. After a city fire in which a great many buildings were destroyed, the king at the time—this was before we became an empire—ordered that the city be rebuilt above sea level. Have you noticed that at the docks and all of Riat's beaches, you have to take a stairway down to the water?"

Marius blinked. That was true, although he'd never paid much attention to it. Riat was the first and only coastal city he'd lived in. "But how did they raise the city above sea level?"

"Concrete, mainly," said Vitala. "The old city, what was left of it, remained where it was. Now it sits below the new one, abandoned and derelict, rather like the hypocaust beneath the imperial palace."

"You believe the Sardossians live underground among this. . .concrete? In the old city?"

"That's what my sources suggest. Not just Sardossians, but ruffians, exiles, and the desperately poor. Anyone who can't afford housing."

How odd that the Riat City Guard didn't seem to know. "You haven't tried to drive them out?"

"I've got more important things to do than chase the desperately poor from their hiding spots," said Vitala.

Marius smiled. He'd always liked the empress. "Do you know how to enter this underground city?"

"I don't," said Vitala. "The entrance would seem logically to be in the harbor district, but let me caution you about seeking it out. This woman—Isolda?—left for a reason."

"She's convinced that Lucien will hate her. And she thinks I'm upset about her fraudulent divorce, which I'm not."

"Perhaps she's just a little intimidated," said Vitala. "But you might give her some time to come to terms with her feelings. Will she not come back on her own if you give her a chance?"

"She might." But he hated the idea of her and Rory being alone in hostile Riat with the writ expiring. Especially if they shared their living quarters with ruffians.

"Just give it some consideration before you go looking," said Vitala. "And remember that you, as a wealthy Kjallan, may not be welcomed by the denizens of the underground."

"I understand," said Marius.

Isolda's new job at Velox Marine Shipping was working out well. The pay was less than what she'd earned at the surgery, but it was enough to be satisfactory. And while her co-workers were not especially stimulating—for the most part, she worked alone in an office—that was, in her case, probably a good thing.

Her overseer was patient and businesslike, nothing like Twitchy Fingers. He was tolerant of her bringing Rory to work as long as the boy was quiet. So she'd set Rory to reading in a corner of her office. He needed to begin studying if he was going to do well at the university someday. They could forgo his small income for a while, and it was necessary she keep him away from the fruit stand temporarily, so that Marius couldn't use him as a means of locating her.

Caz also worked for Velox Marine. While she did bookkeeping in an office, he loaded and unloaded ships. At the end of the work day, he escorted her and Rory home, which she appreciated. The harbor district was rowdier than Marius's south hills district.

She made her last notation in the ledger and closed the book for the day. This was her first experience working for a company that didn't deal directly with customers but instead acted as a middleman between merchants. She'd had no idea there was so much profit in marine shipping. The margins were enormous compared to what she was used to, but then shipping was a risky business. While a good haul brought in hefty profits, a ship lost at sea could be disastrous to the bottom line.

Caz loitered outside her office, chatting with a friend. He seemed to have a lot of friends, far more than she'd been able to acquire since coming to Kjall. Perhaps it was because she was so focused on her work and her plans for Rory; she didn't have time for much else. She could count her friends in Kjall on one hand: Caz, Marius, maybe Drusus. All of them men. She used to have

Emari, but Emari had been deported. Now there was Vora, who'd moved into Emari's old place in the underground, but Isolda barely knew her and considered her an acquaintance.

She needed more friends, especially more women friends. Her experience with her older sisters and then with Chari had made her skittish of other women, but that was unfair: most women were not like Chari. Maybe she should ask Vora sometime if they could get dinner together. There was safety in numbers, and since leaving Marius she'd been lonely.

"Time to go," she called to Rory.

The boy closed his book and rose obediently to his feet.

Outside, Caz was clasping wrists, saying goodbye to his friend. His yellow hair was spiky and his bare, muscled arms shone with sweat. He was an attractive man, Caz. She'd have been interested in him if she hadn't been so fixated on Marius, but she was certain the interest wasn't mutual.

"Ready?" asked Caz.

"Thank you for walking us home."

He grinned. "Anything for a lady."

As they passed through the harbor district, Caz chatted about the ship he'd been loading that afternoon. It was bound for Mosar, and they'd loaded it mostly with timber. "They haven't any real forests on Mosar," he said. "Can you imagine? They send us luxury goods like coffee and silk and lemons, and we send them raw timber."

"Don't lemons grow on trees?" she asked

"Do they?" said Caz. "I never thought about it."

They'd reached the Drunken Wind Taproom, Isolda's usual breakfast and dinner spot, and also her gateway to the Riat Underground. Sometimes Caz had dinner with her and Rory before heading underground, and sometimes he had friends to meet at another tavern. Tonight he seemed to have no other obligation and sat with them for a brief, unappetizing dinner of potato hash. When they were finished, they headed into the kitchen, where the workers gave them a friendly nod, and down the stairs. Caz pulled back the false door, and they headed into the dripping halls of the old city.

The underground smelled of sewage and rot. Shot through with concrete beams, it was also a bit of a maze. Caz lived in an old inn three blocks away. The building Isolda called home was down a concrete aisle not far from the Drunken Wind. It was a two-room dwelling, of which only one of the rooms was habitable. She and Rory used to share it with Emari. Now they shared it with Vora and a sickly old man. She had no idea what the place had originally been called—there was no official sign—but someone had chalked the word *kodon* on the door: Sardossian for "home."

Though it was a little out of his way, Caz accompanied her to the *kodon*.

Vora stood by the door. "There's a man come to see you. He's waiting inside."

Isolda stopped short. "A man?"

"He said he's been looking all over town for you."

Rory tugged at her sleeve. "Mom, it's Marius."

How had Marius found her? She thought she'd taken every precaution this time.

"Want me to go in with you?" asked Caz.

"No." Strange how her heart fluttered at the thought of speaking to Marius again. She'd wanted to stay away—it pained her too much to think about what he'd offered, and how she'd had to turn it all down. But now that he was here, she wanted very much to talk to him. "I think this conversation needs to be private."

"No privacy in the underground," said Caz.

"We'll go somewhere." If Marius was here, he must have something of significance to say. Maybe the situation had changed. Maybe she didn't have to meet with the emperor after all.

Caz gave her a wink. "Good luck."

She clasped his wrist.

Inside the *kodon*, she worked her way around the fallen rafters and the puddle of seawater in the corner. The place smelled of mildew, and from the bedroom she could hear the old man's raspy cough. How shameful, that Marius should see the awful place she lived. The Kjallans called her people sewer rats, and they were not far wrong.

She crossed the crooked doorframe into the bedroom and stopped short.

The man waiting for her was not Marius.

It was Jauld.

29

Not since his days of eating at Lev's Inn and Tavern had Marius encountered a beef stew as bad as this one. He raised his spoon and examined its contents. "Do you think this is actually beef?"

Drusus, who'd already cleaned his bowl, grunted something noncommittal.

It appeared to be meat, but it had tubes running through it. "You want the rest of mine?"

"Sure."

Marius handed it over. It didn't matter that the food was bad; he was finally making some progress at locating the underground city. For several days now, after putting in his workday at the surgery, he'd gone to the harbor district and tried to surreptitiously follow any Sardossians he spotted. His tailing skills were untrained and clumsy. His targets often noticed him, became alarmed, and slipped away.

But he was desperate enough to keep trying, and one thing he'd noticed was that while many Sardossians entered the Sage House Tavern on Fisher Street, not as many seemed to leave it. So he'd tried an experiment. He watched a particular Sardossian enter the tavern. Then he waited fifteen minutes and went inside to look for that person. He couldn't find him.

Marius suspected the Sage House was an entry point to the underground city. Somehow, Sardossians were entering the tavern and, instead of coming back out again, were heading to their evening quarters underground. Tonight, he and Drusus had stepped inside the tavern to have dinner so that they could see the place and perhaps observe the route the Sardossians were using.

"I think it's through the kitchen," murmured Drusus. "See there?"

Marius followed his bodyguard's gaze. A pair of Sardossians were walking around the corner into the kitchen. They paused at the entrance to speak to someone, and then disappeared.

"Now we see if they come back out," said Drusus.

Marius gnawed on a hard, tasteless roll while he watched the spot where they'd disappeared. A minute passed. Then five. "I think they're gone."

"Shall we go over there and have a look?"

"As long as you don't think it's dangerous," asked Marius.

"Shouldn't be," said Drusus with a shrug. "Sardossian refugees don't seem much inclined to violence."

Marius rose from the table, took a final sip of his ale, and headed toward the kitchen. He tried to look casual, though his heart was thumping.

Drusus fell in behind him.

When Marius turned the corner, he saw an ordinary kitchen. A mechanized roasting-jack, the type that a cook cranked up and left to unspool, turned a roast over the fire. A boy was washing up, covered in suds, and two men balanced a cask between them as they poured its contents into a smaller container. Marius had been so certain he'd see something exciting—a hidden passageway, a stairway leading into darkness—that this mundane scene was a disappointment.

"Hey," said one of the men with the cask. "You can't come in here."

Marius ignored him. Looking closer, he discovered that there *was* a stairway, half hidden behind the fire and the spit. It might lead to an ordinary cellar. Or it might lead somewhere else.

The man released his grip on the cask, leaving the other to shoulder the burden, and came at them, waving his arms to shoo them away. "No customers back here."

Though his eyes never left that mysterious stairway, Marius allowed himself to be backed out of the room. He had no legal right to force his way through. But how did the Sardossians routinely get past these men? Was there a password, or was it just that Sardossians were allowed in and Kjallans weren't?

"I think that was the entrance," said Drusus at his shoulder as they left the tavern. "Did you see the stairway?"

"I saw it," said Marius. "Might be a root cellar."

"Those Sardossians we saw had to go somewhere, and there was no other way out."

Marius nodded.

"So what now?" asked Drusus. "Your cousin wouldn't like it if we forced our way in. I suppose you could ask for another writ."

Marius didn't feel that a writ was justified, and he certainly didn't want to bother Lucien again. He looked up at the darkening sky. "It's late. Let's go home for now. When we come back tomorrow, we can see what a bribe will accomplish."

Staring at her onetime husband in the Riat Underground, Isolda felt she must be dreaming, and it wasn't a good dream. This didn't seem possible. Her ex-husband occupied one sphere of her life, the life she'd left behind in Sardos. He was not present in the other. How could these spheres have merged? Jauld could not be here, and yet he was.

"Three gods, Isolda, it's really you." Jauld leaned in to peer at her face and clothes.

Something about her ex-husband always made Isolda feel self-conscious. What was he seeing when he looked at her? She was dressed to blend, in a cheap Kjallan syrtos, and she'd tied her hair back in a braid to keep it out of her face. She imagined she looked rather plain. Back in Sardos, she'd tried face paint, but when it didn't seem to improve Jauld's opinion of her, she'd given it up. Too much trouble and expense.

Never mind what he thought. She didn't care anymore. "How did you get here?"

Jauld ignored her question. "So you live in a moldering sewer."

That didn't deserve a reply. He looked different than when she'd last seen him, thinner and grayer. Was food becoming scarce in Sardos?

"Three gods." Jauld's gaze shifted to a spot beside her. "Is that Rory?"

Rory, oh gods! In the shock of seeing Jauld, she'd forgotten about her son. She turned to see how he was taking this. The boy had come in after her, but was now backing away, wide-eyed. He showed no sign of recognizing his father. She wasn't sure if Rory had any memory of Jauld, since he'd been only four years old when they left, and she never talked about him.

Jauld took a step toward Rory. "Do you remember me? I'm your father."

Rory gasped. Isolda couldn't tell if he was scared or excited, but he maintained the distance between him and his father, backing up a step for every one that Jauld advanced.

Jauld stopped advancing. "Your mother took you from me when you were very young. Do you remember our house at the crossroads? Do you remember your second mother, Chari?"

With an edge to his voice, Rory said, "I have no second mother."

Isolda's throat seized. She could scarcely draw breath. Rory *did* remember their time in Sardos—all too well, it seemed.

Jauld turned back to Isolda. "You've come down in the world."

No, she hadn't. As far as Isolda was concerned, the humble life she eked out in Riat was a step way up from the one she'd lived while under Jauld's thumb in Sardos. But there was no point in arguing. Jauld was too foolish and self-centered to understand how she felt. "Why are you here? Have you fled Sardos?"

"Gods, no," said Jauld. "I'm here with a merchant ship."

Good. When the ship left, he would leave too. If he'd moved permanently to Riat and joined the other Sardossians in the underground, she'd have to spend the rest of her life trying to stay out of his way. But it appeared all she had to do was avoid him for however long the ship was in port. That, unfortunately, might not be easy. She didn't own her home in the underground and had no legal authority to order him away. She took Rory by the shoulders and pulled him close to her, sheltering him with her body.

"Isolda, you don't have to live like this anymore," said Jauld. "I've come to offer you forgiveness for what you've done and take you home to Sardos. You and Rory."

Forgiveness. Her mouth flooded with bile. *He'd* mistreated *her*, not the other way around.

"This is our home, and we're staying," said Rory.

Jauld snorted a laugh. "This rotting pile of concrete and sewage is home?"

Isolda felt her son's shoulders tense. "Sometimes we stay someplace nicer," said Rory.

"Oh?" said Jauld. "Where do you stay?"

Don't mention the villa, Isolda pleaded inwardly. *Please don't mention the villa.*

Rory seemed to realize his mistake, and stayed mum.

"Do you remember our nice house in Sardos?" Jauld asked Rory.

Rory nodded.

"Don't you want to go back there?"

"No," said Rory.

Jauld turned to Isolda, his eyes smoldering with fury. "You've taken my son away and poisoned his mind."

"If there's any poison in Rory's mind, you put it there," she retorted. "We're not going back to Sardos. Not under any circumstances."

"Rory is *my son*," said Jauld. "My flesh and blood. And you're my *wife*. Of course you're going back."

Isolda stepped backward, taking Rory with her. Had Jauld come to Kjall for trading purposes, perhaps to buy goods for the shop? Was his search for her merely a side project? In that case, she might get rid of him without much trouble. Or had he made the journey entirely for the purpose of finding her? "How's the store doing?"

"Well enough, given that the country's at war. It wants your magic touch, of course."

She suspected it was failing. That wouldn't be surprising, given that Jauld had been an indifferent businessman before, and, as he'd noted, economic conditions in Sardos were not favorable. "Did you come here to import Kjallan goods?"

Jauld's brows lowered. "I came for *you*."

A chill ran through her. So he'd made the enormously expensive trip just to retrieve her and Rory. But Rory had never interested him. It was Isolda he wanted. He wanted her to run his business and make him rich again. He wanted to live a life of luxury with Chari while Isolda worked herself to death and enjoyed none of the benefits. And meanwhile, a disinherited Rory would be recruited for the blood wars in a couple of years and die on a battlefield. "We're never going back. Kjall is our home now. And I'm not your wife. I got a divorce here in Kjall."

Jauld blinked. She'd surprised him. "Marriage is for life, Isolda. There's no such thing as divorce. Kjallans might discard their wives and husbands, but Sardossians don't."

No, Sardossians replace them with second wives, thought Isolda bitterly. "My divorce is written in the Kjallans' record books. It's legal." At least, it appeared to be, if one didn't look too closely. "You and I are no longer husband and wife."

"What about my son?" Jauld looked down at Rory. "Is he divorced from me as well?"

"I'm not going back," said Rory.

"There's so much more for you in Sardos than here," said Jauld. "Look at the squalor in which you live. You want to end up like that fellow in twenty years?" He indicated the old man in the corner, who was wordlessly watching the drama, and occasionally coughing into his gloved hand.

Rory said nothing.

"In Sardos, we have a house of our own," said Jauld. "We even have a horse."

One horse? They'd had two when Isolda left. Perhaps one had died, or Jauld had sold him. Since Jauld wasn't one for keeping the books up to date, he could have run up significant debts before discovering that his finances were in trouble.

"Here you'll cough your life away in a sewer," said Jauld. "In Sardos, you could inherit the store your mother and I built together. You could be rich someday."

"Rory's not your heir," said Isolda. "Chari's boy is."

"Who says I won't change my mind?" said Jauld. "Rory's grown into a fine-looking boy."

Isolda refused to be fooled—she knew what he intended. He'd play the boys off each other, picking favorites and changing his mind as whim directed, trying to get each one to impress him in order to be named heir. She'd played that fruitless game against Chari, and nobody won except Jauld. He'd have to kill her before she'd let him take her son back to that.

"Mom's getting me into the university here in Riat," said Rory.

Jauld laughed. "You think your mother, who can't afford a proper place to live, can afford to buy you an education?"

"We're saving our money," said Rory.

"You'd better hope you're still alive at age sixty. It'll take you that long, if not longer."

"Leave us be," said Isolda. "We're not going back to Sardos."

"You can't order me away," said Jauld. "I've a claim over you, no matter what those Kjallan papers say. And I've a claim over Rory as well." He advanced toward her.

Gods—would he try to take her by force? She backed around the corner, afraid that if she turned and ran, he would accelerate, and with his long legs he would easily outrun her. And what about Rory? She couldn't abandon him. Perhaps Caz was not too far away, and she could scream for help.

Stepping backward, her foot landed in a puddle of stagnant water. Icy cold flooded her sandals. She risked a glance behind her to correct her course, and when she turned to face Jauld again, he had abandoned all pretense of civility and was running straight at her.

"Caz, help!" she shrieked.

She turned toward the door and pushed Rory ahead of her. The boy found his feet and ran, and she pelted after him. She made it only three strides before tripping over a beam with her waterlogged feet. Just as she was recovering her balance and preparing to launch herself forward again, a heavy weight collided with the small of her back, and she hit the ground.

The impact knocked the wind out of her, and she gasped for breath like a dying fish.

"Mom!" Rory turned and ran back.

Isolda struggled vigorously, trying to buck Jauld's weight off of her. He was holding her down with one hand and the weight of his body while he did something with the other hand. She saw the glint of metal. "He's got a pistol. Run!"

Rory pounded on Jauld with tiny fists. "Let her go!"

Jauld leveled the flintlock at Rory's chest and pulled back the hammer.

"Leave me. Run!" cried Isolda.

For a moment, Rory stared down the barrel of the pistol. Then he turned and fled.

Isolda was left alone with Jauld. Caz had not come. *"Please* let me go. We're not married anymore. I can't go back—"

The butt of the pistol came down on the back of her head. The pain shocked her into immobility and left her dizzy. She tried to say something, but her throat seized. She felt like she was going to throw up. Then the hard metal came down on her again, and her vision went dark.

30

As Marius approached the villa, light glows cast his shadow, and Drusus's, upon the nearby wall of the surgery. Ahead, on the doorstep, he spotted another shadow. Someone was sitting on the stoop, curled up as if to make himself as small as possible.

A patient in need?

No—as he came closer, he saw that it was Rory.

What a stroke of luck! Rory was his ticket to Isolda. If anyone knew where she was, he did. But what had brought him here so late at night? Could Isolda be in danger? He broke into a jog, and as he came close enough for Rory to recognize him, the boy rose.

"Hello, Rory. Is something wrong?" asked Marius.

Rory was normally a relaxed, happy child, but tonight his posture was tense. His arms were crossed in front of his body, his hair was mussed, and Marius had the impression he'd experienced a great fright. His voice shook when he finally spoke. "My father's here in Kjall."

"Your father?" Marius blinked. "The one from Sardos? He came *here*?"

"He wants us to come back to Sardos with him. Mother said no, we wouldn't go back, and he knocked her down." Rory choked on a sob.

Knocked her down? Marius's neck grew hot, and his hands closed into fists. "Then what happened?"

"I tried to get her up, but he had a gun. . ." Rory began to cry.

Marius shared a horrified glance with Drusus. Turning back to Rory, he saw that the boy was beyond words. "Come here."

The boy took a tentative step forward.

Marius pulled him into a hug. The boy sobbed with abandon into his stomach. "What happened next?"

"I don't know!" cried Rory. "Mother told me to run away, and I did. I said the wrong things. I told him I didn't want to go back to Sardos. I didn't know he had a gun! I think I made him mad—"

"You did nothing wrong," Marius assured him. "Whatever happened was Jauld's fault, not yours, and you were quite right to run away." If he hadn't, Marius would never have known Isolda was in trouble. What did Jauld want from her? If he'd come to Kjall to take her back, his interests wouldn't be served by shooting her. But one never knew. Jealous ex-husbands could do terrible things. He turned to Drusus. "We have to find her. Immediately."

"Of course," said Drusus. "But where is she?"

"Can you take us to her?" Marius asked Rory.

"What if he shoots you?" said Rory.

"I'm not worried about that," said Marius. "You see Drusus here?"

Rory looked up at Drusus, sniffling.

"He's a trained bodyguard, and he's more than a match for a man with a gun. Aren't you, Drusus?"

Drusus smiled wickedly. "I'm looking forward to beating the piss out of that guy."

Marius winced. That was a bit much; they were, after all, talking about Rory's father.

But Rory seemed cheered by Drusus's words. "I'll take you there right now."

As Rory led them into the harbor district, Marius grilled him to get a better sense of what had happened. What exactly had been said? How did Isolda react? What had led to Jauld's pulling a weapon? He feared that Jauld and Isolda would have moved from the place where the confrontation had occurred. There was no reason for them to stay where they were. If Jauld wanted to take her back to Sardos, he might have removed her to a ship somewhere.

Or he could have shot her. Marius's pulse raced at that terrible thought.

He had to stay calm. Panicking wasn't going to help. He would go to the scene of the crime and if nobody was there, he'd look for clues.

According to Rory, Jauld had refused to acknowledge her Kjallan divorce, had referred to her as his wife, and had insisted on taking her back to Sardos with him. At first, he'd tried to tempt the two of them by talking about his nice house and the store that Rory might someday inherit. "But I remember that house," said Rory. "Everybody in it was mean."

Marius had thought Rory might lead them to the Sage House Tavern, where he and Drusus had been earlier, but instead Rory led them to the Drunken Wind Taproom, which lay at the other end of the harbor district. He could only guess that there were multiple entrances to the underground. Entering the underground was easy this time. Rory led them into a back room. The barkeep and one of the servers eyed him and Drusus, but after glancing at Rory, they returned to their business.

Down the stairs into darkness. As Marius's eyes adjusted, he saw they were in a finished concrete cellar smelling of hops and old potatoes. Rory led them around a pile of casks to what looked like a dead end. He stuck his fingers into a gap in the concrete and pulled, and a door swung open.

"How—" began Marius, but before finishing his question he touched the door. It wasn't concrete at all, but scored, painted wood. He probably would have seen the difference in better light, but in the darkness, the textures blended into one another.

Rory ran ahead of them into the hallway beyond.

Marius trotted after him. Right away, he stepped in an unseen puddle of water. Gritting his teeth with the cold, he looked ahead and saw that the ground was riddled with pools of inky blackness, hard to make out against the near-black of the dirt floor. A few light glows mounted on the walls cast enough light to allow them to make their way, but not to see much of their surroundings. What he saw was chaotic: light patches that looked like stained concrete, wooden beams, detritus. Incongruously, a storefront directly on his right, with an unreadable sign hanging on one nail.

Rory appeared ahead, in a patch of light shed by a glow. "Come on."

Marius hurried after him. Behind him, he heard a splash, and Drusus swore. Apparently Marius wasn't the only one finding the puddles the hard way.

As he proceeded through the tunnel, he became aware of the smell: a musty, mildewed scent that carried the tang of human sweat. People lived down here—lots of them. While he saw no other souls in the tunnel, he did see signs of human habitation: a ratty blanket in a dry corner. A tattered rucksack, opened and rifled through.

This was where Isolda had lived for the past four years? He felt an ache in his throat.

"Up here." Rory motioned toward a side tunnel.

Marius followed.

Rory led him to a storefront upon which someone had chalked the word *kodon*. "It happened here. Inside."

Drusus shoved past Marius. "I'll go first."

The thin wooden door swung drunkenly on its hinges. Marius followed his bodyguard into the building.

The room was flooded and littered with broken beams, and it was empty of people.

"Soldier's Hell," said Rory, who'd come in after them. "They're not here anymore."

Marius had never heard the boy swear before, but he supposed Rory had ample reason. "This is where Jauld pulled out the gun?"

Rory nodded miserably.

While Drusus walked about the room, checking every corner and splashing through the puddles to see if anything was hidden beneath the water, Marius looked over the sad scene. He saw no signs of a struggle, although in better light he might see more. "You live here?" he asked.

Rory pointed. "Back there."

Heading in that direction, Marius found a second room. This one wasn't flooded, and there were blankets and packs everywhere. Several people lived here, not just Isolda. And one of them was present, an old man sleeping in the corner.

Marius woke him. "My name is Marius, and I'm a Healer. I'm looking for Isolda."

The man's eyes went wide with fear. He tried to speak, but a fit of coughing interrupted his words.

"Don't be afraid," Marius soothed. Now that he saw the man's face, he recognized him. He'd seen this man at the surgery on one of his Free Days. If he remembered right, this cough was not caused by any sort of evil spirit, which was unfortunate since that would have been more treatable. Rather, it was a chronic condition caused by breathing bad air. Marius could give him some relief, but it would be temporary.

He laid hands on the man, letting his magic seep into the man's lungs. Yes—the trouble was the same as before. No evil spirits, just angry flesh that needed soothing. As the magic did its work, he was aware of long minutes passing; the man's lungs were sluggish in remembering the health of their youth. He had to cajole them into acceptance of his magic, like stroking a timid dog whose skin quivered at his touch.

The man cleared his throat when Marius had finished. "Thank you. I'm feeling better."

"Where's Isolda?" asked Marius.

"Her husband from Sardos took her," said the old man.

"He's not her husband. Where did he take her?"

"Don't know," said the old man. "But Vora followed them."

"Who's Vora?" asked Marius.

"She lives here too," said Rory.

"Where do you suppose she is now?"

"She hasn't come back yet," said the old man.

Marius looked around the room. Perhaps they should wait for this Vora to return. He hated the thought of further delay, but other than going to the docks and looking for Sardossian ships, he had no better ideas. If Jauld had abducted her, would he have taken her personal effects as well? "Which bed is yours?" he asked Rory.

Rory picked his way through the mess toward two makeshift blanket nests. He indicated one of them. "Here."

Marius walked over and joined him. The blankets on the floor were spotless. Despite living in squalor, Isolda somehow managed to keep herself and Rory clean. That had to be a prodigious amount of work. Looking through the packs beside each nest of blankets, he found her clothes, neatly folded within. He recognized each outfit and realized for the first time that she only owned four of them, three of which were here. The other she was presumably wearing. He knew she wasn't the sort of woman who cared a lot about clothes, and he wasn't the sort of man who cared about them either. Nonetheless, he was seized with the desire to buy her a whole new wardrobe—anything she wanted. "Are any of your things missing?" he asked.

Rory shook his head.

It tugged at his heart to see their tiny space and how little they had. "You've lived here for four years?"

"Four and a half," said Rory.

Three gods. He had to save them from this—first from Jauld, and then from this desperate poverty. He had paid Isolda enough at the surgery that she ought to have been able to afford an apartment for herself and Rory, but then she'd always talked about saving for Rory's education. Perhaps she lived here by choice, even though she could afford better, so that she could save more of her money. Maybe she was closer to buying Rory a university education than he had thought. But then she'd walked away from her job at the surgery. How was she supporting herself now?

If he could find her, he would help her. Whether she agreed to marry him or not, she deserved better than this, and so did Rory.

His heart was heavy as he returned to the room where the confrontation had taken place. Drusus was still looking around and splashing through the flooded part of the room. "Where did he knock her down?" Drusus asked Rory.

Rory walked out into the flooded section. "Here."

Drusus went to the spot and swept through the water with his hands. With a grunt of frustration, he straightened. "I can't find a gods-cursed thing."

"A man in the back room says there's a woman named Vora who followed Jauld when he took Isolda."

Drusus's brows rose. "That's a good lead."

"We could wait for her to come back," offered Marius. "Or we could go to the docks and look for Sardossian ships."

"Can you tell just by looking which ones are Sardossian?" asked Drusus.

"I don't know," said Marius. "But there can't be that many of them, can there?"

"Caz will know which ones are Sardossian," said Rory.

"Who's Caz?" asked Marius.

"Mother's friend. He works at the docks and got her the bookkeeping job. He knows everything about the ships in the harbor."

Marius blinked. "Isolda has a bookkeeping job?"

"I know where Caz lives," said Rory. "It's not far. I can take you right to him."

That sounded better than waiting around for a woman he didn't know, and who might not show up at all. "Good. Take us there."

31

Marius was jealous of Caz the moment he laid eyes on him. Rory had said this man was Isolda's friend. How close a friend, exactly? Caz was a handsome fellow, tall and fit. He'd apparently found Isolda a bookkeeping job. And yet Marius had never once heard Isolda mention his name. Could this man be part of the reason she'd walked away from the marriage proposal?

Caz lived in the Riat Underground, in an ancient inn called the Pilgrim. Rory cautioned them to wait outside while he fetched Caz; the residents would be sleeping and wouldn't appreciate a gaggle of visitors. Now the big Sardossian stood in the tunnels with them, outside the inn, blinking bleary-eyed as Rory, in a rapid whisper, caught him up on the evening's events.

"She's missing?" Marius heard Caz say, with a glance around the tunnels as if he might spot her lurking somewhere. Then, after more explanation from Rory, "I thought the man waiting inside her home was supposed to be Marius."

Marius stepped forward. "That's me."

Caz gave him an appraising look. "You're the man she always talks about. You weren't the one waiting for her at her home?"

The man she always talks about—Marius liked that description of himself. "No. She never told me where she lived. The man waiting for her was Jauld, her former husband from Sardos. He knocked her down—so I'm told—and when he pulled out a pistol, Rory ran to find me. When I arrived on the scene, both of them were gone. We think she's in his power and he's taken her somewhere, probably onto a Sardossian ship."

"Soldier's Hell." Caz furrowed his brow. "What Sardossian ships do we have in port right now? The *Amaranthe*, the *Gallant*. . .that one with the brown sails. . .that other one with the name I can't remember. . ." He ticked them off on his fingers.

"Do you know which one he might have taken her to?" asked Marius.

"I'd just be guessing," said Caz. "We should go there and look. Though I don't imagine the sailors will be eager to allow us on board—especially if they're the ones concealing her."

Marius tried to envision how Jauld would have smuggled Isolda onto a ship. She wouldn't have gone willingly. Either he'd forced her to cooperate or he'd carried her on board unconscious. It was likely the scene would have drawn some attention and someone at the docks would have seen them. But even if someone had seen and remembered Isolda, it was now late at night. Any witnesses were likely to be in their beds. "Will you take us to the ships?"

"Of course."

Marius felt his shoulders drop—he hadn't realized he was carrying so much tension.

Behind him, a distant splash echoed through the tunnels. Turning, he peered into the darkness as footsteps thudded on the dirt floor. Whoever approached was winded and panting heavily. Drusus stepped quietly in front of him, resting his hand on his sword hilt.

The runner entered the half-light of the nearest glow, and Marius saw that she was a woman. As she reached them, she staggered to a halt, bending over and pressing her hands against her knees. "Caz," she managed to say.

"Vora." Caz hurried up to her. "Did you see where Isolda went?"

"Jauld took her onto the ship *Frolic.*"

"Is that the one with the brown sails?" asked Caz.

"Not sure," said Vora.

"I think it is," said Caz.

"I can take you there."

"Rest a moment," said Marius. "Catch your wind." Anxious as he was to find Isolda, he could see that Vora was on the verge of total exhaustion, and his healing magic had no answer for that.

"If we go slow," panted Vora, "I can take you there now."

As Marius made his way through the harbor district to the docks, he felt more optimistic. He was in good company. Vora had seen where Jauld had taken Isolda, and Caz knew the docks and the ships in port—furthermore, he looked like he'd be good in a fight. That made three of them who could hold their own if the situation turned ugly, including Marius himself, whose healing magic could be handy in a pinch.

The harbor at night looked otherworldly. Every ship was lit up. Glows mounted on the masts and spars delineated their forms against the inky black of the ocean. Some shone white, others green and orange and red.

"I thought so," said Caz, as Vora directed them to turn left, onto Pier Eight. "It *is* the one with the brown sails."

Marius couldn't see any sails at all in this darkness, only light-glows.

"There may be resistance when we try to board," Drusus said softly to Marius.

"I'm expecting it," said Marius. In his mind, he'd been turning over the option of going to Lucien for another writ. He wasn't worried about bothering the emperor again, even in the middle of the night—this situation was urgent enough to justify it—but the trip to and from the palace would take several hours. If he let the ship out of his sight for that long, he might lose it.

Caz dropped back beside them. "I think I can get us on board without a fight."

"How?" asked Drusus.

"I unloaded the *Frolic* when it came into port," said Caz. "And I helped load it yesterday. It's carrying wine. I can tell them there's a problem with the paperwork and we think we gave them the wrong crates—say, we loaded Orryash wine instead of Evory. They'll be anxious to correct the error before setting sail."

"A good plan, if awkward in its timing," said Drusus.

"Are the wine crates in more than one location?" Marius could imagine their being allowed on board to check on the wine, but not to wander all over the ship.

"Three gods," came Vora's faint voice from ahead of them. "I don't see it anymore."

Marius ran up to her, followed by Drusus. "What do you mean? You don't see what?"

"The ship is gone." Vora pointed. "Look."

"Soldier's Hell," said Caz. "She's right. The *Frolic* has gone to sea."

Gone? Marius felt he was back in the Riat Underground, with the concrete walls closing around him. He'd missed her? If Isolda was on her way to Sardos, he might never see her again. "How can that be? You saw Jauld put Isolda on the ship."

"It was here," said Vora. "And now it's gone."

"A ship cannot leave so quickly!"

"It was a small ship," said Caz.

"But—didn't it just get here?" His skin prickled. How could this have happened?

"It didn't just get here," said Caz. "We unloaded it last week and loaded the wine yesterday."

"Maybe it took Jauld a while to find the Riat Underground," said Drusus. "Maybe he waited until the last minute to snatch Isolda."

Marius's breaths came fast as he stared out into the harbor. Jauld had stolen the woman he loved, and he was going to pay for that crime. "It doesn't matter how it happened. We're going to follow them—and for that, we need a warship."

Isolda awoke with her head pounding and couldn't figure out where she was. She was moving—swaying back and forth. Within some sort of a sling? No, she was lying in a hammock suspended from the ceiling. The room she was in was small, dark, and sealed. A bit of moonlight filtered in through a round window. A porthole! She must be on a ship.

Apprehension knotted her stomach. If she was on a ship, where was she going, and why? She wriggled out of the hammock, wincing as her throbbing head took offense.

Standing on her own feet, she realized the floor was tilted, and she was still swaying. She tottered drunkenly to the porthole. Yes, she was definitely on a ship—and it was moving. The waterline wasn't far below her, and her impression was that the ship was neither large nor small but medium in size. Several miles in the distance, a shoreline skimmed by, silhouetted in the moonlight. She did not recognize any of its features.

Feeling a little steadier on her feet, she went to the cabin door and tried the handle. It was locked. She jiggled it experimentally. The handle and door felt flimsy. Could she break it? Someone like Drusus or Marius could probably rip it off the door frame, but she wasn't sure her own strength was up to the task.

Drusus. Marius. Something flitted about the edges of her memory.

Jauld. The memories struck her with such force she leaned over and almost retched. He'd found her in the Riat Underground. He'd told her he was still her husband. He'd threatened Rory with a gun. And then he'd hit her on the head.

Had he put her on a ship to Sardos?

Infused with new strength, she yanked on the door handle, trying to force it. She felt it give, just a little—but more like the handle was going to break under the pressure than open the door. She released it. *Think, Isolda.*

If she got out of this cabin, what would she do next? She could hardly jump overboard and swim. Was there a boat on board that she could steal? The shoreline looked near enough that she could row to it.

Perhaps she was thinking about this the wrong way. Maybe instead of trying to get off the ship, she should find the captain and tell him what had happened. Would he be on her side? If he was, would he turn the ship around?

Someone knocked at the door, and she jumped.

Could that be Jauld?

The knock was quiet, almost respectful. Perhaps he was trying not to wake anyone.

She looked around for a weapon, wanting something in her hand for this confrontation.

A key rattled in the lock, and before she could find anything hard or heavy, the door opened. She whirled to face the intruder.

It wasn't Jauld, but Chari.

Isolda blinked. Chari had aged visibly since Isolda had left Sardos, and in some ways the changes were agreeable. Chari had been a teenager when she'd married Jauld. Now she was in her early twenties. Her body had filled out, and she looked more matronly. The angles of her face showed a new maturity, but also fatigue. Motherhood did that to a woman. "Get out," Isolda spat.

Chari, ignoring her command, eased herself into the room and shut the cabin door. "I need to talk to you."

Isolda eyed the door. It was unlocked. If she shoved Chari out of the way, she could escape her prison. Although she still didn't know what she'd do once she was out.

"I know you hate me," said Chari. "But please, set that aside for a moment. I think we can help each other."

Isolda's eyes narrowed. That sounded suspicious. "Why are you even on this ship?"

"Jauld doesn't trust me on my own. I tried to run away last year."

"Why would you run away?"

Chari swallowed. "I had a second child—another son. And only one of my boys can be Jauld's heir."

Isolda stifled a laugh. Chari was now in the position Isolda had been in five years ago, seeing a second male child born and wondering if he would dethrone the first. But in Chari's situation, she could not possibly win. No matter which of her boys Jauld chose as heir, one of them would be disinherited and left to the army recruiters.

"I know you've no reason to trust me," Chari continued. "But I can't see one of my sons murdered in the blood wars. I have to get out of Sardos. We could escape to Kjall together."

"You'll never survive," said Isolda. "A spoiled girl like you? Go and sleep with your worthless husband; you haven't the strength to live on your own in Kjall."

"I *hate* Jauld," said Chari, with passion.

Isolda fell silent. Through her bitter lenses, she'd seen Jauld and Chari as a happy couple enjoying an easy life at Isolda's expense. But perhaps her perception had not been entirely accurate. Chari was a scheming sort of woman. Her professed love for Jauld could easily have been false, a strategy to promote the interests of her child over Isolda's.

"When we knew each other in Sardos, I was only a girl," said Chari. "I know you think I can't manage on my own, that I can't earn my own money. But I've grown up since those days. I *can* make it in Kjall. I *will*."

Isolda looked harder at Chari. Perhaps there was more strength in this woman than she'd thought. Still, Chari had no idea what she was getting into. "Life in Riat is harder than you think. We live underground in something akin to a sewer, and it's hard to find work. Most of the jobs are illegal and dangerous. And you'll have two small children to take care of. I can't see how you'll possibly manage."

"I'll find a way," said Chari.

Isolda shrugged. If Chari wanted to take her chances in Riat, so be it. She could learn for herself how hard it was. "What do you suggest we do?"

"Escape on a boat," said Chari. "You and me."

"With your children?" asked Isolda.

Chari nodded.

"I don't know," said Isolda. A woman with no street smarts and two small children could be more hindrance than help.

"At four in the morning, the shift changes on deck," said Chari. "I think we should go around three, when the sailors are tired and less likely to take notice."

"What time is it now?"

"Around midnight."

"If you want so badly to escape, why didn't you try it when the ship was in port?"

"I got caught," said Chari. "Jauld locked me up until the ship sailed."

"Hmm," grunted Isolda. Chari's ambition seemed to be greater than her skills, but Isolda admired her pluck.

"Just think about it—that's all I ask," said Chari. "And here's a gift, to give you some idea of how serious I am." She handed Isolda a bundle wrapped in cloth.

Isolda's hand dropped with the weight as Chari gave it to her—the object was heavier than its size suggested. She unfolded the cloth and gasped as dull metal winked up at her. Chari had given her a pistol. "Is it loaded?"

Chari nodded. "I'm leaving tonight. I'll knock on your door around three. You can decide then whether you want to come along."

32

Since he had only two horses, Marius could not bring the Sardossians on his trip to the imperial palace. Vora returned home to the Riat Underground. Caz refused to leave—he wanted to help find Isolda—and Rory could not be abandoned in the city at night. So Marius offered the two of them sleeping quarters at the villa and bade them stay there until he returned, hopefully with the means to pursue Jauld and Isolda.

How strange that he was leaving his home in the hands of a Sardossian man he barely knew, and he thought nothing of it.

When he reached the imperial palace, he pleaded his case to the night guards at the gates, and they passed him through to the Legaciatti who guarded the imperial hallway. After making it past those hurdles, he then had to persuade the guards who stood in front of Lucien's bedroom door. All the while, he paced restlessly, feeling the clock ticking—Isolda was being carried farther away by the minute. Eventually, the guards capitulated, went inside the bedroom, and woke Lucien.

Marius and Drusus were called into the emperor's sitting room.

Marius's cheeks warmed as he saw that Vitala was with Lucien. She sat beside the emperor on a couch, clad in a dressing gown. He knew he shouldn't be scandalized by the sight. The emperor and empress had a loving marriage, and while Vitala had chambers of her own, of course she would share Lucien's bed when she had the opportunity.

Moonlight streamed in through the windows, casting the sitting room in eerie gray shadow. Here and there, he caught a feature familiar to him—the carved edge of a bookcase, the soft darkness of a damask covering.

Vitala yawned.

Lucien gestured to the settee in front of him. "This had better be important."

Marius sat. "Your Imperial Majesties, I apologize, but it's an emergency. Isolda has been abducted by her former husband and carried away by ship."

Vitala's half-lidded eyes opened.

"When?" demanded Lucien.

"Only hours ago," said Marius.

"Are you certain she was taken by force?" asked Vitala. "For all we know, she might have gone willingly."

"She did not go willingly. He had a gun." Marius told them the story as Rory had related it to him.

Vitala turned to Lucien. "Not much wind tonight. They can't have sailed far."

"Our ships will have the same poor wind," said Lucien.

"Still, they can outrun a merchantman."

Lucien nodded. "Marius, I'm going to give you temporary command of the *Soldier's Sweep*. She's a twenty-eight-gun frigate, nimble and fast, and more than a match for any merchant ship. I'll compose a writ. Once you have it, you can march straight down to the docks, take command of the ship, and send it after—what's the name of the Sardossian ship?"

"The *Frolic*."

"May the gods speed you on your way," said Lucien, signaling the guards to bring his writing implements.

"No need for a writ," said Vitala. "I'll go with him."

"Are you sure?" A line appeared in the middle of Lucien's brow. "You've been working hard these past weeks."

"One of us should go, and you've got that meeting tomorrow," said Vitala.

Marius didn't dare say a word, but he was thrilled and relieved that the empress was coming, especially since he knew nothing about sailing ships. "Thank you, Your Imperial Majesty."

"Oh, Soldier's Hell," groaned Lucien. "Forget the meeting. I'll go as well."

Though it was the middle of the night, Isolda couldn't sleep. Perhaps it was because she'd been unconscious so long, which had disrupted her body's rhythms, or maybe her mind was just preoccupied. Was she better off trying to escape with foolish Chari and her small children, or on her own? Was there more than one boat available?

Since Chari's gift of the pistol, Isolda was taking the woman more seriously. She turned the weapon over in her hand, trying to figure out how it worked. She'd never fired a pistol before, had never even held one until now. Pulling back the hammer, she felt it catch. Now it was cocked and ready to fire—presumably, if someone had already loaded it. Should she leave it in this state? Perhaps not; it seemed dangerous. She uncaught the mechanism and lowered it gently to its resting place.

At least Rory had gotten away. She didn't want to abandon the boy in Riat, but Rory would be better off as an orphan in Kjall than as a stray in Sardos. She hoped he'd run straight to Marius, who would surely take him in once he learned what had happened. She might never see him again, but her boy would have a chance. That was all she asked for him, a chance. But gods, she would miss him.

Someone knocked at the door.

Chari? It was a harder knock than before, and it seemed too early for her return.

Isolda wrestled her way out of the hammock and wrapped the gun back up in its cloth. She dropped it into the hammock, but immediately saw that was a mistake: its weight sank into the netting, making its presence obvious. Quickly, she retrieved the gun and hid it in a dark corner, while the hammock netting bobbed up and down.

A key scrabbled in the lock. Then the door opened.

It was Jauld. She retreated a step, wishing she had not put down the gun.

"Isolda," he said. "I thought I'd see how you were settling in."

"Settling in?" Did he think this was the equivalent of her taking a room at a boarding-house? "This is a prison you've put me in."

"Not for long. Only until you forget about Kjall and remember your duties to me," said Jauld.

Her *duties?* She felt like throwing up. "I don't owe you anything."

Jauld shook his head. "Our marriage contract says you do."

If he succeeded in taking her back to Sardos, she had a feeling the relative freedom of her former life there would end. He'd have her watched all the time. He wouldn't let her handle money. He'd lock her up at night, worried she'd escape again and run home to Kjall. "We're divorced—I told you. Our marriage contract is no longer in effect."

"There is no such thing as divorce." He stepped inside and closed the cabin door, sealing them in.

Perhaps she was wrong to argue with him. Perhaps she should act meek and accepting in hopes that he would go away—so that she might have a chance to escape with Chari. She forced some submission into her voice. "I'm settling in well. Thank you."

He nodded, looking about the cabin. His eyes lit on the cloth bundle in the corner. "What's that on the floor?"

"It's. . .nothing," she stammered. "A blanket."

His brow furrowed, and he stepped toward it. "There was no blanket in here before."

Gods help her, she was a terrible liar; she could not think of a plausible explanation. "But there was. Perhaps you did not notice."

As he took another step, she moved to place herself between him and the pistol.

Jauld folded his arms. "Why do you not want me to see it?"

Unless she could think of a way to divert him within the next few seconds, he was going to discover the pistol, and then he would know she was up to something, and she'd never get away. Diving for the cloth bundle, she scooped it up. "Here," she said, holding it out. "See? It's just a blanket."

Jauld reached for it, and she pulled it away.

"You're hiding something," he accused, stepping toward her.

She backed away, shaking her head.

"What's under the cloth?"

Isolda looked and saw that a corner had fallen away, exposing a bit of metal. She searched for a plausible explanation and came up with nothing.

Jauld reached. "Give it to me."

Isolda took the pistol from the fabric. She leveled it at him and pulled back the hammer.

Wide-eyed, he retreated a step. "Where did you get that?" He hesitated, uncertain. Then he darted forward, reaching for the weapon. He grabbed it by the muzzle.

Isolda pulled the trigger, and a deafening crack split the air. Acrid smoke stung her eyes. Gods, what had she done?

Jauld lay on the floor, unmoving. Had she killed him? The weight of the deed trampled over her like a four-in-hand. She threw the spent weapon away as if it were a hot coal, yanked open the cabin door, and ran out. "Chari!" she yelled. If they were going to escape together, it had to be now.

She was in a narrow corridor lined with alcoves. Within the alcoves were hammocks, some of them occupied. Eyes watched her, uncertain.

A ladder, there! That should lead up to the ship's deck, or at least to a higher level within the hold.

She ran to the ladder and began to ascend.

"Hey," cried a male voice behind her. Someone grabbed her around the waist. She kicked frantically and felt her sandal connect with his nose. With a muffled cry, he fell away. Drawing on strength she'd hardly known she had, she scrambled up the ladder and onto the ship's deck. A square piece of wood lay next to the opening: a trapdoor. She picked it up and slammed it into the gap, hoping to delay anyone who tried to come up after her.

The deck around her was deserted. A roaring noise filled her ears, but after a moment's confused panic, she recognized it as the harmless singing of the wind in the sails. Toward the front of the ship, she spotted three sailors slumped against a railing. Two men were at the wheel and another looked out over the prow.

If this ship was anything like the one on which she'd sailed to Kjall, the boats would be stored near the stern. Ducking down to keep her shadow small, she ran toward the back of the ship, where she found a single jollyboat hanging off the stern, suspended by davits.

She stared at the tangle of ropes and pulleys that hung over the boat. How in the world was she to get the craft free? It looked like one got into the boat first, and then did something with the ropes—it wasn't clear what. As she pondered this, with her blood pounding in her ears, she heard a noise behind her. She glanced back and saw the trapdoor she'd come through earlier pop off the deck.

Soldier's Hell. She ducked around a trio of barrels, putting them between her and the newcomer. Unfortunately, this also blocked her own vision. She heard footsteps approaching and circled around, staying out of sight.

"Isolda?" called a soft voice.

She sighed. It was Chari. Isolda popped her head over the barrels and said, "Here."

Chari came around, and Isolda saw that she was carrying both her children: a four-year-old boy and an infant.

"Are you crazy?" Isolda hissed. "They'll make noise."

"I can't leave without them," said Chari. "Anyway, they're drugged."

Isolda looked again. Both boys were soundly asleep. A trail of drool leaked from the four-year-old's mouth. She shook her head. "How do we get the boat down to the water?"

"We have to get into it first," said Chari. "You go, and I'll hand the children down."

Isolda climbed over the railing, aware of how close she was to the churning sea below. One wrong move, and she'd be in the water. A lee-lurch tossed her sideways, and she clung to the burnished wood as if sticking to the saddle of a cantankerous horse. Her hands shook as she lowered herself into the swinging boat. "We may have company. A sailor tried to grab me as I came on deck."

"I took care of him," said Chari.

Well, that was unexpected. Isolda would not ask how. "Hand down the children."

Chari gave her the four-year-old first. He was heavy, but soft and unresisting—thoroughly unconscious. She lowered him like a sack of meal into the stern of the jollyboat and reached up to take the infant.

Once Isolda had the second boy, Chari swung herself over the railing and began to climb down.

"Ho—avast there!" came a sailor's voice.

"Hurry," Isolda hissed.

Chari's weight dropped into the jollyboat, and it swung.

"How do we lower it?" said Isolda.

Chari went to the pulley on the stern to examine it, and Isolda went to the one at the prow. It was clear the two would have to be raised or lowered together. While Isolda was tempted to simply cut the rope—surely there was a knife on board the jollyboat somewhere—that would leave one side still attached. They'd be dumped into the ocean.

The jollyboat gave a lurch, and the stern side dropped by several feet. "I've got it," said Chari excitedly. "Pull that rope." She pointed.

Isolda pulled, and the prow side dropped.

Sailors' heads appeared over the railing. "There they are!"

Chari raised her pistol and pointed it at them. The heads disappeared.

Isolda pulled her rope again, sending the prow downward a little more, and then Chari lowered the stern. Zigzagging back and forth, they dropped the boat until it just touched the swirling sea. But it was still attached to the pulleys. Isolda was trying to figure out how to detach it when the prow end of the ship suddenly rose several feet.

"No, don't bring us back up," said Chari.

"That wasn't me." The stern side rose, and Isolda realized what was happening. The sailors above them had hold of ropes somewhere and were raising the jollyboat.

"We have to cut ourselves loose!" Chari cried.

Isolda dived to the bottom of the jollyboat, searching. Ropes, oars, waterskins—no, none of that was useful. There it was, a knife! Seizing it, she went to the prow-side pulley and sheared through the rope. The boat's prow dropped into the water.

The stern side rose by several more feet. The jollyboat was now dangerously tilted, and the unconscious children began to slide.

"Cut the rope! Cut it!" cried Chari.

Isolda climbed up the boat from prow to stern. The stern jerked upward still more. Chari grabbed her children and clung to the side of the jollyboat. Isolda reached the pulley and sawed at the rope. It frayed, its fibers parting one by one. On the next jerk upward, the fibers yielded, and the jollyboat fell into the water with a splash.

Isolda grabbed a pair of oars and flung them at Chari. "Start rowing."

33

Marius stood at the prow of the *Soldier's Sweep*, scanning the dark horizon for a sail. Now that his eyes had adjusted to the almost-total darkness, he could just discern the demarcating line between the black sea and the star-studded sky. A brown sail was less visible than a white one, but he should be able to spot it, even if it appeared only as an occlusion of stars.

The *Soldier's Sweep* had the *Frolic* outclassed, so the problem they faced wasn't defeating her in battle, but finding her in open ocean. The *Frolic* had several hours' head start, and no one knew exactly where she had gone.

The triarchus who commanded the ship had suggested to Marius that they sail up the Neruna Strait. That route, regularly swept for pirates, was the fastest and safest way to Sardos and the most likely one the *Frolic* would take. The strait ran northeast along the coastline and was of critical importance to Kjallan shipping. Since the fall of Dori, Kjall had controlled the strait without challenge and built new shore batteries to fortify it. They stood sentinel along the coastline, lit up with glows. Marius could judge the *Sweep*'s progress by counting the batteries as they passed.

The land on the far side of the strait was haunted, gods-cursed Dori. That might scare away the Sardossians, since sailors were often superstitious. But time was money when it came to shipping, and it was unlikely a merchantman, no matter how afraid of ghosts and curses he might be, would go the long way around.

But what if the *Frolic*'s destination wasn't Sardos? The merchantman could be headed to Mosar or Inya first for southern trade goods. Then she certainly would not be in the strait.

Vitala, dark and shadowy in a boat-cloak, slipped up beside him on the rail. "The wind's picking up," she said. "That's good for us, since we're faster than a merchantman."

"If the *Frolic* is in the strait at all," said Marius.

"I'm sure she is," said Vitala. "The triarchus likes this south wind. When we catch the *Frolic*, we'll be windward of her."

"What's the advantage of that?"

"It's better for maneuverability and putting pressure on another ship."

Marius frowned. Watching and waiting was hard.

"Would you like to rest in the imperial cabin? They've a head start on us; we won't catch them for a while yet."

"I'd rather stay here and keep a lookout," said Marius.

"As you wish."

Vitala stayed with him, looking out over the empty ocean. Marius took comfort from her presence. So many people were on Isolda's side, not only Marius and Drusus but Vora, Caz, and

Rory, and now the imperial couple as well. The woman he loved was neither forgotten nor abandoned. He hoped she knew that and did not despair.

Vitala caught his eye. "I understand Lucien talked to you about Maxian."

"Yes." Tension hardened Marius's shoulders as he leaned over the rail. He had been trying not to think about Jamien and Maxian lately, focusing his energy instead on Isolda. The problem between the imperial heirs was not his to solve, but if it were not solved, it would ultimately affect everyone in Kjall.

"Lucien and I have made a decision," said Vitala.

"What decision?"

"To start Jamien in the palaestra."

Marius blinked. "He'll train to be a war mage?"

"That was always the intent—it's traditional, you know, for imperial sons. We normally start them at age ten, but given how precocious he's been, and. . .well, for other reasons, we think he should start now."

"Children training at the palaestra live at the palaestra, don't they?"

"Yes," said Vitala. "That factored into our decision. With Jamien away from the palace, I think we may see a change in Maxian."

"I believe you will." So they were sending Jamien off to the school of war. Marius's feelings were mixed. If Jamien was dangerous now, he'd be even more so armed with war magic. But as Vitala had pointed out, war magic had always been the destiny of imperial princes. Maxian would receive the same training when he came of age—and when that happened, the boys would be on even footing, more or less.

At a military school, Jamien would be far away from the palace servants and sycophants who feared to challenge him. He would, presumably, learn some old-fashioned discipline, which might be just what he needed. Meanwhile, little Maxian needed time away from Jamien, and he would get it. "I think it's a good decision."

"Thank you for saying so," said Vitala. "It's been hard."

"I don't doubt it." His impression was that Vitala and Lucien were capable parents, loving but strict, holding their children to high standards. Yet it was a rare individual who, bowed and scraped to constantly by those currying imperial favor, didn't let the unearned power go to his head. For this reason, Marius was eternally grateful that his mother had raised him far from the imperial seat. Had he been raised here, he might have grown into an entirely different person. Jamien's ill treatment of his younger brother might be a childhood phase; he hoped that was all it was. But if the problem persisted, the stakes were high, not just for the family but for the empire as a whole. This boy would someday inherit the throne.

"I'll tell you something I've told no one yet except Lucien," said Vitala. "I think I've got another one on the way."

"Another child?" He looked instinctively at her belly, and his cheeks went hot. One shouldn't look at the empress in such a way. At least she was covered by the boat cloak.

"It's early, and I'm not sure, so don't say anything yet," said Vitala. "But Vagabond's Breath, two boys is enough. I'm hoping for a girl."

Isolda had never rowed a boat in her life, and Chari's flailing attempts made it clear she hadn't either. The *Frolic* had drawn away from them, carried forward by the wind in its sails, but Isolda was aware the merchantman could come back, if only to recover its jollyboat. They had to reach shore as soon as possible.

When her oar tangled with Chari's for the third time, Isolda said, "Let's take it in shifts. You rest, and I'll row. When I tire, we'll switch."

Chari dragged her oars into the boat and went to the stern to check on her children. The older boy was still sleeping, but the baby was beginning to fuss. She picked him up and bounced him.

Isolda hauled at the oars. Her arms burned. All the walking she had done in Kjall, to and from her various places of employment, had made her legs fit but not her arms and shoulders. "What did you drug the children with?"

"Rum," said Chari.

Isolda raised her eyebrows but said nothing. She shouldn't judge. Chari had done what she had to do to escape Sardos, and if the children had been awake and fussing, the sailors might have caught them more quickly and foiled their escape.

"I'm sorry about how I treated you, back in Sardos," said Chari.

Annoyed by this overture, Isolda gave the oars a vigorous stroke. Did Chari think such treatment could be atoned for with an apology and nothing more?

"I never wanted to marry Jauld in the first place," said Chari. "Did you?"

Isolda said nothing. Escaping with Chari was one thing; strength in numbers justified a temporary alliance. But that didn't mean they needed to have a friendly conversation. They weren't friends.

Chari sighed. "Forget it."

They rowed for a while in silence. Chari sat pensive, looking out over the ocean, idly bouncing the baby, while Isolda wondered. Who was Chari, anyway? Isolda had lived in the same house with her for years, hating her without knowing a thing about her. Grudgingly, she answered the earlier question. "I wanted to marry, but not specifically Jauld."

"Were you in love with another man?" asked Chari.

Isolda shook her head. The truth was that back then, she barely looked at men, having convinced herself that none would want her, and why create a desire that could never be fulfilled? "I wanted to marry somebody, and I wasn't thinking a whole lot about who it should be. And Jauld was the one who offered. I was happy to be chosen—for about a week."

Chari stared out over the ocean. "I was in love with another man, but he had no money. He wasn't his father's heir."

Isolda sniffed. Poor little Chari, who'd loved another man but couldn't marry him. Isolda glanced behind her at the shoreline. It was depressingly far away.

"I envied *you*, though," added Chari. "I had to stay home while you got to run the store. I wanted to work, too—anything to get out of that house!—but Jauld wouldn't allow it. He said you knew what you were doing, and he wouldn't let a stupid girl like me muck it up."

Isolda's rowing rhythm slackened. She had never known that Chari wanted to work at the store, or that she'd been unhappy at home with Jauld. It made sense, now that she thought about it—Isolda would have hated that too. Back then, she'd been so blinded by her jealousy and her fear of losing Rory's inheritance that she hadn't considered that Chari's life was not much better than her own. Possibly it had been worse. "I didn't realize."

"And then you left," said Chari. "How lucky you were to get away."

"It wasn't luck," said Isolda.

"Well, you got away, and I was stuck at home with an infant. Jauld became paranoid that I might leave too. He watched me constantly."

"Then I'm glad you finally got away from him."

"I always wondered," said Chari. "Did your father take multiple wives?"

Isolda shook her head. "No."

"Mine did." Chari sighed. "I had two older brothers, once—they died in childhood."

"Of what?" asked Isolda.

"Fever, supposedly," said Chari. "But that doesn't happen anymore, not when they're warded. You know it doesn't."

"I know," said Isolda. She'd heard the story many times, from different families. Competition among the male children in a Sardossian family, especially a family with several wives, was intense. It was not uncommon for male children to die suddenly, in suspicious circumstances, leaving less competition for those that remained.

"Shall we swap places?" asked Chari. "I can take a turn at rowing."

Isolda's arms were burning; she nodded. Chari put down the baby, and they stepped past each other in the boat, rocking it and sending up an unlucky splash that hit Isolda in the face. Chari took up the oars, and Isolda rested, licking saltwater off her lips, while the baby fussed nearby.

The little one looked so much like Rory had at that age. Gods, how long ago that had been! Now that Rory was half grown, she ached to hold a baby again. "Does he need feeding?"

"Soon," said Chari. "For now he's all right."

Isolda's arms twitched; she hated to watch a baby cry. Finally she picked him up. He hiccupped, and she rocked him gently. He was a cute baby; it wasn't his fault that his parents were Chari and Jauld. Any child deserved a chance to succeed on his own merits.

Including her own. Dear Rory—she missed him with all her heart. Where was he now? She hoped he'd gone to Marius and was sleeping safely in the villa.

Isolda blinked. Were those blue lights out in the channel?

As she squinted at them, trying to determine if they were twinkling stars or something more significant, a tall vertical line of them materialized out of the darkness.

She set the baby back in the stern. "Row faster. The *Frolic*'s come back."

Chari's rowing arms jerked in surprise, and the jollyboat bumped over a wave. She craned her neck toward the approaching lights. "It'll be the jollyboat they want."

"They can have it once we reach shore." Isolda picked up the second set of oars, slid them over the edge of the boat, and stabbed them into the water. But as hard as she pulled, she could not outrun a sailing ship in a good wind. The single blue line became two crosses in the sky, outlining the *Frolic*'s masts and main spars. Then she could make out the prow. The ship was not heading directly toward them, she realized, but moving southwest, parallel to the shore. "They might go by us. Stay silent."

"There's a second ship."

"Where?" Isolda turned in the direction Chari was staring. Orange lights outlined three tall masts—no merchantman at all, but a sleek frigate. "What in the Soldier's Hell?"

"It's got to be Kjallan," said Chari.

"Or it could be a pirate." Isolda backed her oars. The *Frolic* had seen the orange-lighted ship too and was turning around. The blue light-glows illuminating its masts and spars were winking out, one by one. Meanwhile, the newcomer was coming on fast. Already she could see its bright white sails in the moonlight. Its topgallants were set, and its studdingsails reached outward like wings. As the *Frolic* turned her stern to the frigate, colors erupted in the air. Someone from the frigate was communicating with the *Frolic* in the arcane language of pyrotechnics.

"What do you suppose they're saying?" Isolda asked.

"I have no idea," said Chari. "But I don't think a pirate ship would have its lights on. Maybe it's a Kjallan warship asking for information, seeing if the *Frolic* has a right to be in the strait."

"Perhaps." But since the *Frolic* had doused its lights to flee, it clearly saw the new ship as a threat, which meant caution was warranted. Colored lights erupted over the sea, first in one place and then in another. They seemed almost random, and Isolda feared that, purely by chance, they might illuminate the jollyboat. The frigate was searching the darkness for the fleeing *Frolic*. Why? A wild hope sent her heart racing. Could it be that

Marius knew the *Frolic* was the ship that had taken her? Could he have petitioned the emperor and come for her by sea?

As Chari raised her arms to pull at the oars, Isolda stopped her. "Be silent a moment. I want to watch."

Finally a set of pyrotechnic lights found not open ocean, but the stern of a ship. The pyrotechnic lights stayed where they were, popping and scintillating in the sky, illuminating the *Frolic*.

Then the first cannonballs were fired.

34

"I don't understand!" cried Marius, leaning over the railing for a better look at the fleeing *Frolic*. "Why are they running away?"

"I don't know," said Vitala. "They didn't answer our signal."

"Three gods, what did we say?"

"Nothing that should have frightened them this much," said Vitala. "We ordered them to heave-to. We said a woman had been kidnapped from Kjall and we needed to see if she was on board."

"Is Isolda so important to them that they'd risk the lives of everyone on the ship?" She was important to Marius, of course, because he loved her. And she was important to Jauld, who wanted her to run his store. But the captain of the *Frolic* should have no great interest in her, unless he was a personal friend of Jauld's. At the first sighting of the *Frolic* in the strait, the frigate had cleared for action, crowding sail and beating to quarters. The sailors were ready to fight, but the *Frolic* wanted no part of it.

She'd doused her lights and tried to run, and the *Sweep*'s pyrotechnic mage had found her.

"It doesn't make a lot of sense," said Vitala. "I think there's something else going on."

Emperor Lucien headed toward them on the rail, his wooden leg thumping against the ship's deck. "Our warning volley didn't stop them, so the triarchus is going to get serious."

"He can't shoot at them," said Marius. "Isolda's on board."

Lucien laid a hand on his shoulder. "It must be risked. Do you not see? There is no other way to stop the ship."

"But Isolda might be killed!" The ship lurched, and Marius grabbed for the railing.

"Here we go," said Lucien. "Never you worry. Isolda is probably imprisoned in the hold. We won't be firing at the hull at all, only at masts and sails. The intent is to cripple the ship, not to sink it."

The *Sweep* was turning side-on to the Frolic, bringing its broadside to bear. Marius stared at the merchantman, which looked small and frail in comparison. "Cannonballs don't always go where you point them."

"We either do this, or we let the ship take her to Sardos," said Lucien.

Marius closed his mouth. They couldn't let the ship go. Still, he felt helpless to protect Isolda. In desperation, he uttered the Vagabond's Prayer: *Great One, pass her by*.

Someone below them called, "Fire on the upward roll."

Marius tightened his grip on the railing.

The cannon fire began at the stern of the ship, proceeding toward the prow where Marius stood. A rolling boom like thunder rocked the warship onto its haunches. Clouds of black smoke and the stink of brimstone rose from below.

Staring through the smoke, Marius saw that one of the *Frolic*'s two masts had come down. The gunners below them were cheering their success.

"Perfect," said Lucien. "She's crippled now."

All was quiet on the *Soldier's Sweep* as the gunners sponged their cannons and reloaded. On the *Frolic*, Marius saw desperate activity as sailors climbed aloft on the rat-lines, cutting the wreckage free with axes. The *Frolic*, out of control, swung its stern toward the *Sweep*.

"They've lost a mast. Why don't they surrender?" asked Marius.

"I don't know," said Lucien.

"Fire at will," called a centurion below.

This time there was no rolling broadside, but each cannon fired as it became ready, raking the *Frolic*'s stern. Marius's stomach clenched. How much abuse could the merchantman take? Isolda could be bleeding to death right now, and he couldn't get to her.

"Grape," called the centurion.

Marius shot the emperor a frightened look. What did that mean?

"They're switching to grapeshot," said Lucien. "It won't damage the hull or the spars, but it's deadly to the men."

"The men?" cried Marius. Then it would be deadly to Isolda.

"It will prevent casualties when we board," said Lucien.

The *Soldier's Sweep* wheeled ponderously—they were changing direction again.

"*You're* not boarding," Drusus said to Marius. "You're staying here."

"Of course I'm boarding," said Marius, his eyes on the *Frolic*. "Isolda could be dying over there."

Drusus sighed.

The *Frolic* limped northward and the *Sweep*, which had ceased fire with its great guns, gave chase. As it caught up, it bore wide and moved alongside. Meanwhile, sailors with soot-stained faces gathered at the *Sweep*'s prow. A bosun handed out knives and muskets.

"We need to get out of their way," said Lucien.

Marius headed amidships with the emperor, the empress, and their team of Legaciatti. Someone yelled a command, and a horde of sailors who weren't among the boarding party swarmed into the tops. The *Soldier's Sweep* wheeled around and pointed its prow directly at the *Frolic*.

"Three gods, are we going to ram them?" cried Marius. It was clear that they were, so he grabbed the railing. The uninjured sailors on the *Frolic* yelled and gave way as the *Sweep*'s bowsprit drove toward the *Frolic*'s starboard side. More commands from the bosun, and the *Sweep* spilled its wind and slowed.

The two ships collided. Marius was flung forward. His knees buckled, and he caught himself on the railing. Dragging himself back up, he saw that the *Sweep*'s bowsprit hung above the Frolic's deck, and the boarding party was jumping down onto the merchant ship in groups of two and three.

"Let's go," he called to Drusus, running forward to join them.

When Marius reached the bowsprit, he found himself largely alone, as the boarding party was already below on the enemy ship, carving their way through the defenders. He climbed out onto the long spar and hesitated. It was a six-foot drop down to the *Frolic*. But the sailors had managed it.

Kneeling on the bowsprit, he grabbed a rope and let his feet dangle off the edge. Then he let go of the rope and dropped onto the merchantman's deck.

Drusus landed beside him. "Vagabond's Breath." He drew his sword. "Where to?"

Marius sized up his surroundings. Resistance was thin. The grapeshot must have done its ugly work, because the boarding party had cleared most of the deck already. Near the stern, he saw a group of Sardossian sailors lying face down with their hands behind their heads.

"The deck is ours," said Drusus. "If we wait a few minutes, our men will have the hold as well."

"Let's go down now."

Marius found a trapdoor in the floor. Drusus insisted on going down ahead of him. As Marius scurried down the ladder, he heard shouts and banging, as well as an occasional gunshot. The fighting was still in progress.

The merchantman below decks was a maze of narrow passageways. Marius picked a passageway at random and ran along it, checking all the doors.

In one room, he found a sailor who instantly surrendered. Marius left him where he was. In another room, he found a dead body, male. Nobody else in this passageway, so he darted into another.

As he was checking the first door, a Sardossian pelted down the corridor toward him, knife in hand. Drusus ran to engage him. A few quick slashes, and the Sardossian sailor was on the floor, bleeding and crying out for mercy.

Drusus took the man's knife and frisked him. Finding nothing, he abandoned him, and they continued their search.

By the time they'd checked all the rooms on the second corridor, the sounds of fighting had stopped. "I think it's over," said Marius.

"Think so, too," said Drusus, panting.

A Kjallan in the uniform of a principal, one of the ship's junior officers, spotted them and came running up. "Marius—sir—we've searched the whole ship, and we did not find the woman Isolda. Or any woman at all."

"What?" cried Marius. "But she's here! She has to be."

"One of the Sardossians told us she was on board, but she and another woman stole the jollyboat a while ago and escaped."

"Isolda stole the *jollyboat*?" Marius blinked. He didn't know whether to laugh or cry. He could readily imagine her doing something like that. But who was the other woman? And where was Isolda now?

"We found something else," said the officer. "May I show you?"

"All right." Where would Isolda have gone in the jollyboat? Toward land, surely. They were in the Neruna Strait, so if she was uninjured, she should be capable of rowing to shore.

Summoning a ball of magelight, the officer led them down a dark stairway into the ship's storage hold. As Marius's boots hit the ground, a rat squeaked and scurried away.

"See these crates?" asked the principal, sending his magelight ball to illuminate them.

Marius looked around. The hold was packed from stem to stern with them.

"They say they hold wine, but they don't," said the principal. The nearest crate had been opened. The man reached into it and pulled out a bottle. "Be careful—don't strike a spark." He knocked the bottle against the wooden crate, and its glass top broke off. Black powder spilled out.

"Three gods," said Drusus.

"What is it?" said Marius.

"Gunpowder," said the principal. "Thank the Sage we didn't fire at the hull."

"Glaucus," called a sailor from above.

The principal turned to the ladder. "Yes?"

"Is Marius with you?"

"Yes."

"Tell him we're being hailed by two women in a jollyboat, and might one of them be the woman he's looking for?"

Marius scurried up the ladder.

35

As Isolda reached the end of the rope ladder and scrambled over the ship's railing, the first person she saw was Marius. He held out his hand to receive her. Emotion surged, and she felt her heart might burst. Trembling, she took his hand. He pulled her close and hugged her so hard he lifted her off her feet.

"How did you find me?" she asked.

"Rory came to the villa and told us what happened with Jauld," said Marius. "And then we had some help from Caz and Vora."

She raised her head. "You know Caz and Vora?"

"I do now."

Kjallans crammed the deck of the *Frolic.* They'd taken control of the ship from the Sardossians. Marius took her hand and led her away from the crowd. "I can't tell you how happy I am to have you back. I was afraid I'd never see you again."

Isolda's throat swelled, and she could hardly speak. For the past several hours, she'd had to be brave so she could focus on the problem at hand. But now the ordeal was over.

Marius wrapped his arm around her shoulders like a blanket. "You're safe now. We needn't worry any longer."

"Where's Rory?"

"On the *Sweep*—the other ship," he added, when she furrowed her brow.

She glanced at the frigate which loomed nearby, hove-to. Her son was near. Soon her small family would be reunited. And they *were* a family, no matter what Marius's powerful cousin thought. She'd been a fool to walk away from the marriage proposal. Marius didn't seem to worry overmuch about the emperor, so she'd swallow her fears and brave the man's dislike. She would convince him somehow that she and Marius were right for each other.

She'd overcomplicated things, worrying about family, class, her nationality. But tonight she had fought for her life and for the people she loved. Primal acts had a way of stripping away everything that didn't matter. What mattered? That she loved Marius, and Marius loved her. Their love had substance; everything else was but a detail. Issues such as class and citizenship could not be simply ignored; she and Marius would have to deal with them. But deal with them they would, because they loved each other.

"It was Jauld who abducted me," she told Marius. "He wanted to take me back to Sardos."

Marius stroked her hair. "Well, he didn't succeed. How did you manage to steal the jollyboat?"

"Luck, mostly. Our plan was to row to shore and walk back to Riat."

"*Our* plan?"

She'd forgotten about Chari. Glancing back, she saw the younger woman hanging off the railing on the rope ladder, handing her older son to a Kjallan sailor. Another Kjallan already held the baby. "I escaped with Chari, Jauld's second wife."

His brows rose. "The woman who treated you so badly in Sardos?"

"I had a similar reaction when she showed up in my cabin. It turned out she wanted to get away too, and she thought we'd be better off running together. She wants to emigrate to Kjall with her children."

"That won't happen," said Marius. "We'll send her back to Sardos where she belongs."

"Please don't," said Isolda. "I don't like her, but without her I might never have gotten away. She gave me a pistol."

"Was there a fight?"

"Yes. I shot. . .oh, gods." She'd forgotten about Jauld, whom she'd abandoned in the cabin, having no idea if he was alive or dead. "I shot Jauld."

Marius hardly even blinked. "Is he dead?"

"He might be. I was trying to hide the gun from him in a bit of cloth. He tried to take it from me, so I shot him and ran."

"Gods above. Are you hurt at all?" He lifted her chin with his finger to examine her face.

She shook her head.

"Shall I find out if Jauld survived?" asked Marius.

Isolda nodded.

Marius signaled to a young principal, explained the situation, and asked him to search the ship for a Sardossian named Jauld with a gunshot wound.

A well-dressed woman walked up to them and extended her hand to Isolda. "Here she is, the lady of the hour. I'm glad you've returned to us safe and sound."

It took Isolda a moment to figure out who she was: Kolta, the woman who'd spoken to her in the surgery about the gunpowder factories. Which meant that, gods, she was the Kjallan empress. What did one do in this situation? Isolda dropped to her knees, hoping that was correct. "Your Imperial Majesty," she stammered.

Empress Vitala took her hand and pulled her back to her feet. "I heard you might be joining our family soon."

Isolda tried to speak, but her tongue got in the way.

"I believe you'll make Marius a happy man," said Vitala. "It takes courage to run away from everything you've ever known. You remind me of a girl from Riorca I once knew."

"Marius," called a man's voice from nearby.

The newcomer was black-haired and dressed in a fine silk syrtos. One of his shoes thumped on the wooden deck while the other was silent, giving him a syncopated gait. As he approached the group, he slipped an arm around Empress Vitala, which shocked Isolda until she realized he was the man she'd seen at a distance that night at the villa: Marius's cousin, the emperor.

"We've got business to discuss," said Emperor Lucien. "The sailors are transferring the gunpowder to the *Sweep*. After that, I think we'll let these smugglers limp home in their crippled ship. What say you?"

Isolda was lost. Gunpowder? Smugglers?

Lucien caught her eye. "Are you Isolda, whom we've heard so much about?"

Belatedly, Isolda sank to her knees. "Yes, Your Imperial Majesty."

"Rise," he said, and she obeyed. He extended his hand, and after a moment's hesitation, she clasped his wrist. He smiled. "It's wonderful to meet you at last—I've heard so much about you. Marius said you transformed his business at the surgery."

Vitala spoke. "Allow me to thank you again for the information you gave us about the gunpowder factories. We've taken Galbus into custody. He had indeed started a third gunpowder factory, which we shut down only days ago. He faces trial next week. But it appears his people managed to smuggle out one last shipment."

"Smuggle it out—you mean on *this ship*?"

Vitala nodded. "The *Sweep*'s officers found gunpowder hidden within wine crates in the hold."

Isolda's stomach went hollow. "My lady, are you saying that the gunpowder we manufactured was destined for export to Sardos?"

"The final batch was. I can't speak for all of it."

Isolda swayed on her feet. She'd always thought the gunpowder she'd helped manufacture went to supply the Kjallan army, where it did no harm, at least for now, because Kjall was not at war with anyone. But if it was going to Sardos, it was fueling the blood wars. Her work in Kjall had been killing her countrymen at home.

Lucien turned to Marius. "The Sardossians don't have a Healer on board. Do you want to help their people before we give them back their ship?"

"Oh—three gods!—I was so focused on getting Isolda back that I never thought about the wounded sailors." Marius turned his head to look around the deck.

"They're below, in custody. Glaucus can take you," said Lucien.

Marius turned to Isolda. "Do you mind if I spend some time healing the Sardossians before we go?"

"I'll come with you and help."

The hold was full of injured Sardossians. Marius asked Isolda to handle triage, assessing each man's condition so that she could bring him the most urgent cases first.

But before they could begin work, a principal slipped up beside them. "We've identified a man we think may be Jauld."

"Is he alive?" asked Marius.

"No," said the principal. "Shall I take you to the body?"

"Do you want to go?" Marius asked Isolda.

She gritted her teeth. "Later. These men need help."

"If the dead man is Jauld, you're not to blame for what happened," said Marius. "You were only defending yourself."

"I'm not sorry I shot at him," said Isolda. "Last time Jauld had a gun in his hand, he pointed it at Rory and hit me on the head with it. But I wish it hadn't ended this way—if indeed the dead man is him."

Marius squeezed her hand, and they went to work.

He extracted fat splinters of wood impaled in sailors' bodies, pinched off blood vessels, flushed and sealed wounds, dug bullets and bits of cloth out of singed flesh, and closed sword cuts. As he stabilized the worst cases and began to deal with the more routine ones, Isolda sat with him, translating when his patient had a question. Her presence was a comfort, all the more so now that he'd had the opportunity to experience life without her. Before she ran off again, he had to convince her to come back to the surgery—and to accept his marriage proposal.

He spoke to her in Kjallan, knowing that Drusus would be able to listen in but not many of the Sardossians would. "I heard you got a bookkeeping job."

Isolda's face flushed. "I did—at the docks. I'm sorry. It was wrong of me to disappear without saying a word."

"What would it take for me to lure you back? Shall I double your pay?"

"You'd have to raise your rates if you did that."

"Consider it done," said Marius.

"But your patients—" she began.

Marius looked at her. "I saw where you live."

She winced. "You weren't supposed to see that."

"You deserve better," said Marius. "I thought I paid you enough to rent an apartment somewhere. Did I not?"

"You did," said Isolda. "It was my choice to live there. I told you, I'm saving for Rory's education."

Marius blinked. "How much have you saved?"

"Eight hundred tetrals so far."

"Eight hundred? Three gods!" That was a small fortune, enough to pay for Rory's first year at the university. "Where do you keep it?" When she hesitated, looking around the room, he raised his hand. "Sorry, don't tell me. Nobody should know but you."

Still, he was astonished. Here was a woman who took no luxuries for herself, not even the luxury of a home, in order that she might give her son a future. It was remarkable. It was heroic. And it was profoundly sad. "I cannot bear that you should live in the underground any longer. If you won't marry me, please allow me to rent you an apartment near the surgery. And to take you shopping for a new wardrobe—not that you're not lovely in what you're wearing now. But you've done so much for Rory. I think it's time someone did something for you."

Isolda made a choked noise.

At the moment, he could not look at her—he was healing a sword cut, watching the seams of the wound knit themselves together—but he listened, and he soon ascertained that she was fighting tears. "Please say yes."

She spoke softly. "Is your offer of marriage still available?"

"Of course it is," said Marius. "Say yes to that, too. But what about Caz?"

"Caz?" She looked up at him in surprise. "What's he got to do with anything?"

"He says he's your friend, and that he got you the bookkeeping job. I was wondering how close a friend he was."

"Oh—not that close," said Isolda. "I might have liked him if I hadn't fallen for you. But he has no interest in me, not like you're thinking."

"Perhaps you underestimate his interest," said Marius.

"It wouldn't matter, since I want only you," said Isolda. "But he spends his Sage's Days at the Green and Yellow."

"The Green and Yellow?"

"She's saying Caz likes men," growled Drusus.

Marius blinked. "How is it that you two know about the Green and Yellow, and I don't?"

"She lives in the underground," said Drusus. "And I read books."

"Well, then." Marius let his breath out. "Does that mean your answer is yes?"

Isolda aimed that smile at him, the one that made him go weak in the knees. "Of course."

Marius leaned over to kiss her, and Isolda flung her arms around him. He heard a smattering of applause—apparently a few of the Sardossians *did* understand Kjallan. His cheeks warmed, yet he couldn't stop grinning. When they parted, he said, "I believe the only obstacle remaining is getting you a legal citizenship. I think Lucien may grant it. He's met you now, and he seems to like you."

"His wife was friendly," said Isolda.

"If you win over the empress, you'll win over Lucien," said Marius.

36

When they were finished healing most of the sailors, Isolda went with a Kjallan officer to identify Jauld's body. It was indeed her former husband—and he lay exactly where she'd left him, in the room where she'd been imprisoned. Heavy of heart, she went up on deck to look for Marius. Instead she spotted Rory, whom someone must have brought over from the other ship. He stood by the railing, apart from the others. When he saw her, he ran to her.

She took his hand. "I'm sorry to tell you this, but your father is dead. We had a confrontation on the ship after he kidnapped me. We were fighting over a gun, and. . ." She trailed off, unable to finish.

"He should have just left you alone," said Rory. "Do we get to stay in Riat?"

She hugged him. "I hope so."

Together, Isolda and Rory waited for Marius to return from the hold. The imperials were in a tight group, surrounded by orange-garbed guards, talking amongst themselves. Chari stood alone, clutching the hand of her older boy and cradling the younger. She looked frightened but determined.

Boats plied back and forth between the two ships, transferring men back onto the *Soldier's Sweep*. The long night was coming to an end. Low clouds on the eastern horizon were beginning to turn pink. Isolda shivered and clutched Rory tighter.

Finally, Marius emerged from below decks. He looked around, spotted the two of them, and walked over. "The officers told me about Jauld. How are you doing?"

"Well enough." Isolda had thought she would grieve; after all, she and Jauld had made a child together, built a life together. But she didn't. Perhaps it was because they'd never truly forged a bond. She'd never chosen him, and he'd chosen her only because her bride-price was low. There had never been any love, so there was little for her to mourn.

Instead, she felt weightless, free at last, like the seagulls circling the ship's mainmast. Jauld would never again come to Kjall to claim her. She was a widow, a single woman, free to bestow her love where she chose.

"Rory?" said Marius gently. "I'm sorry about your father."

The boy scrubbed his face with the back of his hand. "He deserved to die. For trying to take my mother away."

Isolda hugged him tighter and then reached for Marius, including him in the hug. Her little family, such as it was. "Let's go home," she said.

By the time they had everyone transferred back to the *Soldier's Sweep*, the sun was up. It was morning, and Isolda was exhausted. She'd been up most of the night, as had the Kjallans who'd rescued her. Now that she saw how many of them there were, she marveled at it. Hundreds of Kjallans, including the emperor and empress, had roused themselves and put their lives at risk to chase down the *Frolic* and retrieve her.

Marius had said the emperor would grant her citizenship, and she could not wait for that to become official. She might look Sardossian, but she was becoming Kjallan in her heart. And Rory, who'd been here since the age of four, was more Kjallan than she.

Chari had come over to the *Sweep* with them. Her children had fallen asleep, and she was sitting with them on the deck, leaning against the railing. The four-year-old was sleeping with his head on her lap, and the infant dozed in her arms. Chari herself was wide awake.

Marius had gone to speak to the emperor, and Rory had been invited by the sailors to shinny up the mainmast and learn how the sails worked. Since Isolda was alone for the moment, she went to Chari and sat next to her. "Did you hear about Jauld?"

"What about him?" asked Chari.

"He's dead," said Isolda. "He came at me in the cabin, and I shot him."

"Oh." Chari's brows rose, and she was silent for a moment. "Well, I won't miss him."

"Do you know what you're going to do when we get to Riat?"

Chari shook her head. "I'll figure something out."

"See that man over there?" Isolda pointed at Caz, who had instantly befriended the Kjallan sailors and was now standing amongst a group of them, talking and laughing about something.

Chari nodded.

"His name is Caz. When the ship docks, I want you to go with him. He can show you the place I used to live in the underground. I won't be staying there anymore, so you can have the space if you want it. It's relatively safe. You'd be lodging with a woman named Vora and an old man who doesn't cause any trouble."

"Thank you," said Chari.

"Good luck." Isolda rose, because Marius had left his imperial friends and was beckoning to her.

The return trip was a short one. Apparently the *Frolic* had not gone far before the *Sweep* had intercepted it, and now that the sun was up, the wind had freshened to speed them on their way. By midmorning, they were anchored in the harbor and taking boats back to land. Isolda, because she was with Marius and the imperial party, had the privilege of being on the first boat. Intimidated by the company, she settled in the back row and said nothing.

At the docks, two carriages waited for them—the same two she'd seen that evening when they came to the villa. Isolda and Rory were ushered into the front carriage, along with Marius and the emperor and empress. Here, the confines were so tight that she could not avoid scrutiny by the imperial couple.

The carriage lurched forward. At the sudden movement, she grabbed Marius's hand. He squeezed it. As the movements became rhythmic, Rory's drooping eyes succumbed, and he dropped off to sleep, slumped against her shoulder.

"I know you've been through an ordeal," said Lucien, eyeing her. "But when you're rested and recovered, I'd like to have you up to the palace for lunch. Shall we say, three days hence?"

Her stomach fluttered. "Yes, Your Imperial Majesty."

"*Sir* will do," said Lucien.

"Yes, sir."

"We've much to discuss," said Lucien. "Your citizenship papers, the wedding, and whether you'd like to have private tutors or attend the university."

She blinked. "Sir?"

"If you're going to join the imperial family, you must have magic. It's a safety precaution."

Marius leaned over to explain. "Those who possess magic also possess some immunity to other people's magic."

"Until you soulcast, you're vulnerable to dangerous forms of coercive magic," said Lucien. "Mind magic, for example. We can't have that. It's a security risk. Therefore, you must learn magic, and so must he, in a few years." He nodded at Rory.

Always, she had saved her money so that Rory could learn magic. She had never considered that she might learn it herself. "Aren't I too old?" she blurted.

"Hardly. You can learn at any age," said Lucien.

"What sort of magic shall I learn?"

"Any that you choose," said Lucien. "Do you have a preference?"

She thought about the types of magic she was familiar with. War magic wasn't for her. Mind magic was used in interrogations; she didn't want that. Pyrotechnics—that was an interesting area of study, artistic in nature, but pyrotechnic mages usually worked as signalers, and that would take her away from Marius during the day. Warding magic could be useful. Marius often had to call a Warder into the surgery as an adjunct to his healing. Warding spells had all kinds of uses, from preventing disease and pregnancy to detecting intruders to opening the Rift for young soulcasters.

And yet that wasn't what she wanted either. "Marius," she said. "What if the surgery had a second Healer?"

His brows rose. "We might have to expand the space a bit. But with two Healers, we could help twice as many people."

"And double our income."

He smiled and squeezed her hand. "Always the businesswoman."

"I want to become a Healer," she told Lucien, "and work at my husband's side."

"Then you shall," said Lucien, leaning back against the padded seat and closing his eyes. "We'll work out the details when you come to the palace."

She let out her breath and angled her head to look out the window. They'd entered the south hills district, and the sights were becoming familiar. The carriage wove its way through the morning traffic. There was the flower shop she passed every day, and the fishmonger's cart. A few more blocks, and the surgery passed by her window—closed for the day. It would open tomorrow.

The carriage eased to a stop. A footman jumped down and opened the door.

Rory was still sleeping against her shoulder, but before she could wake him, Marius scooped him up and carried him out. Isolda stepped gingerly down from the carriage, blinking in the sunshine. Drusus waited for them. The drivers slapped the reins, and the carriages rolled away.

Marius, Isolda, and Rory headed up the front steps to the villa. It was good to be home.

Thank You

Thank you for reading <u>Healer's Touch</u>! I hope you enjoyed it. This is book four in the Hearts and Thrones series, which also includes the novels <u>Assassin's Gambit</u>, <u>Spy's Honor</u>, and <u>Prince's Fire</u>, as well as the novella "Archer's Sin." Reviews help readers find books, and I would appreciate it if you'd post an honest review on Amazon or your favorite retailer. Or you can send me your feedback directly at amyraby@gmail.com.

My other series, Coalition of Mages, is set in the ancient Indus valley. It follows the adventures of romantic couple Taya and Mandir as they solve mysteries and struggle with the troublesome Coalition. Book one, <u>The Fire Seer</u>, is out now, and book two will be out in early 2015.

If you'd like to know when my next book is available, you can subscribe to my newsletter at http://www.amyraby.com, or follow me on Twitter at @amyraby, or like my Facebook page at https://www.facebook.com/Amy.Raby.Author.

Acknowledgements

My effusive thanks to:

Copyeditor Kim Runciman of Night Vision Editing and cover designer Ravven for their perfect blend of artistry and professionalism.

Jessi Gage and Julie Brannagh of the Cupcake Crew, for their insightful critique as well as their friendship.

The talented people at Writer's Cramp, who never let me get away with anything: Barbara Stoner, Steven Gurr, Tim McDaniel, Amy Stewart, Thom Marrion, Janka Hobbs, Michael Croteau, and Courtland Shafer.

And my readers, who make this all worth it.

About the Author

Amy Raby is literally a product of the U.S. space program, since her parents met working for NASA on the Apollo missions. After earning her Bachelor's in Computer Science from the University of Washington, Amy settled with her family in the Pacific Northwest. She shares her household with a Golden Retriever, two rosy boas, and an Andalusian horse.

Amy is the author of the fantasy romance Hearts and Thrones series as well as the fantasy/romance/mystery Coalition of Mages series. She is a 2011 Golden Heart® finalist for <u>Assassin's Gambit</u>, a 2014 PRISM winner for <u>Spy's Honor</u>, and a 2012 Daphne du Maurier winner for <u>The Fire Seer</u>.

44878328R00207

Made in the USA
Lexington, KY
12 September 2015